"THIS MISS[   ]
NOT BY A [   ]

Hal Brognola turned aw[   ]
great, painful weight pr[   ][   ][   ] on his chest.
He had to remind himself to breathe.

Rosario Blancanales's death, if that is what had
come to pass, was ultimately his responsibility.
He was the man in charge. Circumstances beyond
his control had forced him to make decisions
based on fragmentary information, under
incredible time constraints.

Under those conditions, unpleasant outcomes
were to be expected. Friends, comrades lost in
the bargain. But in the end, there was one simple,
sustaining truth. Every member of Stony Man,
Able Team and Phoenix Force was expendable if
the fate of the nation hung in the balance. None
of them had any reservations about dying for
their country.

The grieving for the loss of their comrade in
arms would have to wait. As the Bear had said, it
wasn't over.

DON PENDLETON'S

STONY

AMERICA'S ULTRA-COVERT INTELLIGENCE AGENCY

MAN®

RED FROST

A GOLD EAGLE BOOK FROM

W✦RLDWIDE®

TORONTO • NEW YORK • LONDON
AMSTERDAM • PARIS • SYDNEY • HAMBURG
STOCKHOLM • ATHENS • TOKYO • MILAN
MADRID • WARSAW • BUDAPEST • AUCKLAND

First edition August 2007

ISBN-13: 978-0-373-61974-0
ISBN-10:   0-373-61974-X

RED FROST

Printed in U.S.A.

RED FROST

PROLOGUE

Port Angeles, Washington,
6:35 a.m. PDT

When day broke gray and chilly over the Strait of Juan de Fuca, the Chugash brothers were already fishing two miles off Ediz Hook, the long, narrow spit of land that guarded Port Angeles Bay. Their fifteen-foot open boat drifted with the current, rising and falling on the widely spaced swells. To the south, the mill town of Port Angeles was backdropped by the dark, heavily forested flanks of the Olympic Mountains. The snow-capped peaks were hidden in a ceiling of low clouds.

Stan Chugash sat on a seam-split life preserver cushion next to the forty-horsepower Evinrude's tiller; brother Bob sat amidships, facing him. They were "mooching" for spring chinook salmon. As the dead boat rode the incoming floodtide, they carefully reeled up and then lowered spinning, plug-cut herring. A salmon's take on the fall of the bait was often almost imperceptible and required concentration and practice

to recognize. The Chugash brothers had been mooching these waters for more than fifty years.

Stan flipped the dregs of cold, bitter black coffee
from his insulated cup and transferred the sticky white
crust of glazed doughnut from his fingertips to a knee
of his green vinyl pants. Under the windproof rainsuit,
he wore three layers of clothes. "Would you look at that
yuppie asshole," he remarked. "Miles of water to drive
through, no other boats in sight, and he's got to crowd
us."

The twenty-six-foot Alumaweld approached steadily
from the west at four knots, dragging double downrig-
gers behind. To Stan, it looked brand-new. A Furuno
radar beacon swiveled endlessly on the enclosed cabin's
roof. In the hull's forest-green side paint the name
Fisher King was emblazoned in two-foot-high, silver-
flecked, cursive letters. Mounted on the stern were twin,
four-stroke Yamaha engines: more combined horse-
power than Bob's full-sized V-8 pickup truck. There
was only one person in the boat.

"Think he's drinking a gran-day lah-tay in there?"
Bob asked as he glanced over his shoulder.

"Yeah, while he's surfin' the Web."

Both in their late sixties, the Chugash brothers had
retired from the Port Angeles paper mill. They had been
salmon-fishing junkies since they were old enough to
pull-start an outboard.

The bow of the Alumaweld turned slightly, aiming
right for them. It wasn't slowing down.

"You want to reel up and move, Stan? Fish the other
end of the bank?"

"We got a dead boat. We got the right of way. Besides,
if we move to another spot, that twerp will just follow us."

The Alumaweld bore down on the Chugash brothers.

"Shit, we're gonna have to pull up, Stan. He's gonna snag our lines on a downrigger ball."

"If he don't ram us first." With an effort, Stan stood up in the narrow boat. "Get out the way!" he hollered, waving an arm over his head.

The man piloting the Alumaweld cruiser stared at him through the tinted windshield and kept on coming, same course and speed.

"He can't hear ya, Stan. Let's just move."

"He can see me, though, the son of a bitch," Stan growled. He locked his rod in the gunwale holder and held out his hand. "Give me a goddamn sinker, Bob."

Under the visor of his brother's parka hood, Bob saw a puffy, weather-seamed face flushed with fury. "Stan, that's not a good idea," he said, then quickly added, "Remember your blood pressure...."

Stan reached down snatched an eight-ounce slip sinker from the thwart. The star varsity pitcher of the Port Angeles High School Rough Riders circa 1955 cocked back his arm and took aim at the approaching windshield. "I'm gonna knock out every one of those bleached fucking teeth."

"Stan, for pete's sake..."

Then both of the Alumaweld's downrigger rods bucked hard in their holders. The reels screamed like banshees.

"Well, I'll be gone to hell!" Stan snarled. "The bastard snagged a pair of fish right out from under us!"

As the man in the Alumaweld shifted his engines out of gear, Stan yanked the battered Evinrude to life. Gunning it, he circled wide, away from the certain collision, while Bob reeled in both of their lines.

The Alumaweld pilot, in a longbilled cap and hot-orange down vest, exited the cabin, beelining for the pair of bent rods as his boat coasted to a stop. Before he could reach the stern, the Alumaweld lurched violently backward, forcing him to grab for a handhold. In the same instant, a rip current appeared on the surface; the Alumaweld was caught in a swirling seam one hundred yards long. Guitar-string-taut downrigger cables sang and hissed as they sliced through the water.

As the Alumaweld rapidly reversed toward the Chugash brothers, waves of water cascaded over the boat's splash well and onto the deck. The pilot dashed back to the cabin, dropped the engines in gear and pounded down the throttles. The twin Yamahas roared, their props sent up a plume of spray. The bow lifted, but the boat continued to move backward.

"That ain't bottom he's snagged on," Bob said with delight. "Something's dragging him. He hook himself a gray whale?"

The pilot stuck his head out the cabin window and yelled for help as he rushed past them. He sounded like a cat with its tail caught in a screen door.

"Hang on!" Stan shouted to his brother as he opened up the Evinrude's throttle, trying to catch up and at the same time steer clear of whatever was going on.

Two hundred feet ahead of the Alumaweld, the rip current suddenly parted. Black columns thicker than a man's body slid up through the surface, draped with the downrigger flashers, cables and cannonballs. The split in the rip current opened wider, and the huge black sail of a submarine emerged.

"Hoo-hah!" Stan hollered at his brother. "Yuppie snagged a Trident!"

As the submarine surfaced, the angle of the trapped downrigger cables grew steeper and steeper, lifting the Alumaweld's stern from the water and driving down the bow. The Yamahas' propellers bit into air, their three-hundred-horsepower roar became a shrill, frantic whine. The motors' water intakes sucked air, too. Red-lined, overheating, the four-strokes belched white smoke.

From the way they were losing ground on the flat-black painted ship, Bob guessed its speed at close to forty knots, this while dragging the Alumaweld behind. He had seen *The Hunt For Red October* seven times. And Tridents from the Bangor sub base were always passing through the strait on their way in or out of the Pacific. This sail was low in profile and sloped in the rear.

"Stan, that ain't a Trident!" he shouted through a cupped hand.

Stan couldn't hear him over the sustained shriek of the wide-open Evinrude.

"That's a goddamn Russian sub!" Bob screamed at his brother. "And it's headed for the Hook!" Then their boat bottomed out, full length, in a wave trough. The sickening impact slammed Bob's jaws shut, and he nearly bit off the tip of his tongue.

Ahead, the Yamaha four-strokes sounded like lawn-mowers hitting rocks.

Big rocks.

Abruptly, they went silent.

Bob held on to both gunwales as the sub's foaming wake hit them. When Stan swung wide to avoid being swamped, he stole a look over his shoulder. The sub was already a quarter mile away. It was about the same distance from the Coast Guard air station on the end of the spit.

Stan slowed the motor to idle. He and Bob carefully stood up to get a better look. The low, long ship barreled toward land. It showed no sign of turning or stopping.

"Oh, my God…" Bob muttered.

The impact boomed across the water like a thousand-pound bomb, followed by the shriek of an impossible weight of metal grinding over the Hook's jagged riprap. As the vessel grounded itself, its bow angled upward. Dark, oily smoke poured from amidships, enveloping the sail and masts, a slender, greasy pillar coiling into the overcast sky.

From a half mile out, the Chugash brothers could see the beached sub's engines were still running full speed, the screw throwing a towering roostertail. The Alumaweld lay bottom up on the edge of the riprap. It looked like a Cracker Jack toy beside the massive black hull.

The yuppie was nowhere in sight.

CHAPTER ONE

Moses Lake, Washington,
6:48 a.m. PDT

Carl "Ironman" Lyons crouched in a water-filled irrigation ditch, soaked to the waist. A black ski mask covered his face, hiding his short-cropped blond hair, any reflection off his skin and, of course, his identity.

The shallow canal was the only cover on the south side of the target. After three hours in the ditch it was finally getting light enough for Lyons to see the killzone without the aid of night-vision goggles. The ramshackle narco compound was surrounded by flat, tilled farm fields. Whatever was planted in them had barely sprouted.

No perimeter fence or gunposts protected the pair of hammered, single-wide trailers on cinder blocks, the converted SeaLand cargo-container-cum-laboratory, the sagging, unpainted shotgun shack, the collection of junked and rusting cars and the jumble of fifty-five-gallon chemical drums and empty ammonia tanks.

No fence was required.

The site was eight miles from the nearest public road, in the middle of seventy thousand acres of private land.

Lyons's .357 Magnum Colt Python hung in a black ballistic nylon shoulder holster, a foot above the water-line. A pair of suppressor-equipped, 9 mm MP-5 SD-3s sat in quilted Gore-Tex scabbards on the mud bank in front of him. The scabbards' flaps hung open, exposing the machine pistols' black plastic grips and retracted folding stocks.

Lyons methodically clenched and unclenched his big fists to keep the blood flowing to his fingertips. Below the water, his legs were numb, hips to toes, and it felt as if his testicles had retracted up into his body cavity. The former L.A. cop didn't try to block out his discomfort. Just the opposite. In the back of his mind he inventoried it over and over, item by item.

Being royally pissed off was a good thing.

It helped him maintain focus.

Then he caught movement on the horizon to the north. Four sets of headlights cut through the purple gloom. The lights bounced up and down, up and down as the vehicles bounded over the crop rows. Lyons flipped open the cover on his wristwatch and checked the time. The convoy was a little ahead of schedule.

As the vehicles drew nearer, he heard the rumble of the engines and the squeak and rattle of cargo. The minifleet of rental trucks was delivering raw materials and would take away finished product for distribution in Idaho, Washington and Oregon.

The Moses Lake operation produced and transported a couple million dollars' worth of methamphetamine a week, a joint venture of the Mexican mafia and an enterprising southern-California-based barrio gang.

Lyons knew all about bangers from his days with the LAPD. They were the Cub Scouts of organized crime, earning their merit badges fighting other gangs, staking out turf for drug sales, supplying security for shipments and collections. The Mexican mafia, on the other hand, was into some elaborately bad, big-boy shit. Kidnappings. Political payoffs and assassinations. Torture.

One by one, the four trucks' headlights swept over an enormous John Deere combine abandoned in the middle of a cultivated field one hundred yards away. As the lead vehicle rapidly closed on the narco compound, the driver started honking his horn. The other drivers followed suit.

Almost at once, weak yellow propane lanterns came on in the trailers; there was no electricity at the site. Lyons saw shadowy movement behind the newspapers taped up for window shades. Then people started spilling out the trailer doors. Some had guns. Most didn't.

That was the sticky part.

The twenty without guns were barefoot, dressed in rags and not there by choice.

The seven with guns wore *ranchero* jeans and shirts and low-heeled cowboy boots. They carried AK-47s and sawed-off pump shotguns on shoulder slings, and two-and-a-half-foot-long clubs on wrist thongs.

Given the small size of the killzone and the number of structures, isolating the camp's forced laborers from the armed enforcers was going to be flat-out impossible once the attack began.

The rental trucks parked in a daisy chain in front of the SeaLand container. The four drivers and four passengers got out, leaving the headlights on and engines running. The lead driver carried an overstuffed, black nylon gym bag. From the tats crawling up their necks and their superbaggy shirts and pants, Lyons immediately made them as bangers.

The *rancheros* started herding the rag people toward the trucks. It was slow going. The unfortunates had to take short, shuffling steps because their ankles were tethered with loops of plastic-covered cable.

In the headlights' glare Lyons got a good look at the meth zombies. Forced to work in the cargo container lab without respirators or skin protection, they were perpetually stoned from the toxic fumes and the drug powder in the air. They had legions of sores on their faces and arms, and bald patches on their heads. Lyons figured most of that damage was self-inflicted. Unless otherwise occupied, hard-core tweakers picked themselves raw looking for "meth mites."

He also got a close look at the clubs the *rancheros* carried. They were made from a single shaft of bamboo. The business ends were split into dozens of narrow strips, right down to handles heavily wrapped with layers of electrician's tape. Like cat-o'-nine-tails, they could shred skin down to the bone. They were relatively sophisticated enforcement tools, which confirmed his guess that the *rancheros* were all mafia crew. If bangers had been in charge of the narco slaves, they would have relied solely on fists and boots.

The Able Team leader caught a strong whiff of beans cooking inside the trailers. The familiar sweet aroma mixed with the cat urine stink of the meth lab. The effect was like a snap kick to Lyons's solar plexus.

Then another set of headlights appeared on the horizon. These were blue-white halogens, coming from the east, the direction of the farm's main house. Lyons had seen the Feds' aerial-surveillance photos of the building, which looked like an upscale Vegas whorehouse. A sprawling, fieldstone-faced split level with a two-story, five-car garage, a swimming pool, tennis courts and gardens.

The workers, *rancheros* and bangers all stopped and stared as a midnight-black Lexus LX740 pulled up and parked. A pair of tall, fit-looking Mexicans got out of the front of the big V-8 SUV, both in short leather jackets, slacks and shiny, pointy-toed dress shoes. The third man, who exited the left rear door, looked as if he'd just rolled out of bed. He wore a gaudy, striped silk bathrobe that fell to his knees and gray snakeskin, silver-toe-capped cowboy boots. His body was round through the middle, like a spider, his cheeks pendulous with flab. His slicked-back black hair hung down in long coils around his narrow, sloping shoulders. Lyons immediately recognized the mafia underboss from the Feds' mugshot gallery. Don Xavier was greedily smoking his breakfast, a fat, juicy, ten-inch-long Cuban cigar.

All the cards were on the table.

DEA knew about the eastern Washington meth lab, but it was holding back its strike teams while it bargained for the Mexican government's assistance in scooping up the cartel kingpins in Baja. The agency was looking for a really big score, and headlines to match. As usual, negotiations between international bureaucrats were going nowhere. While the desk jockeys made faces at one another over six-course lunches, the criminals continued to rake in drug-trade profits, and their spent, poisoned slaves ended up in the fields surrounding the Moses Lake site, in shallow, unmarked graves.

Stony Man, and specifically its three-man subset, Able Team, had been ordered by the President to land a blow the dirtballs would understand. The kind of blow that conventional law enforcement wasn't prepared to deliver.

AFTER THE CONVOY of rental trucks rattled past, Herman "Gadgets" Schwarz rose from the floorboards in front of the Deere combine's bench seat. He rolled up his ski mask, exposing his face, then decocked and reholstered his silenced Beretta 93-R.

Schwarz shoved open the grimy slider window on the passenger side of the cab, which faced the meth factory compound. The early-morning air that rushed in felt heavy and damp; the sun was just peeking out, a seam of neon orange on the horizon.

He shared the combine's wide bench seat with a .50-caliber Barrett Model 90 rifle. The bolt-action, bullpup-style weapon weighed twenty-five pounds; it was the little brother of the thirty-two-pound semiauto Barrett Model 82 A-1. Its forty-five-inch barrel was sixteen inches shorter than the 82 A-1, making it more portable. Unlike the semiauto Light Fifty, there was no backward barrel movement when it fired, which made for better accuracy. To compensate for the additional recoil, it was fitted with a dual-chamber muzzle brake that dampened the kick to 12-gauge levels. The gun's telescope was from Geodesic Sights; in addition to standard optics, it was factory equipped with a laser range finder to verify target distance.

There was already plenty of light to shoot by.

From his knapsack on the floor, Schwarz took out a pair of Lightning 31 ear muffs and two extra 10-round magazines. He pulled on the ear protectors and set the mags close to hand on the seat. Like the clip already in the Barrett, one was loaded with black-tipped, armor-piercing M-2 boattails. The Model 90 was zeroed at 100 yards. At that range, a 709-grain M-2 slug would penetrate almost two inches of nonarmored steel. The other mag contained blue-tipped M-8s, armor-piercing incendiaries.

Schwarz draped the metal sill with a folded bath towel, then pushed the Barrett's muzzle, barrel and retracted bipod legs through the window, resting the short, ventilated forestock on the pad. He snugged the rifle butt into his shoulder and scanned downrange through the scope. From his elevated position in the cab, he controlled the entire killzone.

His assignment was simple: close the barn door.

NOBODY NOTICED when a gray-haired man in overalls suddenly popped up at the edge of the field. The guards were occupied with the slaves, and the slaves with the guards.

The third member of Able Team wore a stained, holed-out T-shirt under his denim bibfronts, exposing the lean, corded muscle in his arms and shoulders. Rosario "the Politician" Blancanales didn't bother to brush the wet soil from the front of his jeans, dirt he'd picked up crawling along the furrows and over the fresh graves. Only his intense black eyes were visible above a cheap polyester dust mask.

Most of the slaves had the masks on, too, either over their faces or hanging down around their chins on the elastic straps. The masks were a psych job by the mafia slavemasters. They did nothing to protect the workers from toxic chemicals. Only biohazard suits with self-contained air supplies could do that.

His head lowered like the others, Blancanales fell in at the rear of the line, moving in short, shuffling steps as if his ankles were bound, too. But they weren't. The frayed cuffs of his jeans dragged on the ground, hiding that fact. He held his right hand tucked inside the bib. Out of sight against his chest, he held a suppressor-equipped Beretta 93-R, safety off, live round under the hammer.

As Blancanales stepped past the meth lab, he stole a peek inside. There was no proper door, just a single, man-size hole hacked through the rusting corrugated steel. A piece of discolored sheet plastic had been pulled aside to let the caustic fumes escape. Propane lamps hung from a cable stretched the length of the narrow enclosure, illuminating a long sawhorse table cluttered with funnels, rubber tubing, and plastic and glass jugs. Propane burners flickered blue under blackened pots. Bedsheets stretched over metal garbage cans were being used to filter the meth. Empty starter fluid, drain cleaner containers and torn plastic and cardboard from battery and pill bottle packaging littered the floor. Outside the doorway stood knee-high piles of the same. The lab's hazardous refuse had created a dead zone around the camp, clearly visible in the Feds' aerial photos.

The other workers kept their eyes on the ground, their expressions vacant, their faces rimed with dirt. Chemicals involuntarily absorbed through lungs and skin had cooked their nervous systems. The meth cowboys inched everyone forward, using their clubs now and then to speed up progress, or maybe just for the exercise.

There was no morning head count. The cowboys couldn't do anything about overnight escapees, if there were any. And the possibility of an extra worker showing up had probably never even crossed their minds.

The little Mexican guy right in front of Blancanales was a herky-jerky skeleton; he could have been sixty years old or thirty. As the man staggered forward, he muttered to himself, repeating the same phrase over and over. *"Lo siento mucho. Lo siento mucho. Lo siento mucho."*

Blancanales didn't ask him what he was so sorry for.

The lights were on, but nobody was home.

Ahead of him, in the middle of the slave pack, were three very pregnant teenage girls. Their long black hair was matted to their skulls, their short dresses stained and so threadbare they were see-through. From the dossier that Blancanales had read back at the Farm, he figured the don had put them all in the family way. For Xavier, child molestation was one of the job perks.

When the big black Lexus rolled up, cowboys and slaves froze in their tracks. Xavier and his bodyguards exited the SUV and headed straight for the lead rental truck.

The mobster passed so close to Blancanales that under the aroma of cigar he could smell the man's hair tonic. Fruity sweet. Mango-pineapple.

Beretta in hand, index finger resting on the wide combat trigger, Blancanales could have shot the underboss in the back of the head as he walked by. That he held his fire was a matter of fair play, but it had nothing to do with the fact that the don was unarmed. Given the animal's track record, Blancanales didn't want death to come as a big, fat surprise.

Flanked by his bodyguards, Xavier stepped up to the driver of the lead truck. As the bald banger leaned forward to accept the don's patronizing hug and backslap, his unbuttoned gray plaid shirt gaped wide. Against a crisp white T-shirt, Blancanales saw the polished walnut butt of a chrome Magnum revolver hooked over the front of his trouser waistband.

Embrace suffered, the driver handed the bulging gym bag to the don, who gingerly tested its weight on two fingers, then passed it over to one of his bodyguards without looking inside. Last stop for the money train. The driver turned and shouted at the other bangers, who immediately rolled up the trucks' cargo doors and started pulling out the loading ramps.

A few seconds later, a dozen very frightened people stumbled down the first truck's ramp, their mouths duct-taped shut, their wrists bound behind their backs with plastic cable ties.

Replacements for the dead and the dying.

A couple of cowboys used their clubs to drive the new workers over to the SUV, and then made them kneel on the ground beside it. The women wept into the poisoned dirt; the men blinked wide-eyed. One look around, one whiff of synthetic cat urine and they knew they had arrived smack-dab in hell.

The slaves at the front of the line shuffled by the newbies, up the ramps of the two nearest trucks. As Blancanales inched by those vehicles, the workers began to emerge. Using dollies, they off-loaded metal canisters of anhydrous ammonia and propane, and fifty-five-gallon drums of ether, toluene, acetone and isopropyl alcohol. They rolled the heavy drums across the hard-packed dirt and deposited them in front of the customized cargo container.

Blancanales showed a tad too much interest in the proceedings. Out of the corner of his eye he saw a blow coming from behind, but was too late to avoid it. The bamboo club whipcracked between his shoulder blades, making him stumble a half step forward. His flesh went numb. For a moment he couldn't breathe; his chest was paralyzed from the shock. Then his back burned as if it had been blowtorched. He knew he had been cut. He could feel hot blood trickling down his spine.

"¡Rápido!" the man who'd struck him growled.

Blancanales glared over his shoulder at a potbellied thug in a tattered straw cowboy hat. The top three snaps of his faded denim Western shirt were undone, exposing a hairless brown chest. His round cheeks were cratered with pocks of assorted sizes, as if he'd taken a load of birdshot point-blank. His small black eyes were set close together under a single black eyebrow. A tooled leather scabbard riding high on his left hip held a stag-handled, gold-pommeled and cross-guarded guthook sheath knife.

The mafia enforcer took Blancanales's stare as a direct challenge. He raised the bamboo club high overhead. His little eyes glittered with delight when his intended victim didn't raise his hands to protect himself.

Hidden autopistol in hand, Blancanales stood his ground. He was already in position. Lyons and Schwarz both had line of sight on him.

It was as good a time as any to start the party.

Blancanales pivoted his hips, turning sideways to his

attacker, poking the sound suppressor's muzzle from behind the bibfront. The Beretta chugged once in his fist. The muffled gunshot was lost in the clatter of heavily loaded dollies rolling down steel ramps.

The 9 mm round caught the cowboy dead center in his torso, just below the tip of his sternum. Grimacing, he clutched at his chest with his free hand. His mouth opened wide, but no sound came out, just a puff of bright blood mist, propelled by an explosive final breath. His right knee buckled and he crumpled, dropping onto his face, loose and boneless like a bag of beans. There was no exit wound out the middle of his back—the subsonic Parabellum round lacked the power to through and through.

One of the other cowboys saw him drop and rushed over to render aid. The *ranchero* knelt beside the fallen man. When the cowboy grabbed his friend's shoulder and turned him over, the weeping red hole was there for all to see. Putting two and two together, proximity and conflict, the cowboy jumped to his feet, swinging his sawed-off 12-gauge around on its shoulder sling. *"¡Asesino!"* he howled at Blancanales.

This time Blancanales shielded his eyes with a forearm, but not to defend himself from a load of double-aught buck.

A 709-grains boattail slug transformed the cowboy's skull, crown to chin, into pink vapor and hot, wet shrapnel an instant before the hollow boom of the Barrett fifty rolled over the camp.

WHEN THE COWBOY RAISED the club to strike Blancanales in the face, Lyons had the green light. He yanked the MP-5 SD-3s from their scabbards and scrambled out of the ditch. As he straightened his legs, both of his buttocks cramped up. When he broke into a run anyway, it felt as if they'd been speared crossways with a barbecue skewer.

The pain didn't slow him down; it made him a whole lot madder.

Lyons had trained in Shotokan karate, but his natural fighting style was pure berserker. He relied on split-second reactions and survival instinct. Wildman rage and the accompanying adrenaline rush helped to ramp up both.

In squishy wet boots, the big man charged across open ground for the rear of the shotgun shack, forcing his legs to move under him, stomping the feeling back into his feet. He angled hard to the left, out of Schwarz's lane of fire. The tumbledown shack and the meth lab just beyond it momentarily concealed his advance. On the far side of those structures, slaves and slavemasters were preoccupied with the unloading of the still idling rental trucks.

Lyons had assigned himself the task of reaching last truck in line, thereby outflanking the enemy, dividing their fire and compressing the battle in time and space.

It was the only way a handful of attackers could annihilate an opposition six times their number.

As Lyons ran from the front of the shack, sprinting across the strip of hardpan for the corner of the cargo container, Schwarz cut loose with the Barrett. Twenty yards to Lyons's right a round whined past at chin height. Even though he knew it was coming, even though he had heard it many times before, the sound of that much lead flying by made the short hairs stand up on the back of his neck.

Five long strides brought him to the end of the meth lab and gave him a clear view of the last two trucks in line. On the sides of the cargo boxes above a screen painting of a joyous, all-American family in transit was the rental company's ad slogan, Moving Your Way.

No one in Lyons's sights was moving, though. The cannonlike bellow of the Light Fifty had frozen the slaves and their keepers in place.

Lyons broke from cover, rushing trucks 3 and 4. As the Barrett's report echoed off in the distance, the legitimate targets and innocent bystanders started running in all directions. It was like one of those computer-simulated target-acquisition training systems, except instead of one shooter there were more than fifteen, and instead of one hostage there were at least twenty.

A torrent of gunfire roared to his right, out of sight, on the far side of the meth lab. It wasn't directed at him. Somewhere in the back of his mind the weapons' distinctive sound signatures registered: shotguns, pistols and sustained bursts from AK-47s, all of them presumably tracking Blancanales and pouring return fire on the combine.

The quartet of bangers at the last two trucks saw Lyons coming between the bodies of the slow-moving slaves. How could they miss him? Honking big dude, all in black, ski mask pulled down to his chin, silenced machine pistols raised in both fists. The bangers responded in a way Lyons couldn't, not with a firing lane choked by noncombatants. As the cowboys back-stepped to cover between truck 4's front bumper and Truck 3's rear, they opened up with blue-steel 9 mm autopistols, shooting around, then through the panicked, hobbled workers.

Close-range body and head shots blew the stumbling, helpless obstacles off their bare feet.

Almost simultaneously the Barrett boomed again. Truck 4's front end rocked hard as it absorbed a .50-caliber round. On impact, the hood delatched and popped partway up. A piercing metal-on-metal screech erupted from the bowels of the idling V-8 as the AP slug plowed through its block. A fraction of an instant later, the engine let out a final, grinding clank as tie rods and pistons broke loose. Smoke and steam boiled from the engine compartment. Hot oil and antifreeze sprayed over the crouched bangers.

Lyons took advantage of the cleared firing lane. As he charged, he cut loose with both MP-5 SD-3s, 3-round bursts to minimize muzzle climb. Staggering backward, half-blinded and panicked, the gangsters tried to return fire. The one in front, a baggy-pants wide boy with blue tats covering both arms from wrists to elbows took a point-blank round from one of his own homeys through the back of the head. The right side of his face just vanished, revealing a red crater from eyebrow to cheek. Gushing bright arterial blood, braindead on his feet, he toppled to the dirt.

The MP-5 SD-3s stuttered in Lyons's big fists, saturating the killzone as he closed the ten yards of intervening ground. Twisting in agony under the hail of slugs, the three bangers went down hard.

And stayed down.

Lyons jumped over the jerking bodies, slipping between trucks 3 and 4. Slaves were bellycrawling under the chassis, taking cover behind the steel wheels. Through the greasy smoke billowing from the engine compartment, he could see others robot-walking across the fields, stray bullets whizzing around them, kicking up puffs of soil.

When he peeked around the cargo box, two of the remaining four bangers were in full retreat, joining up with the cowboys who had taken cover beside the first truck and the front of the cargo container meth lab.

A couple of the cowboys were facedown in the dirt.

Blancanales was nowhere in sight.

A *ranchero* jumped out of the meth-lab doorway, landed flat-footed and tried to drill him with a hip-leveled Kalashnikov. Lyons's reaction time was faster. The Russian rounds went skyward as the shooter abruptly sat down, driven to his backside by a string of 9 mm rounds to the gut. Lyons ducked back as answering fire ripped along the line of trucks. In so doing, he nearly stepped on the face of one of the downed bangers. Brown eyes stared up at him, not angry, not surprised. Not anything, ever again.

With incoming fire hammering the right side of truck 3's cargo box and ricocheting off the dirt, he dumped the spent mags and reloaded the machine pistols. It took him less than eight seconds to put live rounds under both firing pins. Turning left, away from the meth lab, he burst out from behind the rear bumper and took off along the outside of the line of vehicles to seal off any enemy foot retreat across the fields and allow Schwarz to mark his position.

Before he got halfway along truck 3 the Light Fifty roared again. Twenty feet ahead of him the cab shuddered as an M-2 round slammed its engine compartment, popping off a spawl of paint the size of a dinner plate. An instant later, the V-8 inside exploded with a muffled roar, freed pistons punching through cylinders and valve covers, windshield popping out of its frame, cab doors flying open, front wheel covers suddenly airborne.

Another killshot.

When he reached truck 3's front bumper, a pair of bangers inside the cargo box of truck 2 popped up from behind tall canisters of anhydrous ammonia, autopistols blazing. Slaves lay on the floor of the cargo box all around them, hands protecting the backs of their heads, faces pressed into the deck.

Lyons sprayed one-handed, up-angled autofire across the bangers' chests, whipsawing them off their feet. Their guns went flying and their bodies landed heavily on the backs of the prostrated slaves, who were too afraid to move.

As he ran on, the Barrett cut loose again. Truck 2 shuddered as its engine tore itself apart. Six-foot-high flames shot up around the buckled hood.

The volleys of gunfire from the meth lab suddenly trailed off. Over the scattered gunshots Lyons could hear shouting in Spanish. Trucks 4, 3 and 2 were burning, acrid gray smoke sweeping across the compound like ground fog.

Even drug dealers could read the handwriting on the wall. No transportation, no escape.

With a roar and spray of dirt, the black Lexus SUV sped around the front of the first truck, riding on two flat steel radials on the driver's side. Lyons caught a glimpse of a candy-striped silk robe as the rear door swung shut.

SCHWARZ RODE the Barrett's stunning recoil wave, simultaneously working the bolt to chamber a fresh round. Downrange, beneath a puff of glistening red mist, the headless corpse folded up like a lawnchair. The Able Team commando had a chance for another clear, quick shot at an enemy gunner, but he passed it up, instead swinging the crosshairs hard over to the right, to his assigned first target. Numbers had to fall in order for Lyons's battle plan to work.

No deviations.

As the narco cowboys ran for cover they fired back wildly, spraying bullets his way. The location of his hide was pretty obvious: it was the only elevated position in miles of pancake-flat farmland. At a range of one hundred yards the pistol shots didn't even land close, but the Russian autorifle rounds thunked and rattled the broad side of the combine. As he aimed at truck 4's engine compartment and took up the trigger slack, a slug plowed through the rear of the cab two feet to his right, peppering that side of his face with hot metallic grit. He ignored it.

Schwarz knew Lyons was advancing inside the new firing lane, but he had the Able Team leader's designated route to target down cold. The ex-L.A. cop was protected by two layers of cover—the engine block and the meth lab.

The Barrett thundered, battering Schwarz's shoulder as he touched off the round. His arm was still tender from the forty practice rounds he had fired two days before in Virginia.

"Twelve-gauge recoil levels, my ass," he muttered as he ejected the spent round and reacquired the sight picture. Smoke and steam poured out from under the truck's half-open hood.

Not at all surprising.

The cyberteam at Stony Man Farm never left anything to chance. They had blueprinted engine design and placement, drawing virtual bull's-eyes for him on the sides of the vehicles.

Right on schedule, Lyons darted out from between the last two trucks. As he did so, Schwarz fired another M-2 round. Truck 3's front end shuddered, then rocked when the engine blew apart. The Barrett's bolt snicked back, butter smooth, and a huge smoking brass hull flipped up and out of the action.

Locking down the bolt on the third cartridge, he put the sight post on truck 2's ten-ring and let it rip. Though he thought he was snugged up nice and tight, the Light Fifty's buttstock slammed into him. The stunning impact sent daggers of pain up the side of his neck and down his shoulder.

It did much worse to the rental truck.

When the engine deconstructed, flying shrapnel blew out both front tires. As the axle dropped onto its rims, the hood lurched up and the engine compartment belched flame and smoke.

Before he could snap the cap on truck 1, the drug lord's black Lexus burst into view from behind it, bouncing over the furrows at high speed, making a beeline for the farmhouse. Schwarz took a swinging lead on the target and broke trigger. The Barrett bellowed, its minimal forestock jumping high off the bath-towel cushion.

No way could the Lexus's bulletproof glass deflect a .50-caliber AP slug.

Downrange, the SUV's driver's window vanished from the frame as it imploded. A nanosecond later, the passenger's window exploded. As the passenger's window disintegrated, two sets of brains and skull bones mixed with a glittering shower of shattered, gray-tinted glass.

The Lightning 31 earmuffs didn't completely muffle the sustained bleating of the SUV's horn as the vehicle rolled onward, driverless. To hear better, Schwarz edged the sonic protector off his right ear.

The Lexus rolled slower and slower as it bumped over the furrows. The horn suddenly stopped blowing. On the far side of the vehicle, the rear door opened and Xavier bailed with the black gym bag. Stumbling on his skinny bare legs in his thousand-dollar cowboy boots, he waved for his troops to regroup around him. Four cowboys did so, partially blocking the don from view.

Schwarz could have taken him out by shooting through the others, but he held his fire. Kneading out the .50-caliber whiplash in his neck and shoulder, he kept one eye pinned to the scope. He watched as Xavier and his human shields sprinted for the meth lab where the rest of the crew had holed up. After they had scurried between the barrels of offloaded chemicals and slipped inside the crude doorway, Schwarz replaced the earmuff and resumed work, methodically punching a few big-bore rounds through the corrugated walls. He shot high on purpose, to keep the opposition pinned and unable to return aimed fire. The .50-caliber impacts raised clouds of dust from the metal roof. He could imagine what it was like for the dirtbags inside. Like being sealed in a fifty-five-gallon steel drum while someone beat on it with a sledgehammer.

When the tenth spent cartridge flipped out of the action, clinking on the others lying beside him on the bench seat, Schwarz left the bolt open and stripped out the empty clip. He reached for the mag loaded with M-8s and slapped it home.

As he peered back through the scope's eyepiece, something dark flew out of the lab entrance and landed in the dirt about fifteen feet away. It was the overstuffed gym bag. Schwarz again slipped off the Lightning 31's cup. He could hear someone yelling from the doorway. He couldn't make out whether it was in Spanish or English, but the idea was pretty obvious.

Take the bag of cash and leave me the fuck alone.

Schwarz covered his ear, then slid the Light Fifty's bolt forward, chambering a blue-tipped incendiary round.

Some things money just couldn't buy.

BLANCANALES LOWERED his bloody forearm and pulled the silenced Beretta 93-R from underneath the denim bibfront. He concealed the pistol along the outside of his right thigh. Nobody was looking directly at him. Slaves and slavemasters were either staring at the practically headless guy on the ground or gawking uprange for the source of the stunning killshot.

Global paralysis lasted an instant.

Gunmen unleashed sawing bursts of autofire as they sprinted for the nearest cover. As the bangers and cowboys scattered, Blancanales dropped to a knee beside the freshly made corpses and yanked the guthook sheath knife free of its scabbard.

The meth slaves scattered, too, but slowly because of their ankle restraints. Some headed for shelter under the trucks, while others set off across the fields. The three pregnant girls were moving the slowest of all, cradling their swollen bellies in both hands as they shuffled barefoot in the dust, their backs to the conflict.

The replacement workers huddled in a cowering knot beside the Lexus SUV.

A flurry of tightly spaced pistol shots rang out from the end of the line of trucks, then the Barrett boomed again. The second shot from the .50-caliber rifle sent half of the opposition diving for cover inside the meth lab. Xavier and his two bodyguards were the first through the crude doorway. The pair of single-wide trailers was 150 feet away, across a stretch of open ground. Because the bangers and *rancheros* had all seen how accurately Schwarz could shoot, none of them made a break in that direction.

For his part, Blancanales faced a difficult choice. There was a slim chance he could get some of the forced laborers to safety before the numbers ran down to zero. He couldn't communicate with the burned-out zombies among them; and even if he could have, he didn't have bolt cutters to sever the loops of braided-steel wire around their ankles. The newly arrived slaves' wrists were secured behind their backs with nylon cable ties, but their ankles weren't bound yet. They could run. Their brains weren't fried by toxic chemicals, either, so at least there was a possibility they could understand and follow simple commands.

Saving some was better than saving none.

As always, living and dying was largely a matter of luck.

Blancanales ran for the Lexus and the newbies. In the chaos of heavy-caliber incoming and massed, full-auto outgoing, nobody was paying any attention to him or to them. When the kneeling prisoners saw a blood-spattered, masked man with a wickedly curved blade bearing down on them, their eyes widened in terror.

Caught between gunbattle and guthook, they were too frightened to flee. They didn't resist when he started grabbing their wrists and parting the nylon ties with deft snicks of the hook blade.

As one of the men rose warily to his feet, he jerked violently sideways and went down hard. The front of his stained T-shirt was spotted with dime-sized holes from a load of double-aught buck. The shooter, a cowboy who had been hiding behind truck 1, cycled the action of his 12-gauge pump as he advanced on the Lexus. Before the gunner could cut loose again, Blancanales raised the Beretta from behind his hip and ripped off four rapid-fire shots over the SUV's hood. Two of the silenced rounds went wide of the target, but two hit the cowboy. One struck his left shoulder and the other bored straight through the middle of his crotch. Dropping his sawed-off shotgun on its sling, clutching his groin in both hands, the *ranchero* fell to the dirt, writhing like a worm on a fishhook.

There was no time to free the rest of the prisoners. Blancanales yelled at them in Spanish, "Get up! Help each other! Hurry!"

Tossing the sheath knife aside, he aimed the Beretta at the SUV's driver's side front tire and fired once, point-blank, through the sidewall, dropping it onto its rims. As he ran on, he did the same to the rear tire.

"*¡Vámonos!*" he shouted, waving for them to follow him.

In seconds the Able Team warrior caught up to the slowest of the three fleeing pregnant teenagers. He paused just long enough to scoop up the girl. As he did so, a .50-caliber report rolled over his back and an instant later a truck exploded with a dull whump! The girl was light in his arms, and she didn't twist or struggle in his grasp. She had learned to be compliant when set upon by a male. Which probably explained why she had survived.

The other two girls were stumbling along fifteen feet ahead. "Carry them!" he yelled over his shoulder.

His tone of voice and the gun in his hand left no room for discussion.

Two of the freed men stopped and quickly gathered up the pregnant girls, carrying them as they ran.

Blancanales closed on the trailers with caustic smoke flowing from the burning trucks swirling around him, stinging his eyes. The Light Fifty boomed again, and a car horn started to blow. He didn't look back.

On the far side of the single-wides, Blancanales put down the girl. Her baby face was contorted with fear, but she just stood there, a doe in the headlights. She didn't move even when he turned away. As he roughly ushered the others forward, the car horn stopped and the gunfire dwindled, as well. Someone started yelling from the meth lab. He couldn't make out the words.

"Get down! Quick!" Blancanales shouted in Spanish, shoving the prisoners from behind. "On the ground! Cover your heads!"

Then time ran out.

THE METH SLAVES HIDING under burning truck 2 didn't budge at Lyons's urging. They stared back at him as if he were the bogeyman. The unintelligible shouting of a huge guy in a ski mask with two autoweapons didn't do much to instill confidence and trust.

Lyons slung one of the machine pistols, then lunged forward, grabbing the nearest laborer by the arm. "The rest of you, come on!" he yelled. "You can't stay under there! You're all gonna die if you do!"

The raggedy laborer went limp on him. Deadweight in the dirt. Lyons hauled him out from under the chassis anyway, but as soon as he let go, the man turned and crawled right back.

The heat from the engine fire was getting worse. So was the oily smoke. The situation was flat-out impossible. There was nothing Lyons could do. In the end, self-preservation had to take precedence over rescue.

"Shit!" he snarled in frustration as he bailed. High-kicking, he raced back the way he had come, around the last truck in line, past the end of the meth lab and the corner of the shotgun shack, heading for the irrigation canal. A single gunshot from the Barrett rang out, followed by a massive, billowing explosion. Behind him, at the edges of his peripheral vision, the world turned a brilliant orange. Holding the machine pistols overhead, he jumped for the irrigation ditch. In midair, icy cold slammed his back, penetrating right through his blacksuit. A fraction of a second later the overloaded nerves correctly registered the sensation as heat.

Skin-blistering heat.

As he plunged into the ditch water, the explosion's concussive force pitched him forward, face first toward the far bank.

SCHWARZ NEEDED ONLY ONE API round to send the whole narco compound straight to hell.

He put the M-8 incendiary slug through the middle of one of the fifty-five-gallon chemical barrels lined up in front of the meth lab. On impact, there was an intense white flash. A fraction of a second later, with a resounding boom the targeted drum became a forty-foot-wide, forty-foot-high ball of flame. The initial explosion set off a chain reaction with the other drums and with the cargo container. In a stunning instant, the raw materials of meth mass production—acetone, toluene, ether—were transformed into nothing less than a napalm bomb.

At the center of the seething fireball, the cargo container flew apart; the detonation's shock wave blew off the roof of the tumbledown shack and rocked the single-wide trailers off their cinder-block foundations. As a churning black mushroom cloud erupted from the center of the explosion, the heaviest debris began raining down, a torrent of unrecognizable metallic junk falling through the flaming mist.

Like a string of massive firecrackers, the gas tanks and cargo boxes of the rental trucks exploded one by one.

The initial blast sent the trailer nearest to the lab sliding off its foundation. With a sickening screech it dominoed into the second single-wide and knocked it loose, as well. For an instant the sky overhead was the color of flame.

"Stay down!" Blancanales howled as one of the forced workers broke for the open fields behind them. "Cover your heads!"

The runner got maybe twenty feet before he was cut down by a cartwheeling, six-foot chunk of corrugated sheet steel. Its ragged edge caught him square in the back and pancaked him into the dirt.

Lighter and lighter materials pelted the field, then came a rain of fine, choking dust. Mixed in were burning bits of green paper, the contents of the black duffel. The meth lab had become a smoking hole in the ground.

Dripping wet, Carl Lyons appeared through the drug-profit confetti, a muddy smudge on the forehead and cheek of his ski mask.

Glancing at the surviving slaves scattering in all directions, Blancanales said, "What do you think, should we call INS to pick them up?"

"Not our job," Lyons replied. "Besides, these people have been through enough for one day. Let's get the hell out of here."

The two men quickly dragged the limp bodies out of the blackened, blistered SUV and brushed some of the glass off the leather seats. Lyons then drove it on two flats across the field where Schwarz waited beside the combine. As he rode in the back with the Barrett, Schwarz looked up at the gore sprayed over the head-liner and dash and said, "Man, I really made a mess of this ride, didn't I?"

Lyons flattened the gas pedal and the SUV bounded forward, porpoising over the furrows and slewing through the soft, tilled earth. The designated landing zone was a half mile away from the killzone, just in case the mop-up was incomplete.

It wasn't.

When Lyons stopped the Lexus, nothing but rims were left on the driver's side. At once a gray-and-red helicopter popped up out of the north, swinging in very low and very fast. Because of the ongoing federal airspace surveillance, Jack Grimaldi's landing was touch-and-go. The second the skids struck dirt, Able Team piled in.

No time for small talk.

A half-smoked, unlit cigar clenched in his teeth, Grimaldi vaulted the chopper off the ground with a sickening lurch, then wheeled it around 180 degrees, dropping to fencepost height and really putting the hammer down.

"DEA closing in?" Blancanales asked as he snapped into a safety harness.

"Are you kidding?" the deeply tanned pilot growled over his shoulder. "The Feds' mouths are still hanging open."

"Then where's the goddamn fire?" Lyons asked.

"Two hours away. Just got word from the Farm on the secure line. Shit has hit the fan over on the coast…this one's big time."

CHAPTER TWO

Stony Man Farm, Virginia,
9:49 a.m. EDT

Fourteen minutes after the Russian sub ran aground on Ediz Hook, eight minutes after receiving a frantic hotline call from the White House, five minutes after Jack Grimaldi was notified of the situation via secure scrambled channel, Hal Brognola was still staring at the satellite feed replay on the flat panel wallscreen. He couldn't help himself. The other members of the Stony Man team—mission controller Barbara Price, weapons specialist John "Cowboy" Kissinger, and the elite cyber squad of Aaron "the Bear" Kurtzman, Huntington Wethers, Akira Tokaido and Carmen Delahunt—were all having the same reaction.

Recurring disbelief.

The image on the screen was that shocking.

The bow of the huge black foreign warship jutted out of U.S. waters, its submerged propeller churning up plumes of froth. In the background, not one hundred yards away, stood the little orange Coast Guard air station hangar at the tip of Ediz Hook.

A second flat-panel wallscreen was filled with jerky live-feed video with sound from a circling Coast Guard helicopter. A dense pillar of smoke boiled up from the sub's sail, drifting lazily south over the little mill town.

Brognola knew that at that moment additional Coast Guard and Navy helicopters from Neah Bay and Whidbey Island, respectively, were en route, as was the emergency-nuclear-response unit from sub base Bangor on Hood Canal. ETA on the ENR team was five more minutes. Meanwhile, scrambled A-6s from Whidbey Naval Air Station were already screaming low over the scene, sealing off the airspace.

As the Coast Guard video zoomed in tight on the sub's stern and the churning prop, the head Fed couldn't help but grimace. Nuke-powered boat running full tilt half out of the water, smoke pouring out amidships. Brognola wasn't the only one who visualized dire consequences.

"For pete's sake, why doesn't the crew shut down the engines!" Barbara Price exclaimed.

"It's got to be hotter than hell in there," Hunt Wethers said. The African American, former Berkeley cybernetics professor gestured at the screen with the mouthpiece of his unlit pipe and said, "Why hasn't anyone bailed from the sub?"

"Maybe they can't get out," Akira Tokaido suggested. "Exit routes all blocked…"

"Actually, the damage doesn't look that bad," Kissinger told the young Japanese American. "Like a lot of the Russian subs, the hull is probably made up of two layers, an inner and outer skin with six feet of crush space between them, so even grounded there might not be a full breach. I've never seen that design configuration before, but the ship is similar to the Bars class attack subs—something just over three hundred feet in length. There's got to be at least thirty or forty crew on board."

"Is it carrying nukes?" Delahunt asked. The redheaded former FBI agent and divorced mother of three put her finger right on the hot button.

"It's an SSN, not a ballistic-missile sub," Kissinger said, "but who knows what armament's on board."

"There's a nuclear reactor, though," Brognola countered.

"Actually there are probably *two* pressurized water reactors," Kissinger corrected him.

"They are the critical issue at this point," Brognola said. "Something's already burning inside."

Kissinger immediately picked up the thread. "If sub's reactors catch fire," he said, "their nuclear material will be released into the surrounding air and water. If there are nukes onboard, they won't detonate from the heat, but their payloads will be dispersed."

Aaron Kurtzman pivoted his wheelchair to face the others. "With strong tides running all the way to Seattle and Tacoma," he said gravely, "the scale of the disaster would be unthinkable."

"And for all intents and purposes, irreparable," Wethers added.

The last comment was met by silence.

"The ENR unit is going to have to work quickly," Kissinger said. "They've got to get inside the ship, put out the fires and shut down propulsion. After that, they can start a full damage assessment, structural and nuclear. If it turns out the sub can be safely towed off the point, they have to identify and secure all hull breaches by sealing internal bulkhead doors."

"Do you think they'll meet resistance from the crew?" Price asked.

"A separate SEAL team will deal with that," Brognola answered for him. "They'll handle the initial boarding and pacification, if necessary."

The scene on the live-feed video suddenly shifted as the Coast Guard chopper wheeled to the north, flying around the edge of the smoke plume. The Hook's narrow road curved past the Daishowa pulp mill before joining up with the mainland at the head of the bay. Five Port Angeles police cars were parked across the two-lane road with lights flashing. On the far side of the cruisers, the town's entire complement of fire engines and ambulances sat idling, waiting for an all-clear so they could approach the stranded ship.

Traffic had already started to back up on the road behind the EMTs. It wasn't just night-shift mill hands who'd deserted their posts for a look, or morning-shift workers waiting around for their day to begin. The resounding impact of the sub's grounding had awakened most of the city's population. From virtually every street corner on the hillsides above the bay, if not every kitchen window, the black ship was a visible blot on the landscape. In response, whole families had piled into their cars and vans, heading for the Hook in hopes of getting a closer view of the spectacular accident. As a result, the streets of Port Angeles's tiny downtown were gridlocked, bumper to bumper. The smarter folks, the few who could distinguish imminent danger from free circus, were already streaming out of town in the other direction, on Highway 101.

The Coast Guard helicopter veered to the left and swung out over Port Angeles Bay. Its video feed revealed an armada of small and large boats racing from the mainland shore, all making a beeline for the Hook and the object of curiosity. The chopper pilot flew low and fast on an intercept course.

Stony Man's wallscreen filled with a bird's-eye view of the sixteen-foot runabout leading the pack. Its lone passenger was hanging on to the windshield with one hand, trying to use a digital camcorder with the other. Rotor wash whipped a ring of froth around the little boat, forcing the photographer to sit down. It blinded the boat's pilot, and he backed off on the throttle.

Someone in the hovering aircraft, presumably the pilot or copilot, addressed the oncoming fleet through a loud-hailer. "Return to the harbor at once! For your own safety, return to shore! This is a restricted area!"

A few of the boaters immediately turned back; however, most ignored the command. There was obviously no way to enforce it. There were too many boats and the helicopter was unarmed.

"Where's Homeland Security?" Delahunt said.

"Basically, you're looking at it," Kissinger replied. "There's a Coast Guard cutter on station out at the entrance to the Strait of Juan de Fuca. But that's almost two hours away. A handful of part-time DHS personnel man the international border where the ferry from Canada docks."

"No way anyone could have foreseen something like this," Brognola said emphatically. "This should *never* have happened."

"Okay, John," Price said, turning to the Farm's weapon systems analyst, "give us your best guess. How is what we're looking at even possible?"

"The U.S. antisubmarine—ASW—warfare program consists of layered defenses using different technologies," Kissinger said. "Some of them are cold war era, some more recent. There's SURTASS, surveillance towed array system. RDSS, rapidly deployable surveillance system. LRMP, long-range marine patrol, armed with magnetic-anomaly detectors. There's radar and stationary directional and nondirectional sonar buoys. A more recent development is UDAR, a satellite-mounted laser aimed at the sea. It reflects off and reveals a submerged sub's wake."

"Sounds pretty solid to me," Delahunt said.

"Yeah, but you've got to keep in mind that the surveillance is covering a vast area above and below the surface. For decades, our ASW people have been monitoring the sub bases in the Sea of Okhotsk, the Barents Sea, the Kola Peninsula and Gremikha. At these choke points, Russian subs can be identified and tracked by satellite and by U.S. sub patrols on station. Past the choke points, in the open ocean, the technological net has holes."

"What do you mean by 'holes'?" Tokaido asked.

"There's an overlap of radar bounce-back, called a shadow or convergence zone, that creates a blind channel thirty-three nautical miles wide. Subs can hide in it and evade detection. The Russians have perfected the welding of titanium for their sub hulls, which makes them harder to locate through magnetic anomaly. Some of their ships can make forty-two knots submerged to three thousand feet."

"Our ships are fast, too, and our people are absolutely

top notch," Price countered. "In fact, there's no comparison."

"No argument there," Kissinger said. "Equipment and personnel aren't the problem. It's mission creep. Between the end of the cold war and the start of the second Iraq war, our fleet's patrol duties were reevaluated and redefined. The hostile threat from Russia was downgraded, and some of our subs were taken off SSBN patrol and converted into platforms for launching conventionally armed missiles against military targets in the Near East. Fewer patrols means bigger holes."

"Sorry, it still doesn't compute," Kurtzman said. "Harder to detect isn't the same as undetectable."

"I can't explain why UDAR and resonance scatter didn't pick up that ship well out to sea," Kissinger said. "At this point there's not enough data to know what happened. After Able Team arrives on scene we'll have more to work with."

"Their ETA isn't until 9:15 a.m., PDT," Brognola said. "We can't just sit here and twiddle our thumbs. From what the President told me, the Russians are denying all knowledge of the sub or the nature of the incursion. They are denying it's even their ship."

The chief of the cyberunit spoke up. "Hunt and Carmen, let's search the DOD's secure database and try to ID the ship from the hull configuration. Pull up everything about sub designers and shipyards. I'll check the satellite surveillance library and backtrack all departures from the known SSBN and SSN bases. Maybe we can figure out where this sub came from and when it left its home port."

"We don't know its route after it entered the Strait

of Juan de Fuca, either," Tokaido said. "I'll go over the sat-feed system replays, second by second. That might tell us something about the sub's mission."

"Did the President make it clear why he was calling in Able Team on this?" Price asked Brognola.

"He wants all means at his disposal."

"Able can do things the white ops can't," Wethers said.

"Like shoot reporters?" Delahunt joked.

"Too many talking heads, not enough bullets," Kissinger said.

"John's right," Kurtzman said. "This is going to be a three-ring circus. You can bet news helicopters from Seattle are already en route. There's no way to stop the media even if the Navy seals off the airspace. You can see that wreck from Vancouver Island in Canada, twenty-six miles away."

"Able's mission isn't a cover-up," Brognola told his people. "The President wants someone on the ground who can cut through the bullshit. He anticipates problems with overlapping responsibilities in this crisis."

"Turf wars between Homeland Security, FBI, CIA, Navy, Coast Guard and state and local police?" Delahunt asked.

"You got it," Brognola said.

"Under the circumstances, Able Team is bound to step on some toes," Kurtzman said. "And they never step lightly."

"The President doesn't care about that. He wants the job done fast, and he wants it done right."

Tokaido pointed at the wallscreen. "Here come the good guys," he said.

Live-feed video showed four Navy helicopters descending on the Hook in tight formation. As soon as their wheels touched the Coast Guard air station's landing pad, men in black jumped from the bay doors.

They hit the ground running.

CHAPTER THREE

Port Angeles, Washington,
7:02 a.m. PDT

As Commander Reuben Starkey and his ENR crew
hurriedly off-loaded gear from their helicopter onto a
pair of handcarts, the thirty-two-man SEAL team
closed on the grounded sub with autoweapons up and
ready. Half of the commando unit took up bracketing-
fire positions along the Hook's riprap, the rest leapfrog-
ging each other to the underside of the looming black
bow.

A tight, excited voice crackled in Starkey's communication headset. It was the SEAL team leader, Captain
Bradford Munsinger. "ENR, we've got severe crush
damage forward," he reported. "Background rads are
within acceptable limits. We're going up."

Commander Starkey and his four subordinates
stopped shifting equipment; they turned and watched
the SEALs in rapt silence. Like Starkey, the others were
all career Navy men. In the seven years they had worked

together at sub base Bangor, they had handled various highly classified and potentially catastrophic nuclear emergencies in Puget Sound, along the western seaboard and in the Pacific theater. Despite that experience and expertise, Starkey found himself cotton-mouthed by what lay before them this morning.

Spitless.

As far as Starkey was concerned, the unheard-of incursion into U.S. territorial waters and breach of national defense systems took a backseat to more immediate and pressing problems. A little slice of America, the Olympic Peninsula mill town, stood utterly defenseless behind them. The nuke-powered vessel was on the beach and on fire. There was no way of telling what kinds of armament the ship was carrying. The commander could feel the vibrations of the rampaging engines and prop through the airstrip's tarmac, even though the submarine was three hundred yards away.

Stepping out from under the protection of the hull, the SEALs took turns firing grappling hooks onto the deck, more than four stories above them. With the sub's sail and escape-trunk hatches zeroed in by flanking fire, black-gloved men shouldered automatic weapons and scrambled up the knotted ropes. The first SEAL to land boot soles on the steeply slanted deck was Bradford Munsinger. Following his hand signals, the others covered the forward and aft escape hatches point-blank with their 9 mm H&K machine pistols.

"Radiation is still within acceptable limits," Munsinger announced into his mike. "Come on up, boys, and join the party."

ENR stayed put. He wasn't talking to them.

Starkey and his crew watched the commandos under the bow start shinnying up the ropes. As they did so, Munsinger mounted the sail's exterior ladder with two SEALs following hard behind him. After a rapid ascent, the trio disappeared over the rim of the bridge into the uncoiling black smoke.

A moment later the captain said, "ENR, we have position and control. The bridge hatch is closed."

A head and shoulders appeared above the sail on the windward side, a tiny pimple on the enormous silhouette.

"The view from up here's nice, but the air quality sucks," Munsinger joked, his voice breaking, his breathing hard and ragged.

The man standing next to Starkey shielded his mike with his hand and said, "Cap sounds like he's been huffing helium." Dave Alvarez was a tall, lanky, fish-white nuclear engineer, and he spoke with a heavy New Jersey accent.

"Munsinger's way pumped," Chuck Howe agreed, turning his head to spit a gob of brown tobacco juice onto the tarmac.

"I know just how he feels," Alvarez said. "That sound you hear isn't castanets. It's my knees knocking."

"The smoke seems to be coming through vents in the deck plating up here," Munsinger continued after a pause. "The sail's hull is hot to the touch. Still no substantial radiation."

"Initial rescue procedures are a go, then," Starkey said into his mike.

"Roger that, ENR," Munsinger said.

Then he addressed his men. "Okay, SEALs, let's say howdy to these lost sons of bitches."

The clang of gun butts on titanium plating was drowned out by the dull, sawing roar of the engines and the pounding of the three-story-high prop. SEALs crawled over the exposed deck with listening devices, monitoring any response from the sub's crew.

The reports rattled back, all in the negative.

"What the fuck is going on!" Garwood Shambliss exclaimed.

Starkey shook his head at the black diver and pointed at the open mike under his blocklike chin, reminding him about the open channel. Shambliss could have been a SEAL himself; he was built lean and hard like one, he had the athletic skills, but his interest was in warships, not in the hands-on waging of war.

Shambliss smothered the mike in his big, scarred fist. "What…the…fuck!" he repeated, carefully enunciating each word. "Trapped inside a burning ship and nobody answers a rescue call? There should be forty sailors on that boat, minimum. And there's nobody at the helm?"

"Commander, have we got a nuclear ghost ship on our hands?" Pete Deal asked.

Starkey said, "That makes no sense, Pete." It wasn't the only thing that didn't make sense to him. The sub on the Hook didn't conform to the established Russian fleet standards. It was clearly a design variant, an undisclosed variant, in direct violation of a long-standing treaty.

"Maybe they're embarrassed," Alvarez suggested. "They just beached a one-hundred-million-dollar boat on foreign soil."

"Where the hell is HazMat?" Shambliss said, looking at the sky to the southeast. There were no aircraft in sight.

"They've got more gear and people to deal with," Starkey said. Based in Bremerton, the Navy's regional HazMat unit transported an entire mobile field hospital, operating rooms, decontamination equipment, isolation chambers, mortuary and personnel to handle catastrophic medical emergencies. Washington's only civilian HazMat unit was part of the state patrol and stationed in Tacoma, 150 miles away.

Munsinger's excited voice crackled in their headsets. "I'm going to try the bridge hatch," he announced.

A second later a puff of much thicker smoke erupted from the sail, like a wet blanket lifted from a ridgetop signal fire.

"The hatch wasn't dogged from the inside," the captain reported. "We've got clear access."

"SEAL leader, this is ENR," Starkey barked into his mike. "Do not enter subject vessel. Repeat, do not attempt to enter the vessel. Close the hatch and pull back, get out of the smoke if you possibly can. We're on our way."

To his crew, he said, "Break out the Nomex...."

With or without HazMat, they had a job to do.

Shambliss, Deal, Howe and Alvarez ripped into the ballistic nylon duffels and started yanking out gear on the double. Commander Starkey did the same. He kicked off his shoes and slipped stocking feet into the legs of his fire suit. He stepped into the attached lug boots, rammed his arms through the sleeves, then zipped up the front closure to his chin. After pulling the drawstring hood tight around his weather-seamed face and unshaved cheeks, he donned a super-high-intensity headlamp. He hung the full-face air mask from the Nomex suit's left shoulder tab and, after checking the pressure gauge, strapped the attached miniair tank to his left hip. The suit's heavy gauntlets, also fire-retardant Nomex, were securely Velcroed to the insides of the sleeves.

In their fire armor, the team finished transferring the backpack extinguishers, the cases of electronic gear and hand- and battery-operated power tools to the carts. The much more restrictive antiradiation suits were loaded on, too, in case things suddenly went even further south. With five strong men pushing, the heavily laden hand trucks moved easily along the runway. When they reached the end of the asphalt and the wheels bumped onto the loose gravel path that led to the end of the Hook, the going got difficult. Three SEALs shouldered their weapons and ran over to give them a hand. With four to a cart, they were able to half carry the trucks and gear.

"Looks like the smoke's starting to get thinner," Alvarez said as they neared the sub's bow. His lean face bulged from the pressure of the tight-fitting Nomex hood. "Maybe the crew put it out or it burned itself out."

When no one responded to the speculation, he took the hint and kept quiet. It was nervous talk. And pointless. Whatever was happening inside, they were going to be in the middle of it shortly.

When they were in the lee of the ship, the enormous raised black bow blocked out most of the sky. Crush damage to the forward keel was considerable. It was impossible to tell whether the interior hull had been damaged. As they stepped up beside the hull, the ground trembled underfoot.

Reuben Starkey had learned Russian at the military language school in Monterrey, California. He had visited the Severodvinsk shipyard as an official observer, and had guzzled vodka with Russian submariners, designers and builders. As the ENR's expert in Russian technology, he knew what had to be on board, and what might be on board. His wife, Sandy, and their three kids were in Silverdale, one hundred miles away, on the far side of the Olympics and the Hood Canal. Whatever happened here, even if it was thermonuclear, they would be safe. He took comfort from that, and he was thankful he'd made the time to kiss them all and say goodbye.

The SEALs on deck deployed rope ladders, and Starkey and the others began to climb them. Commandos on the ground hooked up other dangling lines to the assortment of ENR gear, and the men above hoisted it up, hand over hand.

The deck angle seemed even steeper when Starkey was actually standing on it. SEALs had already rigged safety cables to the sail. The vibration was tremendous, as was the noise. Starkey found it disorienting to look downward aft and see the wash deck half-submerged.

He tore his gaze from the white water roaring behind. He proceeded with one hand on the safety line to the sail's fixed ladder, then started up. The Coast Guard helicopter hovered above him at about one thousand feet. As he swung a leg over the sail's rim, he looked back, across the air strip at the cop cars and fire trucks. Seven stories high, he could see the camera flashes going off along the line of backed-up civilian traffic. Rubbernecking idiots, he thought.

The smoke had definitely thinned out some by the time Starkey hopped down to the bridge deck. He wasn't just sweating inside the fire suit. He was lubed, head to foot.

Munsinger's round, tanned face was speckled with soot; it was on his teeth when he smiled and nodded a greeting. In a gloved hand he held his machine pistol pointed in the air, the ejector port resting against his meaty shoulder. Two other SEALs stood on the bridge like statues, aiming their stubby weapons at the closed hatch.

"Still no response?" Starkey asked into the mike so he could be heard over the ambient roar. The smoke had a definite electrical tang to it.

Munsinger shook his head and said, "Maybe they're playing possum."

One by one, in rapid order, the other ENR guys piled over the sail's rim. Then Starkey ordered lines dropped to the wash deck so they could haul up their dry chemical fire extinguishers and other gear. With five of them pulling, it took no more than three minutes to raise the cylinders and gear bags to the bridge. When Starkey put on his air mask, the rest of his team followed suit. They turned on their compressed-air tanks, switched on the headlamps and pulled on gauntlets. That done, they helped one another shrug into the straps of the backpack fire extinguishers. They then armed one another's extinguishers by pulling the safety pins and cranking down the levers that punctured the CO_2 propellant cartridges.

"Open it," Starkey told the SEALs.

When the hatch cover fell back to the deck, it released another puff of smoke, only much less black. With the hatch open, a warning klaxon could be heard belowdecks, its shrill pulsation barely audible over the engine and prop roar. The SEALs retreated a yard or so, still covering the entrance.

As the smoke continued to rise, Starkey lifted his mask, leaned over the hatch and shouted down in Russian through a cupped hand, "You are about to be boarded by the U.S. Navy. This is a rescue operation. Do not resist. We're here to help you."

If anybody heard him, they didn't answer.

If anybody answered, he didn't hear them.

As Starkey straightened, Howe passed him the hand-held NIFTI—navy infrared thermal imager—and power pack.

"We sweep before you go down," Munsinger said as he stepped forward. "Make sure any hostiles are pacified. It's procedure."

"Blow it out your ass, Munsinger," Starkey said. "The situation can't wait for a sweep. We've got to put out the fire and shut down propulsion, ASAP."

"SEALs will take the point, then."

"Without canned air, you'd last maybe three minutes before you passed out. Stand clear, Captain. Do it now."

Reuben Starkey pulled his air mask over his face and descended into the column of smoke.

CHAPTER FOUR

Clallam County Deputy Sheriff Hiram Turnbull hunkered down beside the roadside ditch. The drainage channel was overgrown, but the bright red soles of a pair of short rubber boots were visible sticking up out of the weeds. He gently pushed the grass aside with the tip of his baton. There were legs in the boots, in jeans. The rest of the body was out of sight, head down in the ditch.

A quarter mile north of Highway 112, a squadron of Navy fighter jets screamed over the strait, flying very low just off the coastline.

On any other day, finding a corpse in a ditch would have been a big deal.

Not on this day.

"Was it a hit-and-run?"

Turnbull rose from the crouch and turned to face the speaker. He towered over the dried-up little guy in the leather porkpie hat who had reported the body. The concerned senior citizen wore a white goatee and a red plaid shirt, and carried a leashed, plaid-caped Chihuahua in the crook of his arm.

"Can't tell yet," Turnbull answered. "Why don't you stand back a bit, sir? Or better yet, take a seat in the back of the squad car while I do what I have to do." The sheriff's cruiser stood parked in the middle of the two-lane highway's westbound side, its roof beacon flashing. Turnbull opened the rear door and gestured for the man to get in.

"Am I a suspect, Officer?"

"Sir, I don't want you or your dog stepping on anything, or getting clipped from behind by a log truck. It's for your own safety. When I'm done looking over the scene, we'll talk." After the old guy sat down and swung in his legs, he shut the door.

Turnbull hurriedly pulled on latex gloves, then, baton in hand, skidded down the side of the ditch fifteen feet from where the body lay. The drainage gulch was waist deep; he couldn't see the bottom for all the weeds and blackberry brambles. When he hit bottom, icy cold, flowing water surged over his shoe tops.

"Shit!" he said, remembering the hip boots he kept stowed in his cruiser's trunk, boots he'd forgotten to put on.

Sweeping aside the undergrowth with his baton so he could see where he was stepping, the deputy worked his way down the narrow channel. There was enough water running to wash away any light debris that had fallen in with the body. As he got close to the corpse, he smelled something nasty. Parting the weeds with the club, he stared down at the seat of the victim's pants. The poor bastard had lost bowel control shortly before or at the moment of death. Turnbull tapped the befouled jeans' back pockets with his baton. There was no wallet in either one. From the narrowness of the hips and width of the back, the subject appeared to be male. The head wasn't visible and the arms were pinned under the torso.

There were no obvious injuries that he could see.

"Shit!" Turnbull said again. He was going to have to turn the body over. He sucked in a breath, held it, then bent deeper into the weeds. Because of the angle and the absence of rigor, the victim wasn't easy to roll. For a second after Turnbull had done the deed, he couldn't figure out what the hell he was looking at. Then his brain connected the dots. It wasn't a silently screaming mouth. The weight of the head hanging down made the horrible red gash under the chin gape six inches wide. The dead man's throat was cut from ear to ear all the way to the backbone.

Well, that just fucks me royal, Turnbull thought as he straightened.

The deputy sheriff kicked himself for not turning his car around when he heard the first sketchy report about a ship grounding on the Hook. Now it was too late. He couldn't bag out on an obvious murder in order to get in on even more exciting duty back in Port Angeles. There was nobody coming to back him up out here, either. All available police, fire and ambulance units had converged on the Hook. He was going to have to sit parked on Highway 112 for who knew how long before a supervisor arrived to sign off on the scene and an ambulance hauled away the body.

Turnbull climbed out of the ditch. Tossing down his

baton, he leaned over and grabbed the body by the ankles, then he muscled it partway up the slope, dropping the heels onto the road. He wasn't worried about muddying a crime scene for Clallam County CSI.

There wasn't any such animal.

After wiping his latex gloves and his baton on the grass, he opened the cruiser's rear door. "Come on out, sir," he said. "Have a look at this guy for me."

With the bulgy-eyed Chihuahua nestled on his arm, the old man squinted down in horror at all the blood. It was caked up solid in the nostrils; it coated the staring eyeballs. "Sweet Jesus," he murmured. "His head's practically cut off."

"Do you know him?"

"I think so. No, I know so. His last name's Rudolph. He lives over near Freshwater Bay."

That was a good four miles away. Rudolph was wearing rubber boots, not jogging shoes.

"What's he doing out here on the highway?"

"How should I know?" the old guy said, crinkling up his nose as he caught a whiff of what Rudolph was sitting on. "Never seen him on foot. He drives one of those new four-door pickups. Japanese-made rig."

"Color?"

"Gray or light blue."

"Do you know his address?"

"I don't know the street or the number, but I think I can find the house if we head over there."

"Get back in the car, please. Watch your head."

Technically, Turnbull wasn't supposed to leave the crime scene unattended, but under the circumstances he knew no one was going swing by and check on him. The victim's front pockets were turned out. His wallet, watch and ring were already gone. There was nothing to steal but the corpse itself. Turnbull took a yellow plastic tarp from the trunk and securely covered the body to keep crows from pecking apart the face. He festooned the ditch weeds with crime-scene tape, then set out some road flares.

Satisfied with the job, he got in the cruiser and with lights still flashing but siren off he headed west. The radio was jumping with reports from the Hook. Navy personnel were on the ground. A full platoon of SEALs, evidently. The old guy ride-along didn't understand the chatter. It was all code numbers and jargon.

It sounded like a Steven Seagal movie.

And Turnbull was missing it.

He mashed down the accelerator and the big V-8 laid thirty feet of smoking rubber on the asphalt.

Deputy sheriffing in Clallam County was life in the slow lane. Peeling drunk drivers off telephone poles. Breaking up teenage parties on the beach. Domestic-violence complaints in shabby trailer parks. A case like this roadside body dump would normally have made Turnbull's year, if not his decade. But in comparison to the sub grounding it was nothing. It was worse than nothing.

It was shit.

Following the old guy's directions after they got to Freshwater Bay, Turnbull pulled into the driveway of a modest single-story house set back in a grove of fir trees. "Wait here," he told his passenger as he shut off the engine.

The recycle bins on the concrete front porch were full of empty beer and liquor bottles. He knocked on the screen. He could hear music playing; it sounded like

Shania Twain. After a minute or two a short, stout woman opened the door. She was Native American, either Makah tribe or Jamestown S'klallam. It was hard to guess her age. There were creases at the corners of her eyes, but her hair was still stone-black. He had some real bad news for her. This was the worst part of his job.

"Good morning, ma'am," Turnbull said. "Is this the home of a Mr. Rudolph? Are you his wife?"

"No, I do housework for him once a week. He isn't married anymore. His wife left him almost a year ago."

"Is Mr. Rudolph here?"

"No. What is this about, Deputy?"

Turnbull ignored her question. "When did you last see him?"

"He wasn't home when I got here this morning. I just let myself in. He might have gone fishing. His truck's gone. I didn't look in the garage for his boat trailer."

"Do you know the make of truck?"

"Toyota Tundra. Four-wheel. Four-door. It's gray. You still haven't said what this is about."

"There's been a fatality out on the highway," he told her. "There isn't any ID but it could be your employer."

"Oh, no," the woman said, sagging back visibly shaken. "Was it an accident?"

"It doesn't look like it."

"A robbery, then? You said his ID was gone. There should have been ID in his truck. Registration, insurance and all that."

"We need to identify the person who was killed, ma'am," Turnbull said. "Would you mind coming with me and having a quick look?"

"I *do* mind," the woman said, "but I owe it to Bill, if

it's him. He's been real lonely since his wife left. He likes meeting people. He's always picking up hitchhikers. I don't know how many times I've warned him— this place ain't like it used to be. Let me shut off my CD."

While he waited for her, the A-6s roared overhead again.

"Those jets are driving me crazy," the woman said. "They keep flying back and forth. What are they doing? Is it a Homeland Security exercise?"

"Something like that."

Turnbull didn't feel like explaining it to her. The way things were working out, the sub would be towed off the Hook before he got to see it. He wasn't just missing the chance to be a 9/11-type hero, maybe get his picture on TV. He could already imagine his fellow deputies and the Port Angeles cops laughing their heads off at how he got stuck ten miles outside of town while they had ringside seats for the biggest crisis ever to hit the West Coast.

Ribbing he was going to have to swallow for the rest of his life.

CHAPTER FIVE

Stony Man Farm, Virginia,
10:10 a.m. EDT

For the second time in less than half an hour, Brognola said goodbye to the President of the United States. There had been further developments at the White House end of the secure direct line. Stunning developments. The big Fed hung up the phone and reentered the command center. The Coast Guard chopper's live video feed showed the last of the fire-suited ENR team disappearing down the smoky hole. "What did I miss?" he asked. "Did they blow the hatch?"

"Didn't have to," Kurtzman said. "It wasn't sealed from the inside."

The head Fed scowled. "Did some Russians jump ship after it beached?"

"There's no sign of that from satellite, Hal," Kurtzman said. "No reports from land of exiting crew, either."

"So you're telling me they undogged the hatch from inside, like they were getting ready to abandon ship, like they knew it was going to crash, but then they didn't bail after it ran aground?"

"That kind of impact could have incapacitated or killed the entire crew."

"I'm sorry, Bear, I can't buy that scenario," Kissinger said. "The ship surfaced a couple miles offshore. All they had to do was power down and hoist a white flag. Which begs the question, did the crew ground the ship on purpose, and if they didn't, why did they let it happen?"

"All we've got is a big fat pile of loose ends here," Brognola told them. "We haven't determined why the sub entered U.S. waters in the first place."

"At this point, it doesn't appear to have had hostile intent," Delahunt said.

"I have something here I think you should all see," Tokaido said. He tapped his keyboard and transferred the image on his workstation flat-panel LCD to one of the wallscreens. "I've gone over the spy-in-the-sky data second by second," he said, "working backward from the instant the sub surfaced off Port Angeles. There's no evidence that it surfaced before that. DOD satellites would have caught it for sure. They would have caught it optically. So, I've been looking for anomalies in UDAR laser surface refraction, temperature gradients, sonar signature, anything that would give us a directional vector seaward."

"And?" Kurtzman said.

"Zip, vis-à-vis the sub. At a certain point using these analytical techniques, we hit old Heisenberg—the software filters start distorting the evidence, making its reliability suspect and therefore worthless. That's the point I've reached."

"So we've got nothing?" Kissinger said.

"Not quite," Tokaido said, tapping the keys. "Check this out."

A coastal map of the U.S. side of the strait appeared on the screen, overlaid by a faint green distance grid-work. The map scale was such that the Hook was visible in silhouette at the bottom left. Tokaido tapped on his keyboard again. "This is a real-time-sequence run-through," he told them. "Estimated object speeds are in the bottom right screen."

Three fine, parallel, brilliant orange-colored lines suddenly appeared well offshore. They grew longer and longer as they headed straight for land.

"Wakes," Kissinger said.

"High speed, shallow running," Brognola said. "Was it a torpedo launch?"

"They aren't torpedoes," Kurtzman said. "Or if they were, they didn't detonate."

"Jet Skis?" Delahunt said.

"Damn, they're wave skimmers!" Kissinger exclaimed. "Superfast water assault vehicles. Like riding a Tomahawk missile bareback. They've got a Graphic User Interface, touch-screen controls. Our versions are two-man. SEALs use them."

"And the Russian equivalent to our SEALs is Spetsnaz," Wethers stated.

"Right," Kissinger said.

"Where was the skimmer launch point relative to Port Angeles?" Brognola asked.

"About ten miles west," Tokaido said.

"And landfall?"

"Freshwater Bay. It's mixed rural and residential. Sparse population."

"Any reports of a beach landing there?"

"Not yet, but things are very confused on the ground. At the moment 911 emergency lines are jammed."

"How long before the sub's grounding did the skimmers reach land?" Kurtzman asked.

"Looks like the wakes hit the beach twenty-three minutes prior," Tokaido said.

In an explosion of pent-up frustration, Brognola demanded, "Are we under attack? If so, by whom? And by what? We have to come up with answers, people."

The outburst was met by an uncomfortable silence.

Then Delahunt said, "We haven't been able to ID the ship, Hal. The configuration isn't part of the existing archive. It has elements of two previous designs, the Alfa and the Akula, and other elements that are unique to itself. Hunt and I have assembled a list of all the architects and engineers known to have worked on those programs. It spans almost forty years."

"A penetration like this, however it was accomplished, requires new technology," Kissinger said. "This is way beyond Akula."

"How long have the Russians had it?"

"A long time," Kissinger said. "My guess is it would take a decade or more to actually design and build a ship around it. The question is, how did they manage to hide an entirely new class of vessel from our inspectors? How many more are there? Where are they?"

"And why are they letting the cat out of the bag now?" Kurtzman added.

"DOD is going to have a field day tearing that sub apart," Wethers said.

"Bear, do we know where it came from?" Brognola said.

"We know where it *didn't* come from. It didn't sail out of any of the previously identified naval shipyards or sub bases in the last twenty-four months. The construction site is equally a black hole."

"Why aren't we already at DEFCON 1?" Delahunt asked.

"The President has ordered our missiles retargeted and ready for launch," Brognola replied, "but he is holding back the go-code. He has reason to believe that if this is an attack, it wasn't coordinated by the Russian government or its armed forces."

"Because they're still denying it's their ship?" Wethers said incredulously.

"No, Hunt, because the Russian government and military have just given the President complete access to their most sensitive internal-security material and to crack black-ops units already in the field," Brognola said. "That's what the last call from the White House was about. It appears that today's events may be part of an isolated conspiracy on the fringes of the Russian military establishment. If that's the case, the Russian politicians and generals want to root it out as badly as we do. As an act of good faith, they haven't reprogrammed their launch codes or prepped their missiles. And they've invited us to participate in the ground action, on their home soil."

"Whoa," Kissinger said.

"The details are for our eyes only," Brognola said. "No other clandestine service will be involved—none of the information we receive will be shared. That's the deal the President made. We've got to live with it.

"Able Team's Homeland Security credentials and closed-airspace flight authorization are waiting for pickup at Boeing Field in Seattle," Brognola went on. "Barbara, do we have a live link to Phoenix Force?"

"I just finished alerting David to the necessity of a quick exit from the U.K.," Price replied.

"What about just scrubbing his current mission in light of events?" Kurtzman said.

"David said there's no need, and I agree with him. We're basically still in a holding pattern at this end. The presence of the target at the London location has been confirmed. Phoenix Force is closing in as we speak, about to initiate contact on-site. Mission wrap-up in the next hour."

"With any luck we'll know more by then," Brognola said. "Make sure the Gulfstream at Heathrow is fueled and cleared for a flight east."

CHAPTER SIX

London East End,
2:20 p.m. GMT

David McCarter and Rafael Encizo hustled down the rain-slick East End street, a treeless, winding canyon of two-story, nineteenth-century brick. In the middle of the gray afternoon, it was deserted but for a few mothers pushing prams on the opposite sidewalk. McCarter noted the huge For Sale signs in upper-story windows. This neighborhood of tenement slums was gradually being gentrified. Where immigrants from Eastern Europe had once lived ten to a room without running water, frantically upscale yuppies from the city's financial district cooked on their Jenn-Air ranges under expansive skylights.

The white panel van following behind McCarter and Encizo turned hard right, then angled down an alley that ran parallel to the street they were on.

Phoenix Force was closing in fast.

McCarter and Encizo walked on with their heads

slightly lowered, their stocking caps pulled down over the tops of their ears. They looked like a couple of workmen, painters or plasterers in white-spattered coats, pants and shoes, hurrying to get back to a re-model job after an ale break.

They stopped in front of a take-out curry shop. The shopfront was made up of small, wooden-framed windows and a wooden-framed door that was mostly glass. A Closed sign hung in the window.

Through the glass McCarter could see a guy with his back to the entrance, working at a table on the far side of the service counter. He was small, brown, wiry, and he was wearing an orange-stained white apron. Loud, rhythmic music blared from a boom box on a shelf above him. Manic Punjabi rock.

While McCarter shielded Encizo from street view with his big body, the little Cuban deftly popped the lock with a credit card and put his shoulder to the door. Encizo had cased the front door lock the night before.

The glass shuddered in the door as it swung open and a little bell tinkled, announcing the arrival of new customers.

McCarter and Encizo had already pulled down their ski masks when the little guy behind the counter began to turn around, a big chopping cleaver in his hand. He said, "Damn, I thought I..."

The aroma of concentrated spices—cumin, coriander, garlic, bay leaf, cinnamon and onion—permeated the very walls of the cramped little shop.

The curry guy looked from their masks to their white hands and jumped to the obvious conclusion. "You're in the wrong neighborhood for this game, you bloody skinhead wankers!" he shouted over the music, waving the cleaver in the air. "Do you know who the fuck you're robbin'?"

McCarter reached under his paint-spattered jacket. The curry guy's angry black eyes stared down the muzzle of the dehorned blue-steel pistol that was suddenly pointed at his head. The gun sort of looked like a Luger, but wasn't. IDing the weapon's make and model was the furthest thing from curry guy's mind; he was mesmerized by the size of the bore, which was immense.

He dropped the knife on the counter and held up his hands in surrender.

McCarter fired practically point-blank. The .50-caliber pistol didn't jump in his fist; it didn't boom deafeningly, either. It whacked, as if someone had dropped a metal pan on the scarred linoleum floor.

Like magic, the red plastic tail of a hypodermic dart appeared in the front of curry guy's throat. The impact of the projectile and simultaneous explosive injection of bolus of viscous fluid sent him staggering backward into the edge of his worktable. The one-inch-long, hollow needle was unbarbed. The dart immediately fell out of his neck, but the dose of sedative had already been delivered. A madly pounding heart sped the drug through his system. Grimacing in pain, the curry man clutched his throat with both hands, then his mouth began to sag, his face went slack and his eyes rolled up in his head. His knees gave way and he crumpled down behind the counter.

McCarter took another loaded hypo dart from his jacket pocket, opened the breech of the Benjamin-Sheridan Model 179B CO_2 pistol and chambered it. Then he cocked the single-shot mechanism. The stock Model 179B pellet pistol had been customized, rebarreled and rechambered into a smooth-bore tranquillizer gun intended for close-range injection of large animals, penned livestock. With the right sedative concoction, it worked just as well on people. Cowboy Kissinger had ground off the ridiculous leaf rear and ramp front target sights so they wouldn't hang up on their clothing.

Encizo kicked a metal wedge between the door and its floorplate, then kicked another along the jamb near the knob so the door couldn't be opened from the outside. While he was doing that, McCarter moved beside the bead curtain that separated the storefront from a narrow, windowless hall that led back to the shop's storage room. With the muzzle of his trank gun, he spread the strands of beads. The corridor was lit by a single bare light bulb in the ceiling. At the far end of the hall, the unpainted hollow-core door was closed. On the other side of that door was their target, Dr. Freddy Hassan, a wealthy Jordanian national. Codenamed "Penguin" by U.S. intelligence services, Dr. Freddy was a suspected international terrorist financier, widely known in London's tight-knit Islamic community as a philanthropist and benefactor. He always traveled with a private four-man security team.

Personally, McCarter would have preferred to use 9 mm FMJs and silencers on the lot of them, but dead men don't talk.

And talk was what this mission was all about.

After Encizo joined McCarter at the curtain, the Briton slipped through the dangling beads and took the lead down the hall with weapon raised.

IN MIRROR SUNGLASSES and hooded black sweatshirt, Gary Manning drove the van down the cobblestone alley.

Calvin James rode in the passenger seat, likewise in shades and hood. The third man, T. J. Hawkins, was back in the van's cargo compartment, sitting on a crated junk-yard four-cylinder engine block. The alley was narrow and dotted with puddles of standing water. Empty clotheslines were strung overhead, from the back of one building, across the alley, to the back of the building opposite.

The curry take-out's rear entrance was on the left, and coming up fast. There was enough room for a de-livery truck to pull in, but the space was taken up by two parked cars, both black, top-of-the-line Mercedes sedans with dark-tinted windows all around.

Dr. Freddy's rides.

Manning stopped the van in the middle of the alley, cranked down his window and stuck his head out.

There was a tall, olive-complected guy standing just inside the rear entrance. He was leaning against the closed metal-sheathed door. His arms were folded across his chest.

"I got a delivery to make inside," Manning told him. "How about moving one of those cars out of the way so I can pull in the van?"

"Come back later," said the man in the doorway, who looked like a bodybuilder. His loose-fitting Hilfiger gangsta-wear was open to the navel to show off his pecs and six pack. He had high-top Nike running shoes; all that was missing was the poser, sideways white billcap.

"Can't do that," Manning said, leaving the van run-ning and setting the emergency brake. "Got a schedule to keep."

"Are you deaf, or just stupid? I told you to sod off!" The sentry stepped out of the doorway. With a practiced snap of his wrist, he telescoped a black baton to full length—seventeen inches of spring steel with a weighted steel knob on the business end.

Manning ignored him. He turned on his emergency lights, then got out of the van and headed for the rear doors.

"Hey!" the sentry called at his back.

James and Hawkins exited the far side of the truck. Hawkins, the only one carrying a conventional weapon, covered the shop entrance from the front bumper with a suppressor-equipped machine pistol.

As the sentry rounded the back of the van, Manning raised his trank gun to greet him. The range was three feet and closing.

Manning put the dart between the sentry's lapels, into a bulging right pec.

The hypo hit the guy hard enough to stop him in his tracks. The color and the anger drained from his face, replaced by shock as he stared at the trank gun and the report echoed down the alley.

It took four seconds for the guy to realize he hadn't just been shot in the heart. Then he ripped the dart out of his chest in fury and threw it on the ground between them. He brandished the baton. "What you think you're playing, you fucking bender? Is this some kind of fucking joke?"

In two more seconds, the 250-pound guard was trembling and staggering like a near comatose drunk. Two seconds after that, he went down for the count.

As he fell, he reached out to grab Manning for support. The big Canadian sidestepped out of the way, letting the man topple forward. The sentry banged his head hard on the rear bumper as he went down. He never felt the impact; he was unconscious before he hit the ground.

Manning quickly reloaded the trank gun while James hauled the limp sentry toward the metal door by the back of his jacket collar. A unlocked padlock hung from the door's hasp.

James and Manning burst through the entrance side by side, with Hawkins right behind them.

A fraction of an instant later, Encizo and McCarter kicked the storeroom door off its hinges.

The brick walls were lined with tiers of cardboard boxes and five-gallon plastic tubs. Four guys sat around a card table in their shirtsleeves, drinking mint tea and smoking tobacco from ornate hookahs. Two of the men carried autopistols in shoulder leather.

Before they could reach for them, the trank guns popped out four darts. On impact, the explosive charges in the hypos made faint flashes in the dim light. The flashes were followed by shrill cries of pain. Two of the bodyguards managed to get to their feet before falling on the floor. The other two never made it off their chairs; they slumped facedown on the card table.

"We're clear," McCarter said. He took in the unconscious bodies. "Which one's our guy?"

"This one," James said as he raised a stout, black-turbaned man from the table and held him propped in his chair.

Dr. Freddy Hassan was sixty-one years old, long bearded, grizzled, with spectacular bushy eyebrows. He had large pores and a peppering of brown moles on his cheeks, his bloated nose and his forehead.

"Let's roll," McCarter said.

James and Hawkins stretched Dr. Freddy out on the

floor, belly up. Then Hawkins stripped off the turban, revealing a coiled, bobby-pinned topknot of waist-long, coarse gray hair. He pulled heavy shears and a cordless electric trimmer from his jacket pocket.

The others left Hawkins to it.

Their mission was hit-and-git.

McCarter, Manning, James and Encizo moved quickly, using plastic cable ties on all the downed men, securing wrists behind their backs and tethering their ankles. They confiscated cell phones and ripped the landline out of the wall. After Encizo dragged the curry man into the storeroom with the others, they opened their SOG Auto-Clips and started cutting off the men's clothes. They took their shoes and socks, too, leaving them naked on the floor.

It wasn't strictly part of the job, but a little psy ops never hurt.

"Man, you are really messing him up," James said as he leaned over Hawkins's shoulder.

"What are you talking about? He looks great," Hawkins insisted.

He had already hacked off Dr. Freddy's beard and the long hair, and was going to town with the electric trimmer, crudely shaving his chin, his cheeks and his head. In a final flourish, Hawkins sheared off the dramatic eyebrows, too.

The unconscious financier bled from dozens of tiny cuts where Hawkins had nicked him with scissor points and trimmer blades.

"Looks like he fell into a weedwhacker," Encizo remarked.

"Even his own mother won't recognize him," Manning said.

"DIA will," McCarter said. "They've got his finger-prints."

Phoenix Force had already accomplished two-thirds of its mission. They had live-captured a high-profile, politically sensitive figure, and changed his appearance so he could be spirited out of the country without raising alarm. All that remained was to arrange a pass off of the captive to an on-the-books U.S. intelligence service. Dr. Freddy was going to wake up in a nameless prison in Syria or Dakar with a twelve-volt battery connected to his balls.

They left the boom box booming in the shopfront to cover cries for help from the bound men after they came to. As James and Encizo carried Dr. Freddy to the back of the van, Manning locked the padlock on the rear entrance.

With McCarter behind the wheel, they were out of the alley and back on the main road in a hurry. He negotiated the crosstown traffic snarls and free-for-all roundabouts like the professional driver he was. As they closed on the drop-off location, McCarter took out a disposable cell phone and made the call to DIA's London branch.

"I have a package for you," he said to the man who picked up on the other end. "It's something that's been on your wish list for a long time. Highly perishable, though. You need to pick it up in fifteen minutes or less, and move it out of country within two hours."

"Who the hell is this?" demanded the agent on the other end. "How did you get this number?"

"If you want Penguin, bucko," McCarter said, "you'd better come and get him before he wakes up and walks away. He's in the phone booth near the corner of

Great Russell and Bloomsbury. An ambulance would do the job nicely." Then he hung up, wiped the phone down and threw it out the window.

A long line of traffic inched toward the intersection just ahead.

When the van came up alongside a red phone booth, James and Hawkins slid back the side door and jumped out carrying Dr. Freddy between them by the armpits. They quickly muscled him into the booth and shut him inside. There were pedestrians moving in both directions on the sidewalk, but no one stopped. No one said anything. Up at the corner of Bloomsbury and Great Russell Street, the light turned green. James and Hawkins piled back into the van, and McCarter drove on.

A few blocks down he made a left turn and circled the little park in the middle of Bloomsbury Square. When he was sure they hadn't been followed, he retraced his route on the other side of the street and pulled into a loading zone within sight of the phone booth.

"Now we're going to see just how good these guys are," Manning said as he checked his wristwatch for the elapsed time.

The drop-off was close to DIA's London HQ and a major hospital, where they could commandeer an ambulance.

Despite what McCarter had told the agent, he had no intention of letting someone like Dr. Freddy "walk away." That's what the engine block in the back of the van was for. The fallback plan was to chain it to his waist and sink him in the Thames.

People walked right past the booth where Dr. Freddy sat slumped. Nobody paid any attention; in fact, they averted their eyes when they saw him. Given his rough appearance and the neighborhood's decline, they thought he was an overdosed heroin addict. After about ten minutes, a siren sounded in the distance. A couple of minutes later, an ambulance stopped at the curb beside the phone booth with roof beacon flashing. Two uniformed attendants picked up the unconscious man, loaded him inside, and then the ambulance left the curb, siren blaring.

"Heathrow, here he comes," James said.

"That's where we're heading, too," McCarter informed the others. "The Gulfstream is fueled and ready to go. Looks like we might have another job on our plates."

CHAPTER SEVEN

Port Angeles, Washington,
7:23 a.m. PDT

As Commander Starkey backed down through the sail hatch, particulate matter howled up past him in a black torrent. He descended into swirling darkness, reversing down the ladder with forty pounds of fire extinguisher on his back. On the way down, he counted the ladder's rungs, one by one. Relative to the ground, the ladder canted off to the right. The engine and prop vibration trembled through his hands and arms, as well as his feet. Inside the hollow shell of titanium, the warning klaxon was much louder, contributing to the sense of chaos.

Five rungs down and even with the high-intensity headlamp he couldn't see the backs of his own gloved hands. The concentration of smoke was always thickest at the highest point of the hull—in other words, the sail. He had to be careful, but he also had to move quickly through it. He needed to get his people in and seal the sail hatch shut. An influx of oxygen from the outside could cause a catastrophic flare-up.

Somewhere in the darkness above, his number two, Chuck Howe, was starting down the ladder.

Starkey knew there were twelve rungs from the top of the sail to the control deck ceiling on Akula/Bars-class subs. And there were a dozen more rungs to the control deck floor. With a variant design like this, things below could be altogether different.

That thought gave the commander a sudden jittery-sick feeling in the pit of his stomach.

He squelched it.

Fifteen rungs down, Starkey stopped climbing and braced himself against the ladder. He switched on the NIFTI—his eyes in the dark—and aimed it below him. Even with the shaking screen, he could make out a distinct, bright fluorescent-green blob.

"Got one hotspot on the control deck," he said into his mike. "Seems to be isolated." He continued to swing the NIFTI around. "I'm picking up what looks like body heat in a big clump aft. Nothing's moving down here."

He lowered the thermal imager and descended another four rungs of the ladder. He still couldn't see the deck between his boots, but with his naked eye he could just make out a faint red glow where the control deck ceiling should have been. It wasn't from burning embers—it was the battle lanterns.

When his boot soles finally touched solid deck, he immediately started to ski toward the stern. He hung on to the ladder to keep his feet. The floor was slick, perhaps with residue from the fixed automatic fire-extinguishing system.

Starkey dropped onto his hands and knees. As he looked up, his headlamp beam swept across and reflected off the underside of an impenetrable bank of smoke. It hung at about waist height and obscured everything up to the ceiling; below waist level there was some visibility. He couldn't make out the wall opposite in any detail, but he could see it through the shifting haze. The fact that the smoke was concentrated well above the floor came as a major relief to him. That meant it was possible that the fire was confined to the uppermost deck.

He used the NIFTI to scan the hotspot again. About ten linear feet of console space was involved. There were no erratic superbright flashes indicating arcing from broken power-supply cables. No leaping flames were in evidence, either. Even with the influx of oxygen flowing in from the open hatch, there hadn't been any flare ups. That was another very positive sign.

Shambliss was the last man down the ladder. As he joined Starkey and the others, he confirmed the sail hatch was once again closed.

"Hotspot is aft on the starboard wall," the commander said. "The deck is coated with something slippery."

The black floor plates glistened under their headlamps. Color, if any, was indistinguishable in the poor light and smoke.

"Can't be water, though," Howe said. "Russians wouldn't use that to put out a fire on the control deck unless they wanted to fry themselves."

"We don't know what the electrocution threat is," Starkey said. "Keep a safe distance from the heat source until we have it bagged and tagged."

The ENR team had trained rigorously for years for just such a job under just these conditions: fire-suppression unit working smoke-blind under the direction of the leader holding the NIFTI.

"Let's stay cool," Starkey reminded them. "Follow the drill. Maintain physical contact at all times." The commander then took the point, crab-crawling across the deck toward the starboard side wall. Howe followed, with the fingers of his left hand laced through Starkey's extinguisher straps. Deal, Alvarez and Shambliss formed the rest of the human chain.

As Starkey got close to the wall, through the swirling smoke, he could see red backlit dials and gauges, and small, hooded LCD screens. It looked like the sub's sonar console. Swivel chairs were bolted to the deck in front of it.

Peering aft through the NIFTI, Starkey edged his line of men into position directly opposite the hotspot's core. As they knelt on the slick deck, he moved behind them, turning each man's shoulders square to the target.

"Okay, it's straight ahead about ten feet," he told them. "Let it rip."

Howe, Deal, Shambliss and Alvarez aimed their nozzles slightly downward and started streaming dry chemical from side to side, starting low, working from floor level up to about a forty-five degree angle. Their initial combined discharge wasn't directed at the center of the hot zone; at close range the stream velocity could scatter burning material. They knew their ranges and streaming patterns cold.

In the NIFTI's screen the difference was immediate: the bright green glow began to dim as layers of dry chemical cooled, smothered and shielded radiant heat, breaking the combustion chain. The force of the streams and their propellant blew away the upwelling smoke. Starkey lowered the thermal imager. In the glow of the red battle lights, he could see the bank of ruined consoles. The front panels had been unscrewed and removed from the frames; the cover plates were nowhere in sight.

"Hold it," the commander said. "That's enough."

Howe, Deal, Shambliss and Alvarez shut off their nozzles.

Starkey moved closer; his headlamp and theirs spotlighted the target.

A few thin wisps of smoke leaked out from under the heaps of white powder.

The damage appeared contained within the uncovered bank of consoles.

Starkey took a close look at the join of the wall and ceiling above them, where conduit and bundled cables were exposed. Every circuit breaker along the row had been tripped, either automatically after a fired-induced short, or manually by the person who'd removed the covering.

Even without the coating of dry chemical, it would have been impossible to guess what the consoles' original purpose was. Everything in the ten-foot section— hard drives, motherboards, silicon chips, electronic modules, power amplifiers, hundreds of miles of wire—was melted.

Starkey quickly went over the adjoining, unburned consoles, the deck and the ceiling with the NIFTI, looking for more hotspots. There weren't any. The fire and the damage were all confined to a single location.

"What do you think?" Alvarez said. "Did someone remove the access panels and try and put out the fire?"

"Did it happen before or after grounding?" Howe added.

Good questions, Starkey thought. None had answers, yet. And it wasn't the time to start looking for them. "Open the sail hatch, Captain," he said into his mike. "We've got the fire out."

He touched his crew on the shoulders in turn as he moved past them. "Follow me," he said.

The ENR team crawled across the deck after him.

The ship's control station was on the port side, forward of the periscopes, the same relative position as in Akula class. Starkey stood up behind the pilot's seat and the lane-rudder control wheel, and leaned over the control console. Fanning away the smoke with his hand, he found the engine control telegraph. He turned the big knurled knob until it pointed at All Stop.

Seconds passed and nothing changed.

The engines continued to roar, the deck to vibrate.

There was either no one in the propulsion spaces, or whoever was there couldn't respond to the command. Starkey located the override on the klaxon and shut it.

With hot air pouring out through the sail hatch and no new smoke coming from the fire site, the visibility was already starting to clear. Being able to see changed the limits of procedure.

"Howe," Starkey said, "find the access tunnel to the engine room and shut everything down." He had complete confidence in his number two; he had taught him everything he knew about Russian subs. "On the double."

"Roger that."

"Deal, go with him," Starkey said.

Howe and Deal took the lead, walking upright aft, holding on to the chair backs and edges of the consoles to keep from sliding on the wet, tilted deck.

Starkey and the others came along behind. The commander could see the raised tables that held twin automated course-plotting boards, but he still couldn't make out the control deck's opposite wall. However, the deeper they descended, the thinner the smoke became.

"Shit!" Howe exclaimed. "Ah, shit!"

A second later, Starkey broke through the bottom of the mass of smoke. Twenty feet away, he saw Howe and Deal standing in front of the control deck's aft bulkhead wall, their headlamps shining down on mayhem.

"Oh, sweet Christ," Shambliss groaned.

It was the Russian crew, or a good portion of it. Maybe thirty or forty men. Their bodies were piled up on the deck in front of the bulkhead, either thrown there by the impact, or rolled there afterward.

Starkey didn't say a word. He stared down at a tangled, bloody flesh sculpture. Spotlighted by the wildly jerking headlamps, it looked like a medieval depiction of the damned writhing in hell. The heap of submariners in matching striped boat-neck T-shirts might have been in hell, but they weren't doing any writhing.

The commander moved alongside his number two and said, "Go on, Chuck. Find the propulsion access. We've got this covered."

Howe and Deal gingerly stepped over the intervening bodies and disappeared through the bulkhead door.

Starkey knelt beside the nearest victim who lay on his back—jaw slack, eyes shot red with blood, pupils fixed and unreactive even when hit by the high-intensity light. The sailor was clearly dead. It was impossible to determine the nature of the man's injuries. His face was a mask of weeping gore, his T-shirt sopping with it. Starkey touched a gloved finger to the mysterious substance that greased the black floor and held it in the beam of his headlamp. "It's blood," he told the others. "The deck is slick with blood."

"Shit, Commander," Alvarez said, "I think this one's alive."

"This guy's breathing, too," Shambliss said, "but just barely."

"Move the dead ones off the top," Starkey said, "or the ones on the bottom will suffocate."

Working together, Alvarez and Shambliss began to shift corpses, lifting them by armpits and ankles. The bodies were rigid, joints locked.

"Munsinger," Starkey said, "the Russian crew is incapacitated. Some are dead, some have major injuries. Has HazMat arrived yet?"

"Negative on that. They are still on the ground. When they do get in the air, ETA is twenty minutes."

"And another ten minutes to set up the isolation tent. These sailors aren't going to last that long," Starkey said.

"Command wants to keep them alive at all costs."

All costs. That was perfectly understandable. And reasonable from a national-security standpoint. Survivors could not only explain why the wreck happened, but also how the ship managed to slip through the ASW defenses.

"We can't carry them out by ourselves," Starkey said. "There are too many. To get them up the ladders and out through the sail and forward escape trunk we need ropes and litters."

"The local fire rescue and EMTs are standing by," Munsinger said. "They're ready to help."

Port Angeles, like every little town on the Olympic Peninsula, had a volunteer fire department. Which meant limited equipment, training and experience. The only gear they had would be for fire fighting. On paper, as part of their protocols, civilian fire departments never risked a firefighter's life to try to save people who were already lost, no matter how valuable. In this case, the risk was unknown. It probably wasn't fire and it certainly wasn't radiation.

Military protocol, on the other hand, said human life was expendable under certain circumstances to attain a greater good.

There was a middle ground that satisfied both protocols and the commander claimed it.

"Get the fire trucks and EMTs over here ASAP," Starkey said. "Make sure fire rescue is totally geared up, everything they've got, with air masks and extra air tanks for the men who are down. Don't let them into the sub. Keep them on the wash deck. We'll move the injured onto the litters ourselves. They can pull them up and out, and then lower them to the ground."

"Roger that, ENR," Munsinger snapped back.

"Commander?"

"Yeah, David?"

Alvarez was bent over a body they'd dragged off the pile. "This guy's got a contact gunshot wound to the temple."

"You're sure?"

"See for yourself. Powder burns all around the wound, and the other side of his head's fucking gone."

"Does he have any insignia of rank?"

"Nothing," Alvarez said. "No ID of any kind."

"None of them do, so far," Shambliss added. "Hey, I can see the console covers underneath the bodies."

At that moment, the sub's engines powered down. The mind-numbing vibration stopped. And for the first time since he entered the boat, Starkey heard the frantic rasp of his own breathing.

There were still at least twenty-five still forms tangled up against the bulkhead. They didn't all have to be shifted, just the few lying on top.

"Let's move the last of them," the commander said. The possibility of aggravating the sailors' injuries took a distant second to preventing certain death. He took hold of a man's ankles, braced himself on the slick deck and pulled. The stiff, still warm corpse slid easily off the body trapped beneath. What looked like a bloody rag, apparently part of the trapped man's T-shirt, was dragged along with it. The torso of the sailor underneath was a gory, seeping ruin from collarbones to the trouser waistband.

Blood had pooled along the join of the deck and the bottom of the bulkhead wall. Starkey quickly stepped around the corpse and turned over a man who was face-down in the dark, sticky fluid. He didn't appear to be breathing. It was hard to tell how many of the crew had survived; none were conscious.

"Sir, should we give the live ones our air?" Alvarez said.

"Negative," Starkey said. "Keep your masks on. Administering emergency air is fire rescue's job and they're on their way. I'm going to open the forward escape trunk and guide down the litters and tow lines. Shambliss, climb back up the sail and do the same."

Akula-class subs had escape trunks forward and aft. In this case, because of the angle of the grounding, the aft one was underwater, and therefore useless.

The escape trunk was just aft of the control room, but because the chamber filled the deck space, floor to ceiling, the entrance to it was one deck below. Under the red emergency lights, Starkey hustled down a narrow staircase, then through the deserted, metal-walled mess room. There was no smoke on the second level; the deck was dry.

The escape chamber control room layout was identical to the Akula. A steel ladder led up to an inner hatch in the ceiling. Starkey slapped the big servo button on the control panel beside the base of the ladder. With a whoosh and a whine, the airtight inner hatch popped up, and the interior lights in the chamber above came on. He could see the underside of the outer hatch and it was sealed. Starkey scrambled up the ladder into the escape chamber, then smacked the button that opened the outer hatch. Bright daylight streamed into the escape trunk, and immediately he could hear the sound of sirens, growing louder and louder.

As he started to climb out, Starkey glanced down and saw he was dragging something; it was caught in the lugs of his boot heel. A scrap of bloody clothing or a strip of torn chart paper, he thought. He tried to kick it off and couldn't, so he reached down and pulled it free.

Only when he had the thing in his hand, and saw the sprinkling of short, black, rooted hairs, did he realize what it was.

A crumpled piece of human skin the size of a washcloth.

CHAPTER EIGHT

Seattle, Washington,
8:30 a.m. PDT

When Carl Lyons exited the helicopter onto Boeing Field, his bare feet squished inside wet boots. He had taken off the sopping socks. His body heat had pretty much dried out his pants, if not his underwear. Rosario Blancanales, Gadgets Schwarz and Jack Grimaldi piled out of the chopper, as well. Their reception committee of one was on her way.

A tall, ponytailed woman in mirror shades, a black Homeland Security jumpsuit, billcap and combat boots crossed the field, heading purposefully in their direction. She was blond, trim, athletic, but not as young as she looked from a distance. She wore a Glock belted low on her thigh. A picture ID flopped on a lanyard around her neck. Over her left shoulder she carried a large black duffel.

"Good morning, gentlemen," she said as she stepped up. "I have some things for you."

"Looks like Halloween is a little early this year, Kate," Blancanales said with a grin. "No, actually, the costume is quite becoming."

"Blow me, Blancanales," she replied. Her eyes were hidden behind blue mirrors, her mouth a deadpan seam. She passed the duffel to Lyons. It was much heavier than it looked. "Your uniforms, side arms and IDs are inside," she said.

She gave Grimaldi a single sheet of paper. "Jack, those are your restricted-airspace clearance codes."

"Give us an update on the situation out west, Kate," Lyons said.

"The sub's in our control," she said. "Nuclear danger still unresolved. Dead and wounded sailors are being evacuated. Looks like mostly dead. A real mess."

"What about site containment?" Lyons said.

"Port Angeles is sealed off by air, water and road. Since the event, there's been a flood of official personnel into the area. Highway 101 and all the arterials and back roads are blocked by local and state law enforcement and DHS. No one goes in or out of the city limits without credentials."

"Who else is on the ground?"

"Alphabet soup. FBI, CIA, DIA, NSA. Everyone wants a piece of this."

"Who's in charge?"

"If I said you were, would you believe me?"

"No."

For a split second, a smile twisted her lips, then it was back to deadpan. "Technically, the DHS regional director is the boss of the whole shebang," she said. "All the agencies involved are subject to his authority. Of course, the reality under fire isn't so clear cut. We've got an unheard-of situation on our hands, apparent massive security failures, unknown, perhaps catastrophic dangers on tap, and a half-dozen rival bureaucracies competing for the limelight."

"Limelight equals better funding," Blancanales wisecracked.

"Among other things," the woman said.

"So, Kate, you're saying our brand-new credentials and uniforms are going to piss some people off?" Schwarz said.

"Yep, that's a given. The Bureau in particular."

"We'll be sure and walk on tiptoes," Schwarz said.

"Extrasubtle with cheese," Blancanales promised.

"Kate, we need a place to change," Lyons told her. "We can't do it in the chopper. There isn't enough room."

"This way, gentlemen." The tall blonde reversed course and headed for a cluster of single-story beige buildings that bordered the landing field.

As he followed, Lyons found himself staring at her tight, muscular backside. Kate wasn't Homeland Security—hell, he thought, she probably wasn't even "Kate." She really looked the part, though, he had to admit. The way she carried herself, the confident glide in her step, the way the Glock rode so naturally at mid-thigh, positioned for speed draw. Fluid. Comfortable. You didn't acquire that style writing traffic tickets in Pomona under body armor and trauma plate. He thought that if Kate hadn't lived through some hairy-ass firefights herself, she knew the role inside and out. And she was one hell of an actress.

The tall blonde worked for the Farm as an independent, off-the-books contractor, one of many. No way could Able have gotten credentialed by DHS in two hours, not without Kurtzman's team pulling major electronic strings, and the string pulling would have left an electronic trail that could lead right back to 1600 Pennsylvania Avenue. Stony Man had sent all the necessary documents and photographs to Kate via encrypted e-mail. She had the equipment and raw materials at her disposal to forge foolproof IDs. The air-clearance code was genuine, of course.

"Whew!" Kate said over her shoulder. "Downwind, you guys stink like gun smoke and cat piss. There's a shower inside. You might want to take a quick one before you change. Just leave the old clothes. I'll burn them."

TEN MINUTES LATER, four big men decked out in DHS black exited the building. They moved briskly across the landing field and into the waiting chopper.

After asking for and receiving tower clearance, Grimaldi lifted off, whisper smooth. He climbed the helicopter to five hundred feet, then angled across the industrial plants and port terminal, heading over Elliott Bay.

Below them, Lyons saw a pair of Washington state ferries, three-story, blunt-ended, white ships, crossing midbay in opposite directions. It was the ferry run between Bainbridge Island and the Seattle downtown Coleman Dock. On the horizon to the west, he had a view of the snowcapped Olympic Mountains.

He didn't know what their ultimate mission was, and he didn't waste any energy speculating on it. The current assignment was to set down on Ediz Hook. After that was accomplished, Stony Man would lay out the next task.

"How long?" Lyons asked Grimaldi as he shifted in the copilot seat, trying to get more comfortable.

"Half an hour."

"Wake me when we get close."

Carl Lyons pulled off his headset, closed his eyes and promptly went to sleep.

CHAPTER NINE

Port Angeles, Washington,
8:22 a.m. PDT

Commander Reuben Starkey braced himself against the safety line, breathing through his mouth, sucking down the clean salt air. His Nomex fire suit was spattered with blood and bodily fluids. His neck, arms and back ached as if he'd been in a free-swinging, go-for-broke barroom brawl.

Howe, Deal, Shambliss and Alvarez were a mess, too. Alvarez sat on the wash deck, head lowered between his knees, a clear strand of bile swaying from his chin. At least he'd stopped retching.

Navy HazMat was en route, its takeoff delayed more than an hour by a series of helicopter problems.

Air-masked Port Angeles volunteer firemen in full gear disappeared through the sub's forward escape hatch. The last of the Russian survivors was on deck, strapped in a litter, about to be lowered to the ground; the firefighters were going back down to bring out the dead.

Everything was fine until the ENR team had tried to move the first injured submariner onto a litter. Starkey should have anticipated what was going to happen, but he didn't. As they lifted the sailor from the control deck, he came to with a violent full-body jolt, as if he'd been electroshocked, then he simply went berserk.

Not because he recognized his situation, a soldier captured on foreign soil by foreign forces; it wasn't that kind of fight. The sailor didn't know where the hell he was or who the hell they were. He battled ENR tooth and nail. Blood and nasty fluids flew every which way.

Leaning heavily against the safety line, Starkey shut his eyes tight. Fuck, he thought, they burned, open or shut. And every time he moved them, or blinked, it hurt like hell back inside his head.

Yeah, he should have foreseen the consequences of such massive skin loss. With nerve ends exposed, even the slightest physical contact would send a person into convulsions of excruciating pain.

Bottom line, five in-shape American guys couldn't handle one skinless Russian.

They couldn't get him onto the litter, let alone keep him there. While they skated around on the blood-slick deck, crashing onto knees and elbows, the sailor punched and kicked and tried to rip off their air masks and claw out their eyes.

Starkey had no choice but to call for help from fire rescue.

Their ordeal was just beginning.

When touched, all the wounded Russians came to with a jerk and fought their rescuers like wild animals, thrashing, flailing and biting. They tried to scream, too, but the only sounds that burst from their throats were awful hissing gurgles. It took six or seven men using all their strength to hold down each slippery body and strap it to a litter. Afterward, they had to shake off the remnants of sloughed off skin that stuck to the palms of their gloves.

That wasn't the worst part, either.

Worst were the snapping sounds in the middle of the free-for-alls, like heavy rubber bands breaking. When that happened, the punching, clawing hands suddenly went limp. Dead limp. Skinned forearm muscles bunched in grotesque, bulging knots right below the elbows, no longer connected to the wrists. One of the firemen said it looked as if the tendons had torn out of their anchors in bone. Starkey had never seen or heard of anything like it.

During the evacuation, things were so frantic and so intense that the commander couldn't think straight. The only thing that kept running through his mind was, *Thank God they aren't our guys. Thank God they aren't our guys.* It was all over now, but he still couldn't think straight because of the way his head was spinning. It was hard just to hang on to the safety line and breathe without gasping.

Starkey turned and looked down at the Russian on the litter, about to be lowered.

Shirtless in sunlight he looked as if he had just been spray-painted candy-apple-red and the paint was still wet, his body surface weeping fluid. The whites of his eyes were as red as his stripped flesh. Jaws locked tight, he blew feeble bubbles of blood out of both nostrils. The Russian sailor was alive but he didn't look human.

It was difficult to see how his injuries could have come from the control deck fire, which was so limited in scope. Maybe there had been an unrelated chemical accident while the sub was at sea? Something that got on their skin, into their lungs—maybe something they had ingested in their food? With an effort the commander pushed the subject from his mind. Whatever had caused the casualties, it wasn't ENR's job to figure it out.

"Let's get off this fucking wreck and ditch these sweatsuits," Starkey said.

There were no quips from his team as they started down the rope ladders, none of the usual postmission banter. The silence was an accurate measure of their physical and mental exhaustion.

Starkey's descent was slow and labored. His knees didn't want to bend; neither did his elbows. His joints felt tight and inflated, and they hurt like hell. Deep bruising, he thought, or maybe he'd torn something by bouncing off the metal deck so many times. He wasn't used to mixing it up like that anymore. As he moved down the swaying ladder, the fire suit rasped against his skin, creating an electric, burning sensation. He paused as a cold shiver ran up his spine and crawled across his scalp.

The commander wasn't a hypochondriac. Just the opposite—he was a denier, an old-school hard guy. He immediately dismissed the burning as a psychological after-effect of the horror he had witnessed belowdecks. Nomex always chafed, for Christ's sake. He pushed the idea out of his head. As he stepped off the rope ladder, the EMTs on the ground took charge of the last Russian survivor.

The commander and his team followed them as they rushed the litter across the Hook to the Coast Guard air-station hangar. Before ENR entered the hangar they stripped out of their fire suits and dumped them in a pile. Out on the bay and in the strait, the flotilla of private boats had been chased back to shore by the combined rotor washes of the Coast Guard and Navy helicopters, and the armed threats of the latter.

Inside the yawning hangar, ambulances were parked with their back doors open and headlights on. The makeshift field hospital was in chaos. Men and women in paramedic uniforms, surgical masks and goggles dashed around in near panic, yelling and cursing one another.

So far, the only part of standard protocol that had been followed was "Don't move a problem."

And it wasn't as if they hadn't tried.

Olympic Memorial Hospital had refused to accept the injured submariners without full documentation on their conditions, this to protect the patients already under its care. Federal and military personnel could have commandeered its services and floor space, but there weren't enough ambulances to move the survivors; Marine Drive was clogged shoulder to shoulder with parked vehicles and spectators; the Navy helicopters didn't have life-support equipment on board; and the Russians were dying like flies.

Eight of them lay on the polished concrete floor, covered head to foot under yellow plastic tarps.

That left seven.

The paramedics had placed the litters bearing the still living on top of the wheeled gurneys, so they wouldn't have to bend over or kneel on the floor to administer aid. They worked in a frenzy, tossing used materials and packaging over their shoulders. It was impossible to tell who, if anyone, was in charge.

Four video cameras documented events on the gurneys. All of the cameras trailed cables that led outside, presumably to DOD satellite or Net uplinks. Starkey guessed the cameramen were CIA and Feds. The other guys standing around with their thumbs up their butts had to be the Bureau and Agency intel specialists: interrogation of these subjects was impossible.

Starkey edged in alongside Munsinger for a closer look.

"The bastards are sinking fast," Munsinger said. Inside the hangar it was chilly, but the SEAL captain was sweating like a pig. His voice sounded strange, too; not high-pitched with excitement, but thready and hoarse. "They're going to be history and we won't have gotten squat out of them."

The EMTs were preparing intravenous lines for the last survivor so they could give him replacement fluids and morphine. When the hypodermic needles disappeared into the veins in the crooks of his skinned arms, the pressure ripped the vessels open; they tore like rotten meat, and thick, dark blood oozed out and drooled onto the floor.

The paramedics abandoned the effort and quickly applied compresses to staunch the bleeding.

"Jesus, his body's falling apart!" one of them gasped.

"Uh-oh, he's stopped breathing," said another. A second later, the portable monitor at the head of the gurney gave off a shrill alarm. His heart had stopped, too.

"Paddles!" someone yelled.

Paddles were applied, several times. The defibrillator did nothing to revive the man. The heart alarm continued to sound. It was joined by others, one after another, along the line of gurneys. A chorus of unison tones echoed inside the cavernous building.

After a blast of epinephrine had been injected directly into the Russian's heart, a male EMT jumped on the gurney and straddled him. When he delivered the first chest compression with gloved hands, there was a sickening crunch. Before he could stop his downward momentum, both hands, as if they had broken through a thin film of ice, plunged to the wrists inside the chest cavity. When the heel of his bottom hand hit the lifeless heart, its aorta exploded.

Literally.

Like a water balloon hitting the sidewalk from a great height.

At least a half gallon of blood burst from the caved-in hole and out from between the astonished paramedic's fingers. The EMT jerked back his hands, eyes wide with shock, his goggles and surgical mask drenched and dripping.

"Son of a bitch," Munsinger groaned.

All seven heart monitors were shrieking.

Too fast. It was all happening too fast. Like an avalanche. Starkey turned away. He had to get some air or he was sure he was going to pass out. He wasn't the only one leaving. Some of the Feds were bailing, too, their faces the color of milk. He made it out the hangar door, but just barely. It was *that* hard to bend his legs, and when he did, electric pain worse than anything he'd ever experienced stabbed up and down them. He felt a spreading wetness in his crotch. It hurt so bad he'd pissed himself. Then he got that chill up his backbone again.

Something was definitely wrong.

Staggering to keep his balance, he looked over just in time to see the Coast Guard helicopter splash down along the shoreline on the Hook side of the bay. Not a vertical descent. A full-power dive. The orange aircraft came apart as it cartwheeled across the surface, snapped-off rotor blades spiraling away in all directions.

To the right of the crash, along the line of cars backed up on Marine Drive, the spectators were weaving on their feet, then sitting or falling onto the road and gravel shoulder. An invisible scythe was passing through them.

The sharp boom of an explosion rolled over the water from the mainland.

A fireball bloomed in downtown Port Angeles. It wasn't a missile strike. One of the Navy helicopters had augered in on Front Street. Half a block of real estate was swallowed up in the flames.

The pain behind Starkey's eyes suddenly became unbearable. It made him want to gouge them out to get at the pain. He might have done so, too, had he been able to bend his arms. Behind him, Dave Alvarez collapsed full out on the landing strip, limbs rigid and trembling. The other ENR guys were reeling like drunks.

Reuben Starkey had to sit down or he was going to fall down. He dropped onto the tarmac with his legs thrust out stiff in front of him. Head to foot, his skin was on fire and so tight it felt as if it was about to split. He stared at the masses of angry, watery blisters popping out on the backs of his hands. There was an awful coppery smell in his nose. Then his nose began not to just drip blood, but to spurt it in time with his pounding heart.

No room left for denial.

No alternative explanations possible.

As Starkey fought desperately to breathe, his heart beating faster and faster, what they had done hit him like a straight punch in the face.

They had opened a Trojan horse.

CHAPTER TEN

Black Sea, Republic of Georgia,
7:37 p.m. local time

The briarwood pipe in Dr. Amirani Vorostov's hand had gone out, but its bowl still warmed the center of his upturned palm. His chest felt as if it were glowing. With each shallow inhalation and exhalation, incandescent waves of pleasure coursed over him. Vorostov sat slumped in a wooden wheelchair, a robe across his lap and legs, a shawl draped around his shoulders, his nearly hairless head kept warm by a crocheted cap. The French doors to the balcony stood open, giving him an unobstructed view to the west, from the relatively unvandalized top story of the sixteenth-century cliff-side monastery.

On the far horizon, sunset reflected fire-orange on wind-whipped water.

The vast inland sea and the frail man in the wheelchair had something in common.

Both were dying.

The Black Sea was being poisoned by toxic waste continuously dumped into it by five rivers; the man was succumbing to wounds he'd suffered twenty years ago. Self-inflicted wounds.

Dr. Vorostov's metastasized tumors had started to secrete chemicals that destroyed his appetite, and loss of appetite was rapidly turning him into a living skeleton. To stimulate hunger and delay the inevitable, he chain-smoked thumb-size chunks of the finest Turkish hashish.

In the room behind him, the din of loud talk and the clink of cheap glassware gave way to braying male laughter. He dropped the pipe beside the butane lighter in his lap and weakly raised his right hand, signaling his attendant.

A stout, jowl-faced woman in an olive-drab tailored uniform jacket and calf-length skirt stepped forward to pivot the chair. Druspenskya Sokolova wasn't a real nurse, but as a former military intelligence interrogator she had considerable experience giving injections—primarily scopolamine and heroin. She wore her lank, iron-gray hair in a short bob that did nothing to hide her most notable feature: a gigantic mole in the middle of her right cheek, like the crown of a small, brown head, complete with fuzzy hair, bursting through the pasty, powdered skin.

She turned Vorostov to face an ancient room. Wide and cavernously empty, its high ceilings were wreathed in cigar smoke. The wood-paneled interior walls were painted a sickly pale yellow; peeling and grimy with handprints, they were artifacts of a more recent incarnation. Before the fall of the Soviet Union, even before the fall of the czar, the seaview monastery had served as an insane asylum and political prison.

Many would say the function hadn't changed.

Around a long, littered, makeshift dinner table, in front of the satellite TV, sat two dozen men in military uniform, some current issue, some twenty years out of date and reeking of mothballs. The television screen showed a picture of the White House while a Russian commentator recapped recent, startling events in the United States.

When the scene shifted to a video clip of the American President rushing across the lawn to his waiting helicopter, one of the old soldiers jumped to his feet, his pale face ruddy with vodka, white eyebrows wild and bushy. He wore a black parade-dress Soviet naval officer's uniform with gold-filigreed epaulettes and piping, the jacket breast lined with rows of ribbons and medals. He tipped the extravagantly high peaked, matching officer hat back on his head and put his hands on his hips.

Former Admiral Anatoli Rukov made violent and suggestive hip thrusts at the image on the screen.

"I fuck you, asshole," he announced in his best English.

This wrung a fresh round of delighted howls and foot stomping from around the table. Most of the celebrants were navy veterans, submariners, Spetsnaz. There were some army special forces, as well. About a third of them were Vorostov's vintage; the rest were half that old, in their late twenties to middle thirties. There were more of the young ones stationed around the monastery grounds, and along its only approach, a narrow switchback mountain road.

Young and old had been brought together by the ongoing aftermath of collapse. They were soldiers without a future…or a present. They hadn't drawn their paychecks or pensions for years. Those raised up to great heights by the magnificent Soviet war machine had been cast into the gutter. Those who should have been raised up were left to fend for themselves. Reduced to moonlighting as enforcers for criminal mobs, or worse, begging the arrogant, strutting victor for bare sustenance. Thirty thousand of Vorostov's colleagues in the Soviet WMD programs were on the American dole, paid by the U.S. Congress so they wouldn't sell their lethal expertise to the highest bidder.

The former admiral capered a nimble 360 while his comrades in arms cheered, then he sat down so hard in his chair he nearly spilled a line of half-full vodka bottles like dominoes over the array of well-oiled automatic weapons laid out on the table.

Even the best vodka made Vorostov violently sick nowadays. His cancer-racked body was too compromised to process alcohol. Although he enjoyed the effects of hashish, he still missed drinking.

He missed the abject wildness of it.

The scene on the TV abruptly shifted to the site of the grounding. In the shimmery telephoto shot, Vorostov could just make out figures crawling over the black sub's wash deck. In beige fire suits they looked like maggots feasting on an enormous charred corpse. Bodies in litters were being lifted out of the sub and lowered on ropes to the ground. The picture had to have been shot from Canada, on the northern side of the strait. The U.S. military could only stop the news coverage on its side of the border. CNN, Fox News and MSNBC were buying live feeds from the Canadian stations, and sending them via satellite around the world.

The doctor took comfort in knowing there would be much better pictures to come. Dying as opposed to living proof. And very soon.

Anticipating big trouble after the fall of his nation, he had systematically destroyed all the accumulated documentation on his work. Not just the paper trail, but the filmed laboratory tests on animal subjects and hapless gulag prisoners. The documentation was no longer necessary, and it was highly incriminating. What mattered was that his brainchild functioned exactly as he intended, and that a stockpile of it remained, hidden deep in the bowels of the monastery's cellars. The sum of Vorostov's four-decade scientific career consisted of a clutch of small vacuum vials, the glass melted to points at either end, and inside each less than a teaspoon of grayish-green dust. The weaponized spores were encysted, dormant, packed in nutrients, awaiting only air to awaken, to self-germinate and multiply. Some of his bioweapon had already crossed under the Pacific. That payload—with foam padding—would fit into an airline carry-on.

Enough to infect a minimum of a million people.

With no survivors.

He hadn't used a viral agent for his weapon vector. As a virus traveled from person to person it eventually mutated; in the case of a viral weapons system, to less and less lethal forms. Instead, Vorostov had genetically engineered a bacteria because the more complex structure better protected it from undesirable mutation. A bacterium took in nutrients and excreted waste products. It was a self-replicating, microscopic chemical plant. By manipulating DNA, a bacterial strain could be made to secrete a specific chemical—in this case, a bioweapon.

To develop the chemical and then tailor the bacteria to manufacture it was a herculean task, requiring the training and skills of a geneticist, a microbiologist, a biochemist and an immunologist. All of which Dr. Vorostov either had, or had acquired during the long and arduous process.

The underlying principle was simple: make the body attack itself. The chemical he created triggered an autoimmune response to collagen, a compound present not only in skin, but in joints, cartilage, tendons, blood vessels and elsewhere. The body's rejection of its own collagen turned those components to mush. The skin blistered and sloughed off whole. Joints ballooned up. Tendons snapped. Blood vessels collapsed. Incapacitation and the breakdown of all physical systems leading to death occurred an hour after exposure to the bacteria. A very painful way to go. Quicker but infinitely more painful than cancer. Happily, the larynx and voice box—both chock full of cartilage and therefore collagen—were disabled by the bacterial attack, rendering the agonized victims nearly mute.

Unlike a virus, the weapon's effects didn't get weaker and weaker as it spread. Because that raised the specter of a permanently uninhabitable, ever expanding ground zero, Vorostov built in a genetic terminator. Apoptosis. After a specific number of generations, the bacteria stopped reproducing and died off.

Vorostov wasn't nearly as thrilled as his coconspirators by the more than symbolic, manly penetration of U.S. territory, in part because his testicles—and therefore his libido—had been destroyed by radiation treatment and chemotherapy; in part because the grounding of the submarine, though impressive, was merely a drumroll from the orchestra pit to gather the audience's attention. When the curtain on the real horror show went up, it guaranteed the whole world would be watching.

Also guaranteed was swift and merciless retaliation.

His coconspirators anticipated massive air strikes on the Black Sea compound and a heavy ground assault up the mountainside. While artillery and missile fire was reducing the monastery to rubble, the heroic defenders would be out of harm's way, safe in the winding catacombs and dripping grottoes that lay beneath the six-hundred-year-old structure. In the mountain's bowels, they would don their biohazard suits and use conventional small arms, mined passageways and Dr. Vorostov's bioweapon to make their last glorious stand.

Every one of them was ready to die for the cause. They weren't counting on an uprising of former and active military to back their play. If that came to pass, it would merely be a bonus. Martyrs to an extinct political system, they wanted revenge for the humiliation of what they considered an unnecessary defeat. They wanted the deaths of comrades, of fathers, of brothers lost in the cold war and in the conflicts that came after to count for something. If these rabid hard-liners couldn't have their world back, they were determined to pull the new one down around them. They wanted to demonstrate to history that without question they had had the right stuff all along—the anti-ASW technology, the bioweapon, the ability to make a deep lightning strike inside the borders of the victor—but had been betrayed by corrupt politicians and organized criminals. After this day, and for all of eternity, there would be no more eating of public crow.

The scales of warrior justice were about to be balanced.

The sailors and soldiers refilled their glasses and shattered the empty bottles against the base of the far wall.

"A toast!" cried Captain Yeveshenko. He was one of the young ones. A Spetsnaz. Well over six-four and broad shouldered, he rose to his feet and raised his glass high. His black, vaguely almond-shaped eyes glistened with vodka-liberated emotion. A dangerous man in a dangerous mood.

"To the crew of 7882!" he shouted fiercely.

Then they were all on their feet. All except the doctor, of course. "To the crew!" they shouted back.

In Vorostov's opinion the toasts should have been to strain B39547. The submariners of 7882 hadn't known what they were getting into until it was too late. They were sacrificial lambs, like the gulag prisoners twenty years ago. But he kept his opinion to himself.

Despite his vital contribution to the night's festivities, there would be no toasts in Vorostov's honor. To the other conspirators he was nothing but a glorified poisoner.

An occupation normally reserved for females, or quasifemales like the lumbering, mustachioed Druspenskya Sokolova.

The good doctor didn't care what the others thought of him, or of his profession. He had no medals but he had been wounded in battle, and more grievously than they. His wounds were malignant tumors, brought on by decades spent working in unsafe, inadequate laboratories. Against all odds, and virtually by himself, he had created the perfect weapon of mass destruction. Invisible. Silent. Quick. Utterly devastating in its effect, both on its victims and on those who had to look on helplessly as they struggled and died. The single greatest accomplishment of his life had been written in invisible ink between the lines of history.

Vorostov knew for a fact that the cancer wasn't going to kill him; given what was coming to this ancient, brooding little corner of the world, he had no doubt just witnessed his last sunset. That didn't matter to him, either.

He had lived enough to see his baby walk.

CHAPTER ELEVEN

Stony Man Farm, Virginia,
11:39 a.m. EDT

A live video feed from inside the Coast Guard hangar filled one of Stony Man's wallscreens. The grainy images of frantic medics and their agonized patients were difficult to watch yet impossible to look away from. The camera panned from gurney to gurney in violent jerks, zooming in between the shoulders of the hunched-over EMTs to capture bloody upturned faces.

The seven members of Stony Man stood witness to an unfolding catastrophe they couldn't influence and that was, at least for the present, beyond their understanding. The only information they had to work with was the video coming over on the wallscreen. Though they could see the massive injuries of the Russian crew, the ultimate cause was still a mystery.

And the Russians were dying like flies.

"All their skins are peeled off," Delahunt said, "but they don't appear to be charred or burned in any way.

Good grief, it's like they've been parboiled! What could have done that to them?"

"Maybe a caustic chemical spill," Tokaido suggested. "A ruptured pipe or broken drum in the enclosed space of the submarine. If something like that got into the ventilation system, it could have overwhelmed them."

"That wouldn't have been nearly quick enough," Kissinger countered. "All those guys went down virtually simultaneously."

"How could you possibly know that?" Delahunt asked him.

"I don't know it, Carmen, but it's a safe assumption based on the few solid facts we have. It stands to reason that if they hadn't all been incapacitated at once, some of them would have abandoned ship before the grounding or immediately afterward."

"What about an explosive steam release from the pressurized reactors?" Wethers asked. "Superheated steam could have knocked them down in an instant. It could also have blistered off their skins."

"An explosive release would have cut ship's power," Kissinger said. "To ground itself like that, the boat had to have hit the beach at full speed. Like our sub crews, the Russians routinely run countermeasure drills for catastrophic reactor failure. If that was what happened, they could have easily and quickly sealed off the propulsion section from the forward part of the ship. There would have been casualties, but they certainly wouldn't have been total."

"We've got serious timeline problems here," Kurtzman said. "If the Russian crew was incapacitated all at once, when did it happen? If it happened at sea, how could they have run the ship aground so far inside the strait? Someone had to have been steering the thing all the way in from the Pacific entrance. If it happened closer to the Hook, someone still had to be able to surface it, turn it and ram it onto the beach."

"Aaron," Barbara Price said, "how the sub ended up on the Hook is less important right now than uncovering its original mission inside U.S. territory. Remember, those wave skimmers came ashore before the grounding."

"In my book that's clear evidence of hostile intent," Kissinger said.

"There's a breaking bulletin coming over on cable news," Brognola said. "Punch it up on the main screen, Akira."

On the wallscreen, a blond talking head looked up from her stage set desk and started reading from the prompter, "This just in from the White House. According to a presidential spokesman, the Russian nuclear submarine that ran aground in Washington state earlier this morning was on a scheduled goodwill inspection tour of Puget Sound naval bases."

The scene abruptly cut to the White House briefing room and a chatter of camera shutters. A stout man in a clip-on bow tie and a suit jacket addressed the assembled reporters from behind the familiar, seal-emblazoned podium. "I'm going to read a brief statement about this morning's naval accident," he said, putting unmistakable emphasis on the last word. His high forehead and fat, cleanly shaved cheeks glistened with perspiration. "There will be no follow-up questions at this time.

"Contrary to some initial erroneous reports, the Russian submarine's arrival in Puget Sound was very much anticipated by this government and its military. It was part of an ongoing exchange program with counterparts in the Russian navy. The program was instituted by the previous administration to further our continuing friendly relations. The reasons for today's tragic accident are under investigation by United States military and civilian authorities, and it will be some time before we have all the answers. The Russian crew has been evacuated from the ship and their injuries are being attended to at this moment. I am sorry to report that there were fatalities, and we send deepest condolences to the families of the lost and to the Russian people.

"The isolation of the Port Angeles area is a purely precautionary measure, and will continue until the damage to the vessel is fully assessed and it can be safely refloated to the waters off Ediz Hook. There is no immediate danger to the citizens inside the quarantined area. There has been no radiation leak as a result of the accident. The ship's nuclear reactors are intact. I repeat, there has been no radiation leak. I will have further updates as information becomes available. Thank you."

The spokesman turned away from the podium and made a hasty exit as reporters fired questions to his back.

"The Russians are evidently on board with that prearranged-peace-mission bushwah," Wethers said.

"Talk about lying through your teeth…" Delahunt added.

"There's plenty of precedent for that," Brognola said.

"They're giving out as little information as possible so they can backfill the cover story without looking like complete idiots," Kissinger argued.

"They're just trying to keep a lid on it as best they can," Price added.

"Even though the situation is anything but contained..." Kurtzman countered, pivoting his wheelchair to face her.

"Mass panic is the last thing we need," Price reminded him.

"Obviously," Kurtzman replied. "But you and I both know this situation may not be containable, Barbara. There are too many unknowns, too many loose ends. What are the powers-that-be going to look like when the bottom drops out?"

"Just more work for the spin doctors," Delahunt said.

"Can they really put in the fix on something *this* big?" Tokaido asked.

"Hey, the history books say men walked on the moon," Wethers said.

"You don't buy that load of malarkey about a studio set in Culver City?" Delahunt asked testily.

"No, of course not. But when everything's possible, anything's possible."

"If we do our job right," Brognola assured them all, "the administration's bullshit artists can take the week off. Do we have an updated ETA for Phoenix's rendezvous with the Russian special forces?"

"They'll touch down at the Tblisi military base a little after 9:00 p.m. local time," Kurtzman said. "That's about noon our time. They'll board a Spetsnaz helicopter and fly to the Black Sea coast. They should be on the ground there before eleven, two our time."

So far, the other side had been most forthcoming with highly classified documents. The information was traveling through so many cyber cutouts that Kurtzman had posited they were, in fact, dealing directly with their Russian equivalent. The Stony Man team likewise was covering its tracks to the max. The web of dead ends and endless loops was such that neither side could identify or locate the other.

The Russians had already transferred lengthy secret dossiers on the conspiracy's prime suspects and their connections to the various contemporary military services. They had revealed the current location of the conspirators, and the fact that Russian special forces were already in the process of surrounding and sealing off the site in preparation for an all-out assault well before dawn. When pressed, the other side had claimed ignorance of any of the details of the plot, something Stony Man had to take at face value for the time being.

Phoenix Force's final destination was an ancient cliff-side monastery on the eastern shore of the Black Sea. The monastery had been built on top of a grotto long sacred to the local Christian population. In the fourth century, a mystic hermit named Karamiso was credited with some minor miracles. Subsequently, the spring waters associated with the grotto where he lived became known for their healing properties. During the twelfth century, when the bubonic plague ravaged Europe, people from the area took refuge in the caves. Those who drank the waters of Karamiso's spring reportedly didn't get the fatal disease. The monastery was constructed four hundred years later, in part to defend the holy spring from the legions of Muslim nonbelievers to the south. The steep, forested mountain it perched upon was limestone, riddled with winding caves and deep passages.

In return for the secret files and tactical updates, the

cyberteam was passing on the live video feed hijacked from one of the official U.S. intelligence services. The person behind the video camera panned a dizzying 180 degrees around the Coast Guard hangar, recording the rushed entrance of EMTs carrying the last of the surviving submariners.

They set the stretcher atop a recently vacated gurney. The previous patient lay under a yellow tarp on the hangar floor. So far, all the heroic efforts of the Port Angeles EMTs had been in vain. Three masked and goggled paramedics quickly scissored away the bloody rags of the man's clothing while others prepared plastic intravenous drip bags of hydration and sedative.

The camera zoomed in on the Russian's rigid, skinless arm as an EMT disinfected an injection site in the crook of the elbow with a cotton swab. When the medic inserted a hypodermic needle into the bulging blue vein, backdropped by red muscle and white sinew and tendon, it came apart like rotten rubber tubing, and a gout of purple blood welled up from the rip.

Then the pulse monitor started to squcal.

The paramedics tried and failed to restart the sailor's heart with drugs and electric shock.

The camera caught the horrifying and disastrous result as an EMT tried to give the dying man chest compressions.

"That shouldn't have happened," Kurtzman said, still grimacing from the explosion of blood. "No way that should have happened."

"His chest just collapsed," Delahunt said.

"And his heart burst," Wethers added.

All the other pulse monitors began to scream.

"What in the world is going on here?" Brognola asked impotently.

Nobody had an answer.

On-screen, some of the nonessential personnel started exiting the hangar.

"They're bailing!" Tokaido said.

The person behind the camera followed the others out of the hangar, video rolling; the jolting impact of footfalls and forward movement produced wild, lurching images. Outside, the camera steadied, but those who had left the hangar continued to lurch.

Then, one by one, they began to drop to the tarmac.

As the camera panned upward, the lens switched to telephoto. For an instant, the screen was filled with a shot of the police and fire barricades across the Hook. The officers and the bystanders were dropping, too, cut down where they stood.

The operator then put his own hand in front of the lens and refocused the close-up. Angry, water-filled eruptions dotted the fingers and palm. The back of the hand looked as if it had been inflated. Knuckles to wrist, it was covered by a single huge blister.

The on-screen image blurred as the camera fell, bounced hard, then the screen went black.

"Good God, what is this?" Brognola said.

"Could be a biological or chemical weapon release," Kissinger said. "That's all I can think of. Point of origin has to be the submarine."

"I've been keeping track of the symptoms we've seen on-screen," Tokaido stated. "High fever, skin loss, fluid loss, immobility, blindness, loss of powers of speech, hypersensitivity to touch, fragility of blood vessels, organs and skeletal system. The global database cross-check has come up a blank. If it is a biological or chemical weapon, it's like nothing we've ever seen before."

"Switch to the Coastie chopper!" Brognola said.

The aerial picture was even more horrendous. People were down all over the Hook. And they weren't moving.

"Whatever it is, it's spreading like wildfire," Wethers said.

"It's already spread, you mean," Kissinger said. "What's the elapsed time, from exposure to incapacitation?"

"An hour and a half, tops," Tokaido said. "The first responders and bystanders are all falling sick."

"A chemical or nerve agent would have worked much faster than that," Kissinger said. "Inhale it or get it on your skin and down you go. But ninety minutes is light-speed for a biological weapon."

"Nothing that's been described in the database works anywhere near that quickly," Tokaido agreed. "For anthrax, plague, any of the other known weaponized bacterial strains, we're talking days for toxins to build up, not hours."

"Oh, my God!" Price said, pointing at the wall-screen. "It's going to crash!"

The Coast Guard helicopter was slewing wildly from side to side, deadsticked, as it steeply angled toward the water. Neither pilot nor copilot responded to the crisis. The helmet cam faced straight ahead as Port Angeles Bay rushed up to meet it. The helicopter hit the surface like a pile driver.

Then nothing.

Black screen.

"Is there another video source we can tap into?" Brognola said.

"All live feeds from the Hook just went down," Wethers said. Then he added, "Hal, you've got another hotline call."

Brognola left the room on a dead run.

"There's more Russian info coming in," Delahunt said.

"Put it up on our individual monitors," Kurtzman replied.

"Done."

There was silence as they scrolled.

"Son of a bitch!" Kissinger snarled over Kurtzman's shoulder. "How could they compile all this data so quickly?"

"They had it lined up and ready to transmit, of course," Kurtzman said. "As soon as they saw the people dying on the Hook, they hit Send."

"So they know a whole lot more than they were letting on."

"Why give up something of strategic value if you don't have to?" Kurtzman said. "We sure wouldn't."

"Thirty thousand former Soviet WMD professionals narrowed down to one prime suspect," Delahunt said. "Hey, I'm not going to complain."

"The bioweapon is code-named Red Frost," Tokaido said.

"As in 'killing frost'," Price said.

"The 'red' works on two levels—the politically archaic and the purely descriptive," Wethers said. "From these documents it appears the bioweapon was developed before the fall of the Soviet Union."

"The President has called up the National Guard," Brognola told the others as he returned.

"He can't send troops in there yet," Kurtzman protested. "Not until we know exactly what we're dealing with."

"They're not going to be deployed at ground zero," Brognola said. "They'll replace the civilian authorities at the roadblocks. Under these conditions, the operating principle is no one goes in…or comes out. Small-town cops might be unwilling to enforce that on their friends and neighbors."

"Look at what our new best friends just sent over," Kissinger said.

As Brognola scanned the documents, he scowled and said, "This Dr. Vorostov is a real piece of work. He spent his whole career in WMD research. Trained in several disciplines aside from immunology. He's also a geneticist and a biochemist. Tested his gene-spliced, lethal creations on disappeared Soviet political prisoners and captured Afghani mujahideen. The Red Frost bioweapon had its secret field trials right before Gorbachev came to power. Vorostov's been on the U.S. payroll since the fall. Look, they've even sent us his annual salary."

"Don't do the math on what that adds up to," Delahunt said. "I just did, and it was a big mistake."

"He was under treatment for metastasized bowel cancer," Brognola went on, "but that was discontinued five months ago. The disease is apparently terminal stage. Has Vorostov got the same bone to pick as the military renegades? Bring back the glory days, or die trying?"

"Either that or he's a garden-variety, frustrated evil

genius," Kurtzman replied. "About to kick the bucket and he doesn't want to go to hell all by his lonesome."

"What's Able's ETA?" Hal said.

"They'll touch down in ten minutes," Wethers said.

"Abort Able," Brognola said. "Do it now."

CHAPTER TWELVE

Port Angeles, Washington,
8:51 a.m. PDT

Bob Chugash lay in the bottom of the mooch boat on his back, his head toward the bow, his legs raised up and bent over the thwart seat. He couldn't move; couldn't scream; couldn't see the sky though his eyes were wide open.

He could hear the Evinrude still running, still in forward gear. When brother Stan had let go of the tiller throttle, it had sprung back to idle speed. He didn't know if Stan was alive. The motor was running, but they were going nowhere. The bow banged and scraped against the concrete pilings of the Black Ball ferry dock, lifted and dropped by the waves from high-speed boat wakes.

The jarring impacts were like a flamethrower fanning over him from the back of his head to his heels.

Molten lead dripped onto his defenseless eyeballs.

His joints had swelled up and frozen. Fingers. Toes. Knees. Elbows. Spine. Neck. Everything rigid as stone.

Other boats were still scooting around the bay, chased by the Navy helicopter. When the aircraft zoomed low overhead, Bob couldn't wave for help.

"Down here!" he tried to cry out. From the depths of his throat came a rich, bubbling hiss. His voice box felt like an overinflated inner tube. He could hardly get any air down his constricted windpipe.

He heard the explosion as the helicopter crashed on Front Street, two blocks up.

It was as if the hand of God had reached down and was sweeping everything away.

Not quickly enough, though.

In his fever, he imagined flames a foot long were shooting out his nostrils and mouth. He imagined child-sized red devils, pointy eared, black tailed, cloven hoofed, dancing along the mooch boat's gunwales and thwarts. Greasy-looking little bastards, laughing and pointing at him as he fought to breathe and prayed to die.

Bob Chugash's life didn't pass before his eyes. He didn't get to review the good and bad parts, to add up the sum of his existence, to come to terms with it. He didn't get to hover above, apart from his tortured body, either; he was a prisoner inside it, trapped by the sensations that racked him.

Every pain he had ever suffered was being pulled out of his guts, a stringball of agony unwinding from his navel: unbroken, vibrating, unendurable. With the drag of a dull razor his skin began to split, seams opening up along the sides of his face, his chest, arms, exposing the nerve endings.

The boat's side slammed against a piling. A grinding crunch of concrete and barnacles against fiberglass.

An even bigger swell followed. It lifted the little boat, reared it back and then hurled it bow first into the maze of pilings.

The fiberglass above Bob's head fractured with a re-sounding crack! Cold water poured in through the breach.

Fifty-degree water, only it didn't feel cold to him.

It felt like lava on the back of his head and shoulders. More water poured in as the boat rapidly began to sink. Like lava, it lapped over his chest, then his face. Lava poured into his blinded eyes.

With all his remaining strength and force of will, Bob Chugash sucked water through his narrowed air-way, down deep into his lungs. He was a man eating his own gun, pulling the trigger in slo-mo.

Despite the terrible dull pain in his chest, he breathed water a second, then a third time. The pain inside him crescendoed, but it led to blackness.

And with blackness came blessed oblivion.

CHAPTER THIRTEEN

Discovery Bay, Washington,
8:55 a.m. PDT

Tre Rupert sucked the bone clean on the first of his three pan-fried pork chops. Like the rest of the customers and staff of Large Marge's restaurant, he was watching the exciting doings on the wall-mounted TV. Rupert was a hugely fat, part-time corrections officer for Clallam County jail. Having dressed in a hurry, his gray-and-green uniform was misbuttoned, and one of his shirttails hung out.

Not that it mattered. No way was he going to make it in to work today.

Port Angeles was twenty-two miles from Large Marge's. According to the TV news, Highway 101 and all alternate routes to the county prison were closed by this Russian sub on the beach. Pretty damn good stuff, though. Made him as proud as hell to be in law enforcement. In his opinion, law enforcement was definitely kicking some Russian ass.

The unexpected day off gave him the opportunity to eat much slower than usual, and more methodically. A white ceramic platter of food lay before him. Chops, four eggs, a giant block of crispy hash browns, six pieces of buttered wheat toast. A satellite platter of pancakes—each a foot wide, stacked six high, drenched in syrup—sat at his right elbow. He had slathered maple syrup on the meat and hash browns, too. Rupert shoveled a fried egg onto a triangle of buttered toast, folded over the bread once, and down it went. He chased the mouthful with a delicate sip of canned Diet Pepsi.

Large Marge's really put on the feed bag. It was renowned far and wide among truckers, loggers, commercial fishermen and crabbers, and other miscellaneous big eaters between Quilcene and the Pacific coast. The roadside restaurant sat at a tight bend in Highway 101 at the southernmost end of Discovery Bay.

Rupert always got a charge from the looks on the faces of out-of-state tourists when they saw the size of the portions being dished out. Marge's hamburgers were as big across as a pie plate, and they came with a mound of steak fries six inches high. The sight and smell of all that food sometimes made them go green to the gills.

He always kept his weight up because often he had to sit on prisoners to keep them under control. Sitting on them was a hell of a lot less effort than beating them on the head with a nightstick or applying his fists and boots. Rupert used his tremendous bulk to mash unruly tweakers flat and break their meth-head bones.

The decor of Large Marge's was Pacific Northwest catchall. Worn Indian baskets. Old farm implements. Rusty sawmill shit. Fishing gear, nets, floats, harpoons.

The stuff was nailed to the walls or suspended on wires from the exposed rafter beams. The interior of the café had been painted with high-gloss white enamel about a decade ago. Now it was gray with dirt and smeared handprints, and the rafters were festooned and chandeliered with cobwebs.

Large Marge's was never going to get an A rating from the county health department. That didn't concern the owner-head cook. She subscribed to the belief that high-temperature deep-fat frying was like an antibiotic: it killed everything.

Rupert looked out a window at Highway 101. Despite the closure way up the road, semis and cars whizzed by in a steady stream. Drivers and passengers always turned and looked at the giant chain-saw wood sculpture of Large Marge herself, standing next to an even bigger statue of a Large Marge hamburger, both painted up in bright colors.

The real Large Marge had stopped cooking and was watching the TV, too. They didn't call her that for nothing. She was wider than an ax handle across her behind, and her belly started just under her chin and pooched out a good two feet in front. Her short, chopped-off hair was dyed a funny color of reddish brown, like a rusty steel wool pad. She wasn't a patient woman, from what Rupert had seen. She was given to pushing the help around. She wore nicotine patches on both of her massive, mottled upper arms. Large Marge was always sweating up a storm. Deep-fat frying was hot work.

The other customers this morning were the usual mix of local working folk, local unemployed folk and senior couples about to start their day at the S'klallam tribal casino just east of Sequim. There were two small groups of tourists, too. One Asian. One white. Neither group was speaking American, from what Rupert could hear.

A gold Maxima four-door sedan pulled in and parked in an empty space in front of the restaurant. As Rupert hacked out a wedge of syrup-soaked pancake with his fork, plopped a fried egg on it and, angling from side to side, pushed it all in his mouth, he watched two tall skinheaded guys get out of the car. Youngish, well-built guys in black T-shirts. They both had on what looked like web harnesses, maybe some kind of utility belts. The guy on the passenger side had a heavy-looking black nylon gear bag in his left hand and a small black backpack over his other shoulder. He cut right, and immediately disappeared out of sight around the end of the building. Probably went to throw something in the garbage bin, Rupert thought. The driver headed for the rear of the Maxima. He was carrying something on a shoulder strap.

Rupert assumed it was a camera. People were always stopping to take pictures of the Large Marge statue.

When the guy stepped out on the shoulder of the highway, Rupert saw it was a gun.

And not just any gun, either.

This was a stubby, mean-looking military-style assault rifle. It had a banana magazine, a folding stock and a fat cylindrical gizmo stuck on the end of the barrel. There was a second, shorter, lower barrel under it, complete with a combination magazine-pistol grip, trigger and trigger guard.

Rupert stopped chewing his food and rose from his chair, the paper napkin still tucked in the front of his uniform shirt.

The guy with the rifle walked right out in the middle of the two-lane highway, straddled the center line and opened fire from the hip. There weren't any gunshot reports, but brass arced in a bright stream out of the ejector port, skittering on the asphalt.

He was firing full-auto into oncoming traffic.

Bullets sprayed across the divided windshield of a semitractor hauling a trailer loaded with wood chips. The shooter neatly stepped to the other side of the centerline—matador style—as the truck careened past him. The truck driver didn't make the sharp curve in Highway 101, either because he was shot or because he was ducking to keep from being shot. The big rig roared across the opposite lane of travel onto the shoulder on that side, spraying loose gravel. Before the rig tipped over, it plowed head-on into a telephone pole. The tremendous impact and sudden stop whipcracked the trailer around in front of the cab. When the trailer toppled onto its side across the left lane, it split open, sending a blizzard of wood chips and sawdust sheeting over the road.

The other restaurant customers jumped up from their tables and rushed to the windows to see what had happened.

Rupert was trying to talk with his mouth full, spraying egg and pancake, a fork still clutched in his fist.

The cars coming northbound from Seattle slammed on their brakes to avoid piling into the overturned trailer. The shooter casually turned and stitched them with slugs as he advanced down the center line. Still walking, he dumped the empty magazine on the road, took a fresh one from his harness, reloaded and fired practically point-blank through each of the windshields into the still belted-in drivers and passengers.

A white, full-sized Ford pickup barreling down the grade in the other direction saw what was happening below, tried to swing a hasty U-turn and fishtailed out of control on the shoulder gravel. With a squeal of brakes, the truck skidded to a full stop, then the engine stalled out.

The shooter turned. He shouldered and sighted his weapon this time, and fired up the road. A single spent shell casing flipped onto the asphalt.

Rupert caught a glimpse of a silvery object a second before it hit the pickup's passenger window. The truck rocked as the cab exploded with a hard boom and a flash of bright white light. The front and back windshields disintegrated, the doors popped open, and the sheet-metal roof bulged up. Smoke and fire boiled from the white wreck.

Rupert swallowed hard.

Large Marge elbowed her way through the customers and staff to the front window of her establishment. Hands on hips, she took in the overturned wood chip trailer and said, "Muh-thur-fuck!"

But the guy in the black T-shirt wasn't done yet.

He took another silvery tube from his combat harness and fitted it to the underbarrel. As southbound cars and trucks descended the grade to the bay and hit their brakes, he blasted them with autofire and rifle grenades.

In two minutes the north- and southbound lanes of Highway 101 were blocked off with burning or deserted vehicles and dead drivers and passengers.

The guy stripped out his empty mag and tossed it away. As he headed for the front door of Large Marge's, he slapped in a fresh clip and snapped the actuator handle, chambering a live round.

"He's coming this way!" someone along the window cried.

Astonishment and horror gave way to panic among customers and staff.

It was as if the Terminator had gotten loose in Discovery Bay.

"He's gonna get what's a-coming to him," Large Marge said. She stormed behind the service counter and came back out carrying a 12-gauge riot pump. It had no buttstock, just an electrician's tape-wrapped pistol grip. The ancient Stevens looked like it had been cut down with a hacksaw by a seven-year-old. There was no blueing left on the barrel or receiver. The proprietor jacked a high brass shell into the gun's chamber.

"Everybody get down on the floor!" she bellowed, "I'm gonna blow up this asshole..."

Rupert and other customers scrambled for cover, tipping over tables and chairs, as the guy in the T-shirt marched up the wheelchair access ramp leading to the roadside café's front door. Though Rupert was a corrections officer, he was unarmed. He worked minimum security at the county jail.

Large Marge stood with her massive legs spread apart, the scattergun's crude pistol butt braced upward on the point of her wide hip, her finger resting on the trigger.

Only when a shadow appeared behind her did Rupert remember the other guy who had gotten out of the car.

By then it was too late.

There was a coughing stutter from the entrance to the kitchen.

Large Marge jolted forward as if she'd been snap-kicked low in the back. The bib of her grease-stained apron exploded outward, sending glistening red chunks hurtling across the room. The 12-gauge boomed in her hand, bringing down wood splinters, dust, cobwebs and blistered paint from the rafters.

She dropped to both knees on the floor, jaw gaping, eyes wide with shock. The hem of her faded flower-print dress was scrunched up, revealing the nylons rolled down around her swollen ankles. The second guy in black stepped up behind her, put the muzzle of silenced assault rifle to the back of her head and fired once.

Large Marge's head exploded, her skull and brains a pink fan that sprayed half the room. She crumpled forward, falling onto her ruined face.

The first guy kicked open the restaurant's front door.

Both of the psychos were in serious bodybuilder shape. Not an ounce of fat on either of them. Short hair, clean shaved, tanned, they had a military bearing. And they killed almost nonchalantly, as if it were a day in the park.

Were they whacked-out neo-Nazis from Idaho? Rupert wondered.

No, he decided. He couldn't see any swastika or Aryan Nation tattoos. The tats he could see were weird. They both had the same one on the inside of their fore-arm: a black silhouette bat with wings spread over a stylized globe. Maybe they were part of some psycho killer vampire cult?

"All of you, get in the corner," the first guy said. "Crawl…"

He had a funny accent, as if he were gargling marbles.

Then it dawned on the Clallam Bay corrections officer who the guys were and where they were from. They were Russians off the grounded sub.

Rupert tried to make himself as small as possible behind the overturned table. No mean feat.

No one stepped forward to speak up for the hostages, or for themselves for that matter. Under the circumstances, it was understandable.

The man kneeling right next to Rupert was a lanky guy in logger bibfronts, rubber boots and a long john top. He had a hinky, wild look in his eyes like a squirrel caught in a live trap.

Rupert knew the fool was going to make a break for it, knew it was going to be suicide, but he didn't say anything and he didn't reach out to stop him.

The logger bolted up from the floor like a sprinter, head down, arms pumping, legs driving for the café's kitchen door.

The second black shirt made a precision pivot from his hips, a narrow arc that brought the sights of his assault weapon in line with the running man. The rifle stuttered and he put four shots in the middle of the runner's back.

This was no dinky machine pistol. It fired high-velocity rounds. Tumblers. As they penetrated they didn't just cut holes, they carved slots in bone, muscle and organ.

The logger never even made it to the service counter. Parts blown out of him splattered wetly across the far wall. Like Large Marge, he ended up on his face, in a dead heap.

Then they all heard the sound of a siren, coming from the left, from up the grade. It was getting louder and louder.

Rupert's heart leaped. There was a state patrol station about a mile up the hill. The cavalry was coming.

While the second guy guarded the hostages at gunpoint, the other one stepped back out through the front door.

None of the huddled captives could see what was going on from their position on the floor in the back corner.

The siren kept wailing, but after a few seconds it didn't get any louder. Rupert figured the state patrol car had to have stopped on the far side of the Russian's roadblock. Then came a string of rapid-fire pistol shots. The state trooper was opening up big-time on the Russian. After eight shots, Rupert lost count.

"Get 'im! Get 'im!" he muttered through clenched teeth.

A now all-too-familiar sound rolled over them. Familiar and ominous. The sound of another rifle grenade exploding.

The automatic pistol abruptly stopped firing.

"Just be reloading," Rupert pleaded with eyes shut tight. "Just be reloading."

The siren continued to whoop, but there was no more gunfire from the roadblock.

Another explosion erupted, then the siren went silent, too.

CHAPTER FOURTEEN

Port Angeles, Washington,
9:01 a.m. PDT

When Grimaldi banked the helicopter hard, the g force woke up Lyons. He rubbed his face with both hands, then pulled on his intercom headset. "What's up?" he said, looking out the aircraft's wraparound front window. They were flying over the strait, heading west, more than a mile offshore. "Where are we?"

"We've got a new destination, Ironman," Blancanales told him. "Port Angeles is a no-go."

"What happened?"

"Apparently there's been a bio- or chemical-weapon release on the Hook," Grimaldi said. "It's related to the sub beaching. Could be an accident. Could be a planned attack. But it's looking more and more like an attack."

"There are mass casualties on the ground," Schwarz said. "Two choppers have already crashed, one Coast Guard, one Navy, with no survivors. Stony Man thinks whatever was released from the sub caused the crashes.

The pilots must've gotten dosed or infected as they circled over the site."

"They didn't have protective suits on board," Blancanales said.

"Neither do we," Grimaldi said. "Only Navy Haz-Mat has those and they just landed on the Hook."

"So, what are we into here?" Lyons said.

"Hard to say at this point," Blancanales told him. "Everything's still fluid. We've been ordered to give Port Angeles a wide berth. We're going farther west to check out a possible landing by personnel from the Russian sub. Stony Man tracked three wave skimmers running ashore before the ship grounded itself. An apparent carjacking with a homicide took place in the area where Aaron figures they came ashore. The Cowboy thinks they could be Spetsnaz, and that they could be carrying additional stocks of the weapon that was released on the Hook."

"This isn't exactly a sneak attack, is it?" Lyons said.

"Just the opposite," Schwarz said. "It guarantees maximum media coverage."

As the entrance to Port Angeles Bay came up on the left, Grimaldi banked the helicopter again, heading upwind, moving even farther out over the strait and climbing to an altitude of two thousand feet.

All patrol aircraft had pulled away to a safe distance.

Lyons picked up a pair of image-stabilizer binoculars and looked southwest. He could see huge fires burning out of control in downtown Port Angeles. Skipperless boats bobbed along the bay shoreline; some of them had been run aground. There were bodies strewed around the Coast Guard air-station hangar and down the length of the Hook. Firefighters, EMTs, police, SEALs and civilians. The only sign of life was the HazMat team. They were walking on the landing strip in moon-suits.

Even from two miles out, the Russian sub looked enormous.

The comm unit crackled with an update from the Farm. It was yet another change of plans.

"We just got word of a 911 request from the town of Sequim that may be connected to the shore party," Brognola told them. "It's a home-invasion robbery. The responding officer is down. There are multiple civilian fatalities."

"What makes you think this has anything to do with the sub?" Lyons said.

"The Toyota truck belonging to the homicide victim from Freshwater Bay is parked at the scene," Brognola said. "We also have an unconfirmed report of a Russian-made, suppressor-equipped assault weapon."

"We're on our way," Grimaldi said. He abruptly changed course, turning a tight 180 and heading back the way they'd come.

"The Sequim PD is stretched very thin," Brognola told them after he gave Grimaldi the crime scene's GPS coordinates. "A skeleton crew is all that's left there. The rest are helping man the roadblocks outside Port Angeles. The Bureau has personnel on the ground. They just arrived."

"And if Russians from the sub are involved?" Schwarz asked.

"Pick up the trail and hunt them down," Brognola said. "We have to assume that they've got more of the bioweapon and that they intend to use it. They have to be found and neutralized before they reach Seattle or Tacoma, or we're going to have an unheard-of catastrophe on our hands—multiply Port Angeles by a factor of ten thousand. Be careful, as always, but take these bastards out."

After the connection was broken, Schwarz said, "Talk about needle in a haystack! We don't know how many opposition there are. We don't know what their primary target is. We don't know if they have sleepers already in position to give them tactical support. We don't know if they're suiciders."

"Do you get the feeling the wheels are coming off?" Blancanales said.

"If that's the case, we're going to screw them back on," Lyons said.

SEQUIM, WASHINGTON, sat nestled in the rain shadow of the Olympic Mountains. From the base of the Olympic foothills, broad, sloping meadowlands stretched to the shoreline of the strait. Able Team flew along the water at fifteen hundred feet until they got close to the coordinates, then they turned inland. Grimaldi angled across the narrow two-lane road that paralleled the strait.

"That's it ahead," he said as they approached a cluster of buildings in a tree-bordered meadow. He circled the target location. The sprawling two-story house had to have been at least five thousand square feet. The RV garage and the barn were two stories, too. A Toyota pickup, two Sequim PD cruisers and a black Ford Crown Victoria without a light bar were parked on the long horseshoe driveway. A hatless man in a cop uniform was bent over double, leaning on the front bumper of the Crown Vic; he didn't look up as their aircraft began to descend.

Grimaldi set the chopper down in the pasture next to the barn. After he shut off the engine, all of them bailed onto the dewy grass.

As they hopped the split-rail fence and started up the driveway, an FBI agent came barreling out the double front doors and down the flagstone stairs. He had on a dark blue nylon windbreaker with big block letters in yellow on the back; his billcap had the same lettering embroidered across the front: FBI. The untrimmed, adjustable plastic hat strap stuck out a good three inches from the side of his head, which made his skull seem a lot smaller than it was and gave him a decidedly goofy look.

As the man approached them with arms spread, palms out, Schwarz told the others, "Let's not forget what Kate said about making waves."

"Hey, we're the big dogs in this yard," Blancanales replied. "If we don't lean on their buttons, they'll know something's fishy."

"Makes sense to me," Lyon agreed.

"The Bureau's got everything covered, gentlemen," the agent informed them, holding out his arms to gather them in and block their path to the house. "No need for you to be here. You have much more pressing matters on your plates this morning."

"We have to take a look," Lyons told him. "It's our job."

"Sorry, I can't let you do that," the man said. "No one goes in the house until after our crime-scene techs get through processing it. That's Bureau standard procedure in a homicide."

"And when are your techs going to show up?" Schwarz asked.

"Frankly, I have no idea. Sorry."

"Don't be," Lyons said as he brushed past him.

Schwarz, Grimaldi and Blancanales followed.

The unhappy FBI agent was forced to bring up the rear.

When they got to the Crown Vic, the Sequim cop was still bent over the bumper. His face was ashen. He kept spitting over and over, trying to get the taste of vomit out from his mouth. Strands of bile draped over the toes of his black brogues.

"You okay, buddy?" Blancanales asked.

The cop shook his head.

"Sit down a minute," Grimaldi told him, "get your breath."

The special agent paid no attention to the local cop; he rushed into the house to warn his fellow agents that DHS was coming.

Grimaldi stayed outside to help the officer while Lyons led the others up the stairs, through the double doors and into the wide flagstone foyer. On the right it opened onto a sunken great room with a skylighted, two-story ceiling and a wall lined with long, narrow windows to catch the afternoon sun. Another wall was covered by an enormous stone fireplace. The plaster was pocked with lines of bullet holes; some of the windows were shot out.

It reeked like a cross between a slaughterhouse and a shooting gallery.

The four agents stood in a row at the end of the foyer, presenting a unified front and a wall of bodies between Able Team and the rest of the murder house. They were all wearing the field jackets. They had powder-blue protective booties over their street shoes and white latex gloves on their hands.

"You were told to stay out of here," a rangy, bald-headed guy said. His official Bureau windbreaker was so fresh from the package that it still had rectangular creases in the front.

"Couldn't do that," Lyons said. "We've got our orders, too."

The bald special agent in charge glanced at their ID tags. A token check. As if he couldn't be bothered reading their names.

"Have you ever been through a crime scene before?" the special agent in charge asked.

He didn't say, "you DHS turkeys," but it was there in his tone.

"We've seen a few," Lyons admitted, his expression deadpan.

"Well, this one's a real mess. Multiple gunshot homicides. I can't have you puking all over my evidence."

"If we have to hurl we promise to swallow it," Blancanales assured him.

"Is that supposed to be funny?" the SAC said. "We drove up here all the way from the Tacoma branch. This is *our* crime scene."

"This *was* your crime scene," Lyons said. "Face the facts. You can't stop us. We're going through the scene whether you like it or not. If you're that worried about the integrity of the evidence, give us your booties and gloves. Come on, make it snappy. We're on the clock here, Agent…."

The SAC's face suffused with hot blood. The look in his eyes said he wanted to give the trio of johnny-come-lately glory grabbers a piece of his mind; it said he wanted to defend the Bureau's turf by protesting the intrusion up the chain of command. But in the new pecking order all that was a waste of breath. "Go on, give them your booties and gloves," he told the others.

The agents took off their shoe coverings and gloves. After Able Team had put them on, the SAC warned his men to stay where they were.

Lyons led his teammates down into the great room. The furniture had been shot up, as well as the walls and windows. Gaudy and expensive hand-blown glass lamps were blown to pieces. The stuffing had been knocked out of leather-upholstered armchairs. There were scads of empty shell casings scattered on the off-white Berber carpet.

Lyons bent down and picked one up.

"Son of a fucking bitch," the SAC muttered loud enough for all to hear.

"Five point four five, Russian," Lyons said. He let the casing drop back onto the rug.

Blancanales and Schwarz had crossed to the other side of the room and stood over a dead uniform cop. At the foot of the two-story-high wall, he was face up in a puddle of dark, sticky blood that had soaked into the carpet. His blue-steel Beretta 92 lay where he had dropped it, inches from his outstretched hand. There were multiple bullets impacts to his body armor. He had been hit in the left arm, and had taken a rifle slug to center face. The 5.45 mm Russian round had a specially designed hollow tip that deformed on impact, making the bullet tumble, which created a devastating destruction track and a keyhole-shaped exit wound. The back of the officer's head was gone. It had hit the wall behind him along with a plume of brains and blood.

Across the wide room, on a built-in conversation-pit couch, another body lay sprawled on its side. Presumably it was one of the perps. He was a big, sandy-haired guy in black T-shirt and black jeans. Late twenties. His eyelids were half-closed, his face slack in death, the mouth drooping from the pull of gravity.

"Look at the tat," Schwarz said. He reached down and turned the dead man's forearm into view.

It was a stylized black vampire bat with spread wings covering a stylized globe.

"Looks like Cowboy was right," Lyons said.

The Spetsnaz sailor had a significant gunshot wound to the upper left quadrant of his chest. The exit track came out through his right shoulder blade. But what had killed him was a high-velocity, close-range gunshot to the base of the neck. With both hands, Lyons carefully lifted the dead man's head. The bullet had through and throughed into the bloody couch cushion. The Spetsnaz was already down when he'd been shot.

"Maybe it was a mercy bullet? Coup de grâce?" Gadgets speculated.

"Check out this dropped piece," Blancanales said pointing at the rug on the other side of an end table.

As Lyons and Schwarz joined Blancanales, the SAC said to their backs, "We've never seen anything like that. We're going to have to send that weapon to firearms division for identification."

"That won't be necessary," Lyons said. "It's a Russian AKS-74U Shorty Assault Rifle. Eight-inch barrel. Thirty-round plastic mag. With PBS silencer and BS-1 silent underbarrel grenade launcher."

"The 74 Shorty is one deadly little package," Schwarz told the head agent. "With the stock folded up, it's the size of a machine pistol, but it has a mil-spec rifle cartridge wallop. We're talking about two and a half times the muzzle velocity of a 9 mm Parabellum round."

"Very interesting," the SAC said, without meaning it. From his fixed, hooded expression it was obvious that he was still going to send the assault rifle out for official Bureau identification.

"Is this all of it?" Blancanales asked him.

"No. There's plenty more bodies. The home owners got themselves killed, too. Come this way."

The special agent led them to the other side of the house, and the laundry room. The door was open and five people were dead on the quarry tile floor. Four of them were senior citizens; the fifth was a very short, dark-skinned latina in her thirties. All had been head shot at close range from the rear, execution style. Their wrists were taped behind their backs. High-velocity spatter clung to the walls and ceiling, and the front of the washer and dryer. Laundry hanging up on an interior clothesline was no longer clean. From the spray pattern it looked as if they had been shot on their knees.

"Who were they?" Lyons said.

"According to the next-door neighbor," the SAC said, "there were two full-time residents, two guests and a live-in cook and maid."

"How many perps were involved?" Gadgets said.

"Unknown," the SAC said. "The neighbor saw a couple of the family cars pull away. He couldn't see inside them."

"How long ago was that?"

"Fifteen minutes."

"Have you got an APB out on them?"

"Not yet. We're still trying to get the model and license plates from Washington state DMV."

"Let's talk to the neighbor," Lyons said.

"We've already got all his information."

"Good for you," Lyons said.

The house next door was a modest late-fifties bungalow on a small lot. The postage-stamp front yard was surrounded by a low chain-link fence. Inside the fence was an elaborate and cluttered miniature garden, complete with droves of ceramic gnomes and rabbits, concrete birdbaths decorated with mosaic tile and a couple of fish ponds with tiny, electrically powered waterfalls. As Lyons started to open the gate in the fence, an old guy in an electric golf cart whirred down the driveway at high speed. He tooted his horn at them and waved. He had on a straw Panama hat and thick-lensed, aviator-style glasses. A thin, clear plastic oxygen line was looped over his head and clipped into his nostrils. The oxygen tank sat on the bench seat beside him.

"You guys are Homeland Security?" the neighbor asked, looking at their sleeve patches after he brought his cart to a jolting halt. "Is what happened next door connected with that mess over in P.A.?"

"That's what we're looking into now, sir," Lyons said.

"Did you call the police?" Schwarz asked him.

"Yeah, around 8:00 a.m. I was out back, watering my rosebushes. I saw some guys in a Toyota pickup pull up the driveway. White guys. They broke in through the front door. Cop car showed up at eight-fifteen."

"How many guys got out of the truck?"

"I couldn't see them too well. I was looking through the tree branches along the property line. Right after the cop went in I heard a couple of pistol shots. I'd have gone over there myself, but I'm kind of bunged up these days."

Lying across the rear platform of the golf cart was a scoped Remington 7400 semiauto rifle with a leather shoulder sling. A .270-caliber. The checkered walnut grips of a Government Colt .45 hooked over the waistband of the old man's yellow-and-white-plaid golf slacks.

"You're loaded for bear there, sir," Lyons said.

"Haven't used the rifle since my lungs went to hell," the neighbor said. "I brought the side arm home from Korea as a souvenir. Figured what with all the Russian crap going on in P.A. I'd better be prepared. I killed Commies when I was in the Army. They were Chinese, though."

The old guy paused, then said, "Are the Weavers okay? They're nice people. Rich but not stuck-up. Retired from Los Angeles. Had some relatives visiting them from down south."

Lyons didn't answer. He asked another question. "What happened after you heard the pistol shots?"

"A few minutes later the garage door opened up and some cars roared down the driveway."

"How many?"

"Two cars. The Weavers have three, if you count the Suburban."

"The SUV is still there," Schwarz said. "I saw it."

"They have a gold Maxima sedan and a white Volvo station wagon," the neighbor said. "Both of them are a year or two old. You didn't say if they were all right."

"Thanks for your help," Lyons said. "Sir, you can put your guns away now. Everything's under control."

When they got back to the entrance of the murder house, the FBI agents were ganged up on Grimaldi and the SAC was giving him a hard time. The Stony Man pilot looked faintly amused by it all.

"This is an emergency," the bald SAC was telling him. "We're all on the same team here."

"What's going on?" Lyons said.

"We're all on the same team now," Grimaldi said as he carefully inspected the unlit end of his stub of a cigar.

"We just picked up an officer-needs-assistance call from a state trooper," the SAC told Lyons. "There's a shoot-out in progress down at Large Marge's in Discovery Bay, about ten miles east of here on 101. It's a major incident. Automatic weapons. Grenades. Multiple fatalities. Hostages. Got the highway blocked off in both directions with wrecked cars and trucks. Sounds like the same guys who did this have moved their act down the road."

"Could be our boys," Schwarz said.

"Most definitely our boys," Blancanales agreed.

"What's Large Marge's?" Lyons asked.

"It's a funky restaurant at the end of Discovery Bay, right on 101," said the agent with the goofy hat strap. "Big chain-saw sculptures out front of a fat lady and giant hamburger."

"Not ringing any bells," Lyons said. "What does the Bureau want from us?"

"Give us a ride to the action over there," the SAC said. "You've got room in the chopper. We can be your backup."

"Sorry, no can do," Lyons told him. Then he added dryly, "This is a job for Homeland Security."

The SAC's face went all red again. "What? You're turning down our help?"

The second question was shouted at their backs as they ran for the split-rail fence.

In two minutes, Grimaldi had the helicopter and Able Team lifting off from the horse pasture.

Blancanales's very amused voice crackled in the intercom headsets. "Ironman, you went and did it. You really pissed off those Feds. The SAC was hopping mad. Pop-a-blood-vessel mad."

"I just saved their lives," Lyons said matter-of-factly. "This is Russian special forces, not some pimple-faced jerk pirating DVDs in his basement."

As the chopper circled to the east, they saw the FBI's black Crown Victoria peeling off in the direction of Highway 101.

"With lights and siren," Grimaldi said, "it'll take them at least fifteen minutes to get there."

"With any luck, by then all the fun will be over," Lyons said.

CHAPTER FIFTEEN

Stony Man Farm, Virginia,
12:14 p.m. EDT

After Able Team broke off the scrambled, in-flight debriefing on the Sequim murder house and the ongoing shoot-out at the Discovery Bay café, Hal Brognola addressed the assembled Stony Man cyberunit. "The tattoo and the weaponry are confirmation that our hostiles are a Spetsnaz unit that came from the submarine," he said. "Most likely on the three wave skimmers we tracked."

"We know they've taken the lives of at least seven Americans so far this morning," Delahunt said.

"And the day is young," Wethers added. "From the description of the shoot-out on 101, that number is going to go a lot higher."

"They abandoned one of their crew at the Sequim house," Kurtzman said. "Safe guess is the cop shot him before he went down himself. Spetsnaz couldn't take the wounded guy with them, and they couldn't risk leaving him behind because of what he knew about the mission. So they executed him on the spot."

"If there is a rational plan here," Tokaido said, "the point of it escapes me. It's like…helter-skelter."

"They are continuing to draw as much attention to themselves as possible," Brognola said. "And you're right, Akira, they're acting like spree killers."

"It's like they want to get caught," Delahunt said.

"Or they're taunting us in full view of the news cameras," Price said. "Daring us to stop them."

"We know they're down one soldier," Wethers said, "but we still don't know how many are left."

"We know there are at least two," Kissinger said. "Because there are two missing vehicles from the Sequim house."

"They left the stolen Toyota pickup at the scene," Tokaido said. "They changed vehicles to throw off pursuit, and so they could divide their force and increase the chances of accomplishing their mission, whatever that is."

"Do we have the carrying capacity of the wave skimmers?" Brognola asked.

"According to the Russians, they hold a maximum of two passengers," Kissinger said.

"A total of six possible hostiles," Price said.

"But as few as three in the landing party," Kurtzman said. "And one is dead. Which would leave just a pair."

"There were two cars taken from Sequim," Wethers said. "That could mean there are two Spetsnaz left. Or maybe it's just supposed to *look* like there are just two left?"

"My guess is, they intended to lay low at the Sequim house for a while," Brognola said. "With all the hubbub in Port Angeles, they didn't count on that uniform cop showing up so quickly."

"Either that or they're just making it up as they go, guerrilla style," Price said.

"Working without a net," Kurtzman agreed.

"They could all be holed up in the restaurant right now," Kissinger said. "Wouldn't that be sweet?"

"Sweet, but it's not very likely," Brognola said. "The question is, why did they pick that particular restaurant?"

"Maybe something went wrong?" Delahunt suggested. "Maybe one of the cars they stole broke down. Maybe they got into an accident on 101."

"There's no way to tell," Price said. "As it stands, we've got no eyes and ears on the ground."

"We won't get any, either, not until Able has the situation under control," Brognola said.

"There are some other possibilities, purely strategic, I think we have to consider," Wethers said.

"We're all ears," Kurtzman told him.

"The hostage taking could be a diversion by part of the Spetsnaz team. Meant to draw attention away from the others. Intended to sow more confusion among the pursuit and panic among the general population. That would buy time for the remainder of the unit to get into position in a population center."

"Are they carrying a bioweapon?" Delahunt asked.

"We won't know what they have until they release it or until Able Team sorts through the bodies at the scene," Brognola said.

"Better that they turn it loose in Discovery Bay, population maybe seventy-five people, than Seattle or Tacoma with millions," Kurtzman said.

"They haven't threatened to use a bioweapon so far," Tokaido said.

"They haven't made any attempts to communicate with the state troopers and county sheriffs on the scene," Price said. "No demands. No public proclamations. No manifestos. Nothing like that."

"Even if it turns out the hostage takers at the restaurant don't have this Red Frost bioweapon," Wethers said, "it doesn't prove anything. The Spetsnaz soldiers still on the loose—if there are others—would be the ones transporting the weapon, and tasked with deployment against specific high-value targets."

"Thanks to our new Russian e-mail buddies, we've got details of the weapon's appearance and likely applications," Kurtzman told Brognola. "The weaponized bacteria is sealed in glass vials along with nutrients. They melt the ends of a glass cylinder and draw them into closed points at both ends. The high temperature creates a vacuum inside the container that keeps the bacterial spores in hibernation mode. The vials are about the size of a cigar tube."

"How many people can one of them infect?" Delahunt queried.

"The number is virtually unlimited," Kissinger said. "Each of the vials could contain millions of the microscopic weaponized spores. Theoretically just a few of them could lead to the kind of awful death we saw on the live video feed. As the bacteria infects, it reproduces, rapidly making more copies of itself outside and inside the victim. According to the Russians, once inside a victim it secretes a chemical that causes the body to attack its own collagen. After it is released into an environment it spreads via person-to-person contact—inhalation, ingestion and through breaks in the skin."

"The applications of this thing are off the chart," Wethers said. "Take a dry day like today in Seattle, and drop one of those vials from an overpass onto the freeway at rush hour. It would shatter on the road, and the cars and trucks driving through the dust would whip the bacteria into the air, and transport it all through the city's central core along the highway. The commuters would carry the bacteria home to the suburbs with them."

"It could also be taken up to the roof of a downtown skyscraper and broken there," Kissinger said. "A strong wind would lift it high into the atmosphere and spread it for miles across the city."

"This stuff is easily dispersed by any number of means," Kurtzman said. "The only bright note is the death gene."

"What?" Delahunt said.

"Dr. Vorostov built in a genetic off switch," Kurtzman said. "After a certain number of generations the weapon stops reproducing and dies off. Otherwise any place that was infected would never be inhabitable again."

"We don't know that the designated target is the Pacific Northwest," Brognola said, "but it stands to reason that it is because of the time element. The longer the renegade Spetsnaz are on the loose the more likely it is they'll be caught and stopped."

"The Russians sent us a potential target list," Price said. "But it's twenty years out of date. It looks like the original list developed by the weapon designer. It isn't much, and the targets listed are all pretty obvious, but it's a starting point."

"With what we've got, we can't advise the President put out a code-red alarm," Kurtzman said.

"A code red would really be letting the cat out of the bag," Delahunt said. "And there'd be no getting it back."

"More to the point," Price said, "what would a maximum security warning accomplish at this stage? People just got to work in the three most likely target states. All DHS could do would be to tell them to go back home and stay indoors. Panic and chaos is what these bad guys want. Clogged streets and freeways would make their weapon a whole lot more effective."

"You're right," Kurtzman said. "We don't have any of the specifics nailed down. We don't know what the mission's goal is."

"What about the victims in Port Angeles?" Brognola said. "What's the word?"

"The latest update is grim," Tokaido said. "Everyone downwind of the sub grounding is either dead or dying. The people on the outskirts of town, and those higher on the slopes of the foothills, seem to be doing okay for now. Navy HazMat medical personnel have taken over the local hospital. More federal and state decontamination teams are on their way. The only good news is, the symptoms seem to be confined to the immediate Port Angeles area. There are no reports of illness to the west or the east."

"That is good news," Brognola said.

"Are we being led down the garden path here by Spetsnaz?" Kissinger asked, returning the discussion to a previous topic. "Could this spree business be a total misdirection? Up to this point, our hostiles have acted as if they have no resources to draw on, no sleepers in position to help them accomplish their mission. Hey, a sleeper agent could just have picked them up at Freshwater Bay with no one the wiser. No murder, no stolen truck. They could have gotten themselves to their target without risk of discovery, delivered the bioweapon and then disappeared."

"But they couldn't have spread the maximum amount of panic that way," Price said. "Anticipated disaster is the key here, anticipation and dread."

"The lack of ground support does seem fairly unlikely, given the complexity of the operation," Kurtzman agreed.

"What do the 'good' Russians have to say about that?" Brognola asked.

"They say they are unable to provide us with information about sleepers at this time," Wethers said.

"Unable or unwilling?" Price said.

"We have to take them at their word," the big Fed said. "Bottom line, they have as much at stake here as we do."

"Maybe Able can find something at the restaurant that will fill in some of the blanks," Delahunt said.

"Don't get your hopes up, Carmen," Kurtzman replied. "These Russian special forces guys are well-trained and well-prepped. Just because we don't know what they're doing doesn't mean they don't."

"Press the Russian intel source harder, Bear," Brognola said. "In case they are holding back what they think they can get away with."

"Assuming the Spetsnaz at the restaurant are carrying the bioweapon, how is Able going to deal with it?" Wethers asked. "They don't have protective gear. They're putting themselves at grave risk."

"The stand-off could go on all day," Tokaido said.

"That can't happen," Price said adamantly. "The longer it gets dragged out, the greater the risk of a catastrophic and unthinkable disaster. The situation has to be resolved ASAP."

"Don't worry about Able," Brognola said. "They'll find a way to get in and a way to get out. They always do."

"We can't count on capturing any of the Spetsnaz alive," Kissinger said. "Essentially, the hostage taking at Discovery Bay is a suicide mission. Think about it. They've shut off the highway at a single point. The reinforcement routes by land, sea and air are still wide open. They've boxed themselves in. There's no way they're coming out of this alive."

"It's another opportunity to draw media attention," Price said. "And it exposes to the world the fact that the situation vis-à-vis the submarine incursion isn't anywhere near contained."

"These conspirators don't care about engendering sympathy for their cause in the U.S.," Kurtzman said. "They don't even care enough to make their cause public. Why would they? We're the sworn enemy of their fallen nation. We're the reason for their suffering and humiliation."

"Frankly, I don't think they give a damn about engendering sympathy in the former Soviet Union, either," Kissinger said. "I think their goal is to force the respective governments' hands through a single cataclysmic attack, thereby reviving the old cold war suspicions and hostilities, and ultimately bringing about some reincarnation of the Soviet war machine."

"And to turn back the hands of time," Price added, "they're willing to take down hundreds of thousands of innocent people."

"We can't let that happen," Brognola said. "Not on our watch."

CHAPTER SIXTEEN

Discovery Bay,
9:18 a.m. PDT

As Grimaldi skimmed the tops of tall firs and spruce that bordered Highway 101, Lyons looked down on the two-lane road below. More than a mile from the scene of the shoot-out, traffic was already backed up in the southerly direction. Some cars at the end of the line were K-turning and heading back the way they'd come, toward Sequim. Other than that, there was no traffic coming north. Beyond the fringe of trees on the left, the hillside dropped five hundred feet to the long, relatively narrow bay.

Farther on, people were out of the stopped vehicles—a lot more people than there were cars and trucks to carry them. When Grimaldi followed the highway around a dogleg right turn, it became obvious what was going on. The downgrade that led to the bay was clogged with abandoned vehicles. They were parked on and off the road, left behind in haste, if not panic. The drivers and passengers had hurried up the highway, around the bend and out of the line of fire.

Grimaldi overflew the state patrol station on the right and whipped down the grade. A mile ahead, the highway flattened out and curved around the end of bay, where it necked down to nothing.

The makeshift roadblock closest to them was a jumble of burning cars and trucks. A pall of greasy black smoke drifted over the mud flats of low tide. There were bodies on the highway, as well—and sprays of glass from chain-reaction rear-end collisions.

"Goddamn mess," Blancanales stated.

"Looks like a Monday afternoon in Baghdad," Schwarz said.

Climbing to two hundred feet, Grimaldi did a quick flyby.

As they hurtled south, Lyons took in the little commercial enclave nestled at the head of the bay. On the left of the highway was a kiddie park with a six-car, gaily painted, antique passenger train. The right side of the road was shared by a shambling secondhand store, a chain-saw sculptor's workshop, a fish market in a rusting, WWII metal Quonset hut and a tiny, drive-through espresso stand. On the far side of the espresso stand stood the red-sided, single-story restaurant with cartoon-figure statues out front.

Just beyond the café, the highway forked. The left fork led up around the east side of the bay to Port Townsend; the right continued on to Hood Canal. The grassy hillside above the split in the road was dotted with a row of dollhouse motel cabins and a ramshackle Victorian farmhouse.

As they swept by the restaurant, they passed over the

overturned semitrailer and the beige fan of wood chips across the road. Beyond, more cars were burning. Cars with shot-out windshields.

Around the next bend, the local cops were out in force. There were more a dozen squad cars and a couple of ambulances, all with lights flashing. Human-shaped forms lay on the road under sheets of bright yellow plastic. Road flares littered the pavement. The police were turning traffic around, sending it back toward Scattle.

As Grimaldi made a hard right turn, starting to circle back, something spanged on the skid under Lyon's seat.

"Whoa!" Schwarz exclaimed.

"That's incoming!" Blancanales said.

There was no gunshot report.

Just the slug's impact.

Grimaldi took evasive action, dropping low and crossing over a vegetation-choked creek bed. He skirted the forested slope as he continued the spiral to the northwest. The fast, tight pivot prevented the sniper from getting off a second shot. At the top of the grade, the Stony Man pilot swung back over the highway just to the west of the dogleg. He carefully set the chopper down in a clear-cut field on the side of the road.

Lyons, Schwarz and Blancanales exited the aircraft, lugging their fighting gear in padded cases. With Grimaldi bringing up the rear, they jumped onto the highway's shoulder and jogged downhill to the bottleneck bend.

Motorists stood on the side of the road and sat inside their vehicles. Some looked dazed; a few were bleeding. They greeted the men in black with cheers, clapping and horn honking.

Just before the highway made the right turn out of the killzone, a lone state trooper was trying to contain an unmanageable situation. He was tall, young, ramrod straight and clearly overwhelmed by what had landed in his lap. He had either lost or discarded his uniform hat.

"Man, am I glad to see you guys," he said. "How many more of your people are coming?"

"For the time being, we're it," Schwarz said.

The incredulous trooper said, "Oh, man…"

"What's the situation?" Lyons asked him.

"I tried to move the civilians trapped between here and the pile-up out of their cars and up the hill," the trooper told them. "But I'm not sure I got them all. I came under some heavy fire and had to pull back before I could check the vehicles at the front of the line. It just got too hairy."

"How many hostages down at the restaurant?" Lyons said.

"I don't know," the trooper admitted. "When I rolled on the scene, the shoot-out was already in progress. From the cars parked out front, there could be fifteen or twenty people in there, counting the hired help. There've been no demands. No word from inside. They just keep shooting at anything that moves."

"Do you know how many shooters?" Blancanales asked.

"It's hard to say. We're not hearing gunshots. There are no muzzle-flashes, either. But bullets keep whizzing past, real close. They're firing this way and down the highway in the other direction. They're using silencers."

"Definitely," Schwarz said.

"So you've got no idea what the shooters took in with them?" Lyons queried, making double sure of the facts.

"The only people who saw that are the hostages inside the café. And they sure aren't talking." The trooper shook his head. "They could all be dead, couldn't they? We wouldn't even have heard the shots."

"Say, are you hit?" Lyons asked, looking at the man's back. His uniform shirt was scorched and there were horizontal tears in the fabric. His armored vest was showing through the rips.

"No," the trooper said. "Just bruised, thanks to the trauma plate. I was the only one on duty up at the station when all hell broke loose down here. The rest of my unit was out west, helping deal with the situation in P.A. I heard the first explosions and got down the hill as fast as I could. I arrived just in time to get grenaded. Man, oh, man, I've never been through anything like that. Blew the holy hell out of my cruiser, but I had already bailed. The blast and shrap knocked me down, but I was lucky. It didn't knock me out, and I managed to crawl to cover before the shooter could finish me off."

"Who's on the far side of the restaurant?" Lyons said.

"There's Jefferson County sheriffs and city cops from Port Townsend. They drove around on 104 to come up on the south side of 101. All available personnel are on the scene at that end. They've got the highway sealed off. Neither department has a sharpshooter. The sheriff's detective has been trying to make contact with the bad guys, but they aren't answering the phone or responding to the bullhorn."

After a pause, the trooper said, "This is connected

to what's going on in P.A., isn't it? These guys are Russians?"

"Could be," Lyons said. "We need to reconnoiter the site and make sure."

"Is that a good idea?" the trooper said. "Won't it put the hostages in even more danger?"

"Like you said," Blancanales told him, "they could all already be dead. We know what we're doing. We're not going to screw up."

Lyons then pulled his three team members aside, just out of the state trooper's earshot.

"I'll take Jack and head down the bay side of the highway along the shoulder," he said. "We'll try to draw fire from the shooters and keep them occupied. Pol and Gadgets, you take the other side of the highway, keep close to the buildings and stay out of sight of the hostiles. When we flew over down there, I saw a creek bed that dumps into the bay. It crosses under the highway near that little espresso stand. Jump down into the creek and follow it behind the café. Pol, see if you can get close enough to the restaurant's back door to use the tactical video-audio system to peek inside. We need hard info on the number of hostiles, the number of hostages and the location of the bioweapon, if it's really in there. But don't go kicking down any doors until I give the word."

Blancanales nodded, then began digging around in one of the duffels for the covert-spy-cam kit.

"Gadgets," Lyons continued, "you keep following the creek. Swing around past the end of the building and hook up with the sheriffs on the highway on the other side. There's some high ground on the slope where the motel is. It should give you a good shot angle with the

Barrett. Find your hide and wait for my signal to fire at will."

"And what if these guys do have more of the damn bioweapon stashed inside?" Blancanales asked.

It was the six-thousand-pound elephant in the room.

"Bear said the glass vials would be kept in a well-padded case, a backpack or a suitcase," Lyons said. "We've got to separate it from the hostiles before they can use it."

"But we can't just blow them out of their socks," Schwarz protested. "They're our only source of intel on the mission's primary targets and the number of Spetsnaz still running around."

"We can blow all but one of them out of their socks," Lyons said.

"That's walking a mighty fine line," Blancanales said. "These guys aren't going to shoot to wound— they're going to shoot to kill. If one of the glass vials breaks while we're inside that restaurant, we've had it and so have all the hostages."

"Better us than half of Seattle," Lyons said. "Better it all ends right here. Based on what Spetsnaz has done so far today, we're the hostages' only chance. Here are the priorities, so we're all on the same page. Get control of the bioweapon, even if it means killing every one of the hostage takers. Wound the targets if you can, but make sure you put them down hard."

Lyons waved the trooper over to them. "Are you in radio contact with the sheriffs and PD?"

"Yeah," he replied, patting the small black radio looped through his uniform shirt's shoulder strap.

"Then tell them that DHS is coming their way on a search-and-destroy. Four guys in black uniforms with weapons moving down the hill from the north. Tell them not to shoot at us. Don't return fire at the café, either. Even if the hostiles open up on us. Stand down and let us handle it. Got that?"

"Got it."

As Able Team began breaking out its weaponry and donning combat vests and communication headpieces, the trooper transferred the information via radio. When he was done, he said, "I want to go along with you guys."

"Sorry, Trooper," Lyons said, "that just isn't going to happen. You're way undergunned for this op. Besides, someone has to handle the civilians up here. That someone is you."

"I feel like I owe the bastards down there something personal."

"You already dodged the reaper once today," Grimaldi said. "Best not stretch your luck, son."

"Don't worry about the payback," Schwarz assured the trooper as he slung the massive, scoped .50-caliber rifle. "We got that covered."

Lyons shrugged into shoulder leather and snugged his .357 Colt Python into his left armpit. As he checked the mag on an H&K MP-5 SD-3 machine pistol, Grimaldi did likewise on an M-16 carbine. The H&K had a fat, blue-steel sound suppressor threaded onto the muzzle. Lyons made sure the seal was nice and tight. From years of experience in close-quarters hostage situations, he knew that a sound suppressor could mean the difference between success and failure; an unalerted enemy was a vulnerable enemy. A suppressor offered an opportunity for multiple killshots.

"Let's do this," Lyons said, waving Blancanales and Schwarz across the road.

Blancanales took the lead carrying another silenced H&K machine pistol. Burdened with twenty-five pounds of Barrett rifle, plus its extra loaded mags, Schwarz kept his hands free and his Beretta 93-R clipped into its hip holster.

Pol and Gadgets, Lyons knew, had a lot more room to work with on the landward side of the highway. The commercial buildings had been dropped onto a wide flat spot chopped from the forested hillside and back-filled out of the bay's intertidal zone. They slipped behind the rear of the first structure, the chain-saw sculptor's roadside workshop and gallery, and disappeared from Lyons's view.

On his side of the road, the shoulder dropped off sheer to the left. Below, there was a small, circular, mucky-looking tidal flat. On its outer edge stood a shambling, mostly imploded wooden structure. The decrepit warehouse had collapsed across an abandoned railroad line that ran along the bay's perimeter.

Lyons took the point, staying low and moving fast. He led Grimaldi on a weaving path through the line of ditched cars and trucks, trying as much as possible to keep auto bodies and engine blocks between them and the red restaurant downrange.

As they descended, he and Grimaldi quickly checked the insides of the vehicles for survivors, popping the doors when they could get them open, peeking over the windowsills when they couldn't. The front ends of some of the smaller cars looked like accordions from chain-reaction collisions. In some cases the air bags had deployed. They didn't start finding bodies until they were almost all the way down the grade.

There were dead people on the ground between the

vehicles, apparently shot from behind as they tried to run away, and there were dead people inside the burning wrecks. A few of the victims were still belted into their car seats, their charred heads enveloped in flame.

Way beyond hope.

Lyons and Grimaldi moved rapidly through the billowing heat and pall of caustic smoke.

The Able Team leader crouched beside the slider door of a metallic-red Chrysler minivan. The windows were tinted so dark he couldn't see inside. He pounded on the door with a balled fist. "Anybody in there?" he said.

A faint whimpering sound came from within.

When Lyons cracked back the door, he found himself staring into the terrified, bloodied face of a brunette woman in her early thirties. She was clutching her blond son, aged four or five, tight to her chest, protecting him with both her arms. They sat hunkered on the floor of the van between the front bucket and rear bench seats. The blood was coming from her nose. It looked bruised and broken.

"Are either of you badly hurt?" he said.

The woman shook her head. "No, but my husband…in the front…I couldn't leave him. He's been shot. I don't know what to do…."

"Easy, now, ma'am," Lyons said. "Just let us help you."

As he pulled the slider all the way open, Grimaldi tried the driver door, but the collision with the car in front had pinned it in the frame.

Lyons climbed into the rear compartment, alongside woman and child. The minivan's driver lay on his side across the console, his head toward the passenger seat. His safety belt was still attached. His breathing was labored, but he was alive.

Lyons stuck his head between the front seats. Both front air bags had popped. And deflated. Bullet holes pocked the corner of the passenger side of the windshield. From the low entry angle, the Russian had walked up the middle of the road, potshotting anyone he could see.

"Help them out of the van," Lyons told Grimaldi over his shoulder. "I need some room to work back here."

As Grimaldi assisted the woman and child out the door, Lyons's serrated SOG Auto-Clip made short work of the safety belt. As carefully as he could, he dragged the unconscious man between the bucket seats and onto the carpeted rear deck. When Lyons rolled the guy over onto his back, he saw the front of his shirt was soaked with wet blood, and there was a bullet hole just below his collarbone on the right side. There was no exit wound out his back. The windshield had absorbed some of the round's momentum. The driver was in shock, his face and his lips dead-white.

Lyons used his multitool to hack long strips from a polyester baby blanket that was lying on the rear seat. As he shoved a stuffed toy, a droopy eared, red-and-white puppy dog against the entry wound and lashed it in place, Grimaldi reappeared at the slider doorway.

"We've got to get this guy up the hill," Lyons told him. "Do you think you can carry him?"

"No problem," Grimaldi said. "But there aren't any ambulances up that way. No medics, no nothing."

"His wound calls for more than basic first aid," Lyons said. "No telling what the Russian tumbler cut through. He could be bleeding out internally. Get him up the hill and fly him out. Anybody else in bad shape, get them out, too. There are ambulances and EMTs to the south, behind the police barricade."

Lyons helped Grimaldi shift the wounded man to the edge of the slider doorway, then the pilot hoisted him over his shoulder in a fireman's carry.

Grimaldi straightened and turned for the rear of the van. As he started toward the mother and child crouching beside the back bumper, a flurry of bullets spanked the asphalt, kicking up sparks and puffs of dust on both sides of the vehicle. A single round zipped through roof and headliner and keyholed into the bench seat, missing Lyons's shoulder by less than eighteen inches. At one thousand yards, they were well outside the accurate range of an AKS-74U. The burst of autofire spanned fifteen feet, a tight shot group with an eight-inch barrel at that distance.

There were no gunshot reports, just the zip and whine of incoming rounds, followed by deathly silence.

Lyons guessed the shooter had to have caught the movement beside the vehicle; someone was watching the roadblock upgrade with high-power binocs or a spotting scope. Returning covering fire for the family and Grimaldi was out of the question. The targets were too far away for his machine pistol, and because their position was as yet unidentified, Jack's M-16 wouldn't work, either. Anything less than precisely aimed fire would put the restaurant's hostages at risk.

"Get going!" he shouted at Grimaldi as he scooted out of the van. "Stay low!"

Lyons took the only course of action available to him: he gave the Russians something else to shoot at.

An easy target. Fully upright, in clear view of the café, he jogged along the highway's shoulder.

Before he got ten yards, bullets started zipping past. But too high. The autofire burst ricocheted off the gravel well behind him; to his right, the slugs spanged into the asphalt and rattled the hoods of the wrecked cars.

Lyon was playing the odds.

At a range of nearly a mile, hitting a stationary target even with a scoped 74 Stubby was almost impossible; hitting a moving target *was* impossible.

There was an obvious downside to the strategy: he was running uprange, running into enemy fire. The closer he got, the better the accuracy, guaranteed.

The gunfire stopped.

Lyons really picked up the pace, striding for all he was worth. He put one hundred yards behind him, dashing across the bayside flatland without drawing another response from the Spetsnaz. He knew what they were waiting for, and he was giving it to them, teeth clenched, arms pumping.

All at once bullet fall became a minihailstorm. The impacts weren't just behind him, but ahead of him, too. More than one autoweapon was cutting loose. The shooters at the restaurant were combining fire, trying to bracket him, to force him to run headlong through the ten-ring.

Lyons broke hard left, cutting across the gravel shoulder, away from the highway, and onto the kiddie train's wide parking lot apron. There were no cars parked out front, and there was no cover until he got through the hurricane-fenced enclosure. At least the gate was standing open.

With Russian rounds skipping at his heels and kicking up loose rock in front of him, Lyons dived behind the unmanned cotton candy and peanut stand. The kiddie park was in line of sight from Large Marge's front windows. The bend in Highway 101 put the five-car train broadside to the café.

Before the Spetsnaz could zero in, he darted beneath the old-time passenger cars, all painted unlikely colors: Day-Glo yellow, green, orange. They sat on a short stretch of track, an artifact of the abandoned railroad.

Lyons scrambled out from under on the far side and got behind a massive, solid steel carriage wheel.

As he gasped for air, he heard a moaning from the railroad car above.

"Somebody in there?" he called.

"Help me," said a strained, high-pitched voice. "Please…"

Lyons grabbed the handrail and pulled himself up onto the metal platform between the dinky cars. He dived through the open doorway onto the aisle. There were wooden bench seats on either side. Below the framed windows, the walls were wood, too. A couple of the windows had been shot out, and there were splintered bullet holes along the wall that faced Large Marge's.

"I'm over here," said the weak voice. It was coming from behind the seats on the right.

When Lyons crawled closer, he saw a white-haired guy with a full white beard sitting on the floor between the seats. From the way he was dressed, Lyons guessed he was the conductor and cotton-candy maker on the kiddie train.

He was also wounded in the head.

"Let me have a look at that," Lyons said. With his thumb and forefinger, he spread the wound track that ran the length of the man's temple, lifting the bloody mop of hair out of the way. Waxy white bone showed through the deep gouge in the skin, but the skull looked intact. Dark blood coated the side of his face, and his beard was wet and glistening to the tips.

Another inch or so to the left and his brains would have been blown all over the interior.

"What's your name?" Lyons asked him.

The conductor opened his mouth, but no sound came out. A blank look came over his face. Vapor lock. He closed his mouth.

When Lyons repeated the question, he still got no answer. It was clear the old guy had a concussion, if not some even more serious brain swelling. Before Lyons could get a good look at his pupils, bullets began zinging into the side of the railroad car, blowing out chunks of the wooden wall and crashing through the glass.

"Come with me," Lyons said, pulling on the conductor's arm, "let's get you to some better cover."

Pushing the old guy in front of him, Lyons crawled back the way he had come. When they reached the doorway, he pushed the old guy out first, onto the open metal platform. Lyons really didn't have much choice in the matter. If he had gone out first, he couldn't be sure the dazed conductor would follow him, and his going first would have alerted the shooters and given them a zone to concentrate fire in.

"Go left, down the steps," Lyons told him.

The old guy crawled out on the platform just beyond his reach, the space of maybe a yard, then froze. He just stopped cold on his hands and knees.

Before Lyons could move, before he could do anything, there was a wet slapping sound.

The conductor's head and neck whipped to the left, as if he had been hit with a baseball bat. His arms and legs crumpled and he toppled, curling up and rolling off the back side of the platform, out of sight onto the ground below.

Lyons stared at the blood trailing across the metal plate.

Back splatter.

One bullet.

An eight-hundred-yard head shot.

With an AKS-74U's stubby little barrel that was an inconceivable feat of marksmanship, as well as an improbable stroke of luck. Able Team was inside the killing range of something infinitely more accurate...and deadly.

Lyons got on the horn at once.

"YEAH, I THOUGHT THAT last shot sounded different," Schwarz said after Lyons had told them the news.

A second Russian round whined from right to left in front of them, across the highway in the direction of the kiddie park. It was followed by a resounding hollow *thwunk,* the impact of lead on wood.

"Definitely a long gun working," Blancanales said.

"With a pro at the other end of it. Let's not give him any sucker shots."

"Deal."

As they approached the peeling, lime-green-painted Quonset hut, Schwarz unholstered his 9 mm Beretta, dropped the thumb safety and flipped the fire selector to 3-round burst. When Blancanales went through the fish market's back door with his machine pistol up and ready, Schwarz followed. The shop had a polished concrete slab floor, crazed with cracks. Over the sights of the 93-R, the only living things Schwarz could see were the Dungeness crabs and Hood Canal oysters and clams in glass-walled, aerated tanks. The shop reeked of bleach and iodine. The portable TV above the service counter was still on, tuned to breaking news from Port Angeles. The Discovery Bay fishmonger had evidently hightailed it over the hills.

They retraced their route out the back door, exited the market and headed for the rear of the secondhand store, about one hundred feet away. As they got closer, they both could hear the low, steady rumble of a car engine.

"Maybe someone's trying to make a getaway," Blancanales said.

Trotting to the near wall of the secondhand store, they high-lowed around the corner. Schwarz went high with the Beretta, Blancanales low with the H&K. Two sets of gunsights swept over the waste ground behind the junk shop.

A dented, gray-primered, full-sized Chevy pickup truck was nose first into the crumbling bluff, smoke puffing steadily out of its tailpipe. No driver was in evidence in the cab. Over the engine noise, a male voice was talking a mile a minute.

The two men approached the driver and passenger doors from the rear, weapons up and ready to rip. Through the open side windows the truck's dashboard was visible. It was covered with a heaps of fast-food refuse, yellowed newspaper, empty pop cans, candy wrappers and cigarette packs, all held in place by a pair of greasy pipe wrenches. The tinny voice came from the radio. It was Rush Limbaugh.

Dirt from the face of the bluff showered down on the hood, grille and bumper, adding to the load already deposited there.

"I think it's still in gear," Schwarz said.

Holding the Beretta aimed at the center of the driver door, he peeked over the top of the windowsill. A man lay sideways on the blanket-covered bench seat. He wore a red do-rag and bibfront jeans, and he had long grizzled hair and a ratty-looking beard. There was a small round hole in his left temple.

"He didn't get far," Blancanales said.

Schwarz reached in through the window, turned the ignition key and killed the engine.

Another heavy-caliber round sailed toward the kiddie park and Carl Lyons.

"Dragunov?" Blancanales speculated.

"Could be," Schwarz agreed.

The one-barista, eight-by-eight-foot portable espresso stand was deserted, the back door ajar. Behind it, a creek fed into a corrugated metal culvert under the two-lane highway. A trickle of water flowed through it. The stream bed ran perpendicular to the road until it reached the foot of the hillside to the right, then it bent around to the left, running behind the café. The roof gables of Large Marge's could just barely be seen over the top of the wall of scrub alder, devil's club and blackberry bushes that sprouted high along the bank.

The two Able Team commandos eased down into the narrow gully, which quickly became a tunnel of backlit, overarching branches—a tunnel roughly five feet high. Both men had to hunch over. Schwarz holstered his Beretta and unslung the Barrett to keep the muzzle brake from dragging across the undersides of the branches.

When they reached the bend in the bed, they saw another, smaller culvert, which directed a feeder creek coming off the hillside into the larger channel. It was only about three feet in diameter.

Big enough to hide someone.

Moving as quietly as possible, the two men approached the pipe. When they got within five yards of it, something moved inside. Something scraped on the corrugated metal, then it stopped.

"Raccoon?" Schwarz whispered.

Blancanales shook his head. He bent down and fished an object from the creek in front of them. He held it looped over his index finger for Schwarz to see. It was one of those elastic scrunchies used to hold ponytails in place. Bright bubble-gum-pink.

He moved alongside the bank, closer to the culvert's mouth, covering it with his MP-5 SD-3. He stopped just short of the opening.

"Come out of there with your hands in front of you," he said in a soft voice.

No response.

"We're Homeland Security," Blancanales said. "Don't make us pull you out."

"Don't shoot me, please," said a faint, high-pitched voice from deep inside the drain pipe.

"We're the good guys," Blancanales said. "Come on out of there."

They heard the scraping noise again, then a girl's head appeared at the mouth of the culvert. Beneath the tangle of shoulder-length blond hair was a muddy, tear-streaked, baby-fat face. The girl was on her hands and knees; she had backed into the pipe. In the process she had lost one of her pink dangly earrings as well as the scrunchy. Blancanales bent and helped her climb out of the culvert. Her T-shirt and low-rise, studded belly jeans were soaked from the creek water. A high-school kid, she looked to be no more than seventeen or eighteen.

The girl took in their uniforms and ID badges. "Is it all over?" she asked, clutching herself and shivering. There was desperation in her voice.

"No, afraid not," Schwarz said.

The girl glanced at the pipe, as if she were considering crawling back inside.

"Don't do that," Blancanales warned her.

"Just try to relax a minute and get your bearings," Schwarz said.

"Jeez, I can't stop shaking," the girl said. "I got out of the espresso stand as quick as I could. I fell down in the creek. I didn't know which way to go. I was too scared to go past Large Marge's. Guns were going off inside. Bombs were going off outside. I didn't want to crawl into that pipe. It's so disgusting in there. But they were killing people. It was so horrible."

"What's your name?" Schwarz asked her.

"Sissy."

"You're going to be okay, Sissy," Blancanales said. "This is a safe spot. You're out of the line of fire. You don't have to crawl back up the pipe. Just stay here until someone comes back for you."

"And what if no one comes back?"

"Someone will," Schwarz assured her.

"Can't I go with you?" she cried.

"That's not a good idea," Blancanales said. "We're going to help rescue the people in the restaurant."

"Oh."

"I'll tell the county sheriffs where you are," Schwarz said. "When it's all over they'll come and get you, I promise. Just sit still and stay low."

Sissy's nose was running. Her blue eyes brimmed with tears. At that moment she looked five years younger than she was, but she nodded.

Schwarz figured as soon as they were out of sight she'd be back up the pipe. Disgusting, maybe, but safe.

He and his teammate continued along the streambed, working their way to within one hundred feet of the rear of the café. They crawled over the top of the gully and peered through the base of the alder thicket. Between them and the rickety back door screen was a swathe of unmowed grass. Thirty yards of open ground to cross. In the middle of it stood a redwood picnic table. Next to the building was an overflowing garbage bin. They could smell fried food and rotting garbage.

"Great spot for a picnic," Schwarz whispered.

"Can't see anything from here," Blancanales said. "I've got to get closer."

"No engagement. This is just a reconnoiter."

"Yeah, yeah, I know," Blancanales said.

"I'm moving on."

Schwarz headed up the creek, careful where he stepped to avoid a fall. As he humped it along the green tunnel, he couldn't help but compare this mission with the one Able Team had already completed that morning. It had also been a hostage situation, but there the similarity ended. Compared to this stand-off, Moses Lake was a cakewalk. The odds they faced here were better, but the limitations on their actions and the stakes were much greater. And the likely presence of the bioweapon inside the café changed the equation, big time. Probably not for him, personally, because he was going to be a distant rifle shot away. That didn't give Schwarz any sense of relief—just the opposite. He wasn't the one who was going to charge through the doors with machine pistol blazing. Because he was more skilled with the long gun, Ironman and Rosario had once again drawn inside duty, the face-to-face. And their fates depended on his ability to hit a target much, much smaller than a rental truck.

After he had traveled another one hundred yards up the creek, Schwarz heard voices and radio squawk above him. He figured he was on the far side of the official roadblock. He slung the Barrett barrel down over his shoulder and came out of the stream-side brush with his hands up and empty.

As he stepped out onto the shoulder, he startled the deputy sheriffs standing behind their cruisers. Seven or eight surprised officers immediately drew their handguns and zeroed in on him.

"Hey, I'm DHS," Schwarz announced.

"On your knees!" one of the deputies shouted. "Don't touch those fucking guns. On your knees now, or you're dead!"

The Able Team commando took in the row of muzzles pointing his way. He knew that if just one of the excited deputies accidentally touched off a round, the rest would join in out of pure instinct. They wouldn't stop until their guns were locked back empty. Seven autopistols, fifteen rounds each. Even if only a quarter of them hit the target; that was a lot of bullet holes. He kept his hands high in the air and knelt on the gravel, cringing as he scraped the Barrett's muzzle brake on the ground.

"Hold it, goddammit!" a female voice shouted from the other side of the line of parked cruisers.

A tall, frizzy-haired, bottle blonde with a bullhorn stormed toward the deputies. In her other hand she carried the jacket to her green pantsuit. She wore a white silk blouse and a Walther 99 in a black, custom-molded hip holster. She was a hard-looking woman. No amount of makeup could conceal the coarseness of her complexion. "Put those guns away!" she snarled at the deputies. "I warned you that guys from Homeland Security were coming our way."

At her command, the deputies stood down. Some looked sheepish at their mistake. The rest tried to hold on to their dignity by shooting Schwarz lingering, sidelong, suspicious looks.

"Are you in charge here?" Schwarz asked her as he rose to his feet and brushed off his knees.

"I'm Detective Dewitt. Sorry about the reception," she said, extending her hand to him. "This is an unusual situation."

When he shook it, her skin felt rough, like a man's. "No harm, no foul," he assured her.

She nodded at the scoped Barrett in his hand. "What are you going to do with that thing?"

"Whatever I'm told to do, ma'am. Are the hostages still alive?"

"As far as we know, they are," Dewitt said. "We haven't seen or heard them since we arrived on-scene. Bad guys are definitely alive and kicking, though. They keep shooting at us. I sent a deputy up to the cabins on the slope with binoculars. Better vantage point up there. I figured he could see inside the restaurant. The shooters pinned him down before he got halfway there. He had to retreat around the back side of the hill. He's okay. He's still working his way around to the cabins."

"That's where I'm headed."

"You'd better go around the back of the hill, too. Keep inside the tree line. Keep to the shadows."

"That's what I'd planned on doing. Who's the sheriff's department hostage negotiator?"

"That'd be me," Dewitt said. "I took a three day seminar last year. In a county of twenty thousand we don't get much call for the specialty. It's hard to negotiate when the perps won't say boo to you. Won't even pick up the phone. Maybe I'm doing something wrong. Maybe they don't understand English."

"Maybe," Schwarz said.

"Come on, let me show you."

Schwarz followed Dewitt around to the front of the roadblock, where they crouched behind the protection of a squad car. Down the slight incline he could see the front corner of the red café, about five hundred yards away. Because of the angle of view, the windows facing Highway 101 were not visible. Still crouching, Dewitt leaned around the back bumper and activated the bullhorn.

"You in the restaurant," she shouted. "This is the Jefferson County Sheriff's Department. We have you surrounded by land, water and air. There is no escape. Talk to me. Tell me what you want. Maybe we can work something out."

A second after the detective stopped talking there was a solid whack at her end of the squad car. And the bullhorn exploded in her face.

With a moan, she fell backward, landing flat on the road on her behind. As she clutched her left cheek, bright blood leaked through her fingers and down the side of her neck.

Schwarz was the first to her side. At first he thought she had been hit in the head by a sniper round. But it was a near miss. The bullhorn had taken the killshot. She had been cut by shards of the shattering plastic.

Scrambling to her feet unassisted, Dewitt clamped a handkerchief to her torn cheek. Blood had dripped down the front of her white blouse. As the EMTs pulled her back to the nearest ambulance, she was swearing a blue streak.

"Don't try to talk to these bastards," Schwarz warned the sergeant who was now in charge of the barricade. "Don't give them a target."

Schwarz crossed the highway and jumped a barbed-wire fence. He didn't attempt to head up the pasture's grassy slope toward the motel cabins. Instead he jogged to the right, staying well out of the Spetsnaz killzone. The handful of brown-and-white goats browsing in the field hardly paid him any notice.

He hopped another fence and slipped into the woods that ran up the side of the hill. Just inside the verge was a deer track. Even though it was cool in the shadows, he humped it up the steep grade fast enough to break a sweat. When he reached the ridge top, he turned left and followed it back toward the cabins. He was almost at his destination when he heard someone on the trail ahead.

"Deputy! Wait up!" he called.

"I'm waiting," a voice replied.

Nobody walked that slowly, Schwarz thought. The

deputy sheriff had to have taken some private time to regroup and reflect on almost getting killed, or Schwarz could never have caught up to him. To his credit, the deputy had decided to press onward instead of lying low back in the trees until the danger had passed.

The deputy leaned against a tree trunk, sweat steadily dripping off the end of his nose. He was a big man, tall and wide, but he looked at least thirty pounds overweight—definitely not in hill-climbing shape. A pair of binocs hung on a strap around his neck.

"Goddamn, that's a big bore," he remarked as he took in the Barrett Model 90. He wiped the perspiration from his face with a hand, then wiped the hand on the seat of his pants. "You got any water?"

"Sorry," Schwarz said as he moved to the edge of the trees. He uncapped the scope, shouldered the heavy rifle and looked downrange. The shot angle at the crest of the hill was marginal. He could see the smashed front windows, but he couldn't see very far into the restaurant. Between the tree line and the protection of the nearest of the six tiny cabins there was a gap of about seventy feet of open ground, a gauntlet that he was going to have to run in order to do the job. The deputy had other options. "I've got to get lower on the hill," Schwarz told him. "You can stay here."

The deputy lowered his binocs. "I can't see anything from here," he said. "I'll tag along."

"We've got to go together when we go," Schwarz said, "and we've got to get out of the shooters' line of sight as quickly as we can. If we catch a break they won't see us slip into position down there."

"Okay."

They broke from cover side by side, sprinting down

the steep slope. Schwarz skidded against the rear wall of the motel cabin. The deputy hit it with both hands to stop himself. They didn't draw any fire from the restaurant, but they did attract the attention of the cabin dweller.

Almost at once, one of the little wood sash windows slid up and a hollow-cheeked, pasty-faced guy stuck his head out. "What's going on, Officers?"

Four little words that lit up Schwarz's radar like Fourth of July. It wasn't just the phony, cringing deference in the man's tone. Or the fact that he was trying so hard to sound casual—and innocent. He wasn't the least bit surprised by an unannounced visit from law enforcement.

Cabin guy had served some jail time.

When the resident got no immediate response, he added, "What's all the racket down on the highway, Officers?"

"None of your business, you goddamn perv," the deputy said. Then he hit the transmit button on his two-way radio. "This is Baxter. I'm at Perv Central. I've got the guy in black with me. We are a go."

"What's all this 'perv' stuff?" Schwarz asked after he signed off.

"Skullface in there was convicted of abusing his thirteen-year-old stepdaughter," the deputy said. "He got eight years. He refused treatment the whole time he was in prison. He's out because he served every damn second of his sentence. This is where the county dumps released sex offenders. The state pays for their room and board."

"That's who's in all the cabins?"

Baxter nodded. "Some of the pervs have electronic

monitoring. You know, the ankle collars. At least we've got them all in one place. And it's fifteen miles from the nearest school in any direction."

The motel cabin was only slightly bigger than the espresso stand down on Highway 101. It had no foundation. It stood on a graded patch of slope on a set of wooden skids that kept it a couple of feet off the ground. Schwarz and the deputy crawled underneath the cabin, squirming forward on their bellies in the cool dirt until they reached the front of the structure, beside the wooden front steps.

It wasn't much of a sniper's hide. It didn't have the hard-site defensive features that Schwarz would have liked, but the shooting position was far enough back in the shadows for concealment. He shouldered the Barrett, uncapped the Geodesic scope and looked downrange, checking the laser distance-to-target readout. It was 1,115 yards to the front of the café.

Sheriff's Deputy Baxter had to edge farther forward on his elbows to get a decent look through the binocs.

Schwarz opened the comm link to Ironman and Rosario and described the view he had from Perv Central. "I'm looking at the front windows along 101. They've been kicked out to provide shooting access. From the angle I've got, I can see about a third of the restaurant closest to me. The tables and chairs are overturned. There's some movement by the front wall, but no muzzle-flashes. Wait a minute. Yeah, there's people along the wall. I see heads. Oops, got a gun. Long barrel. From the regulator and forestock it looks like a Dragunov with a silencer. Ah, shit…"

"What is it?"

"A shooter is sitting in the middle of the hostages. Got them packed in all around him like sandbags."

"What about a shot?" Lyons said.

"A near miss or a through-and-through is going to kill some hostages for sure," Schwarz told him.

"And the dry goods?"

"No sign of it. No backpack or suitcase in sight. But my field of view doesn't take in much floor space."

"Rosario? Are you hearing this?" Lyons said.

"Roger that. Can't talk. Too close to the target."

Looking through the scope, Schwarz caught a faint flash at the other end of the line of windows. Before he could retreat, a heavy-caliber bullet ripped into the clapboard siding, angled up through the cabin and crashed out the back wall.

"We got incoming," he told Lyons as a second round thudded into the siding, then he broke off the comm link. Maybe the deputy's binocs had flashed in the sun and given them away.

Inside the cabin above them, the lone occupant let out a shriek when it dawned on him that he was coming under fire. The front screen door slammed back and the wooden steps creaked as he rushed down them.

A third round slammed the structure, splintering the screen door's frame.

"Don't!" Schwarz called out to the running feet in ratty, sheep-wool-lined house slippers.

There was no stopping the ex-con. Trouble was, he was moving in slo-mo. Maybe because he was out of shape. Maybe because the electronic collar on his ankle slowed him down. Either way, he never made it around the corner.

A fourth round slapped into something soft and resilient.

Flesh.

A fraction of a second later, like an echo, something wet smacked into the side of the cabin.

The slow runner let out an "Oof!" and slammed facedown in the grass. His unbelted, baby-blue bathrobe wadded up under his armpits as he began to roll downhill on hips and shoulders, pale legs flopping rubbery loose, his slippers flying off.

Schwarz glimpsed a fist-sized exit wound high in the side of the rib cage, a ragged, dark crater through which a macerated kidney and liver had been blown. The limp body twisted head downward as it rotated, then it picked up momentum, sliding face first down the grassy slope.

"Get back!" Schwarz told the deputy.

As the officer squirmed around, there was another solid thwack!

"Oh, no..." the deputy gasped.

Dumping the Barrett, Schwarz grabbed him by the elbows and pulled him away from the front edge of the cabin. There was a bullet hole in his uniform shirt. A heart shot. The steel trauma plate in his armored vest had saved his life.

"Oh, fuck, it hurts," Baxter moaned.

"There's no penetration," Schwarz told him. "The plate's deformed by the bullet strike. The shock might have broken a couple of your ribs."

After he had dragged the guy out behind the cabin, Schwarz went back under to retrieve the Light Fifty. The shooter's target had been no more than eighteen inches high. The shot was uphill. And the distance was the better part of a mile.

Then bullets from the highway started punching random holes through the cabin, from one end to the other.

Searching rounds.

CHAPTER SEVENTEEN

Blancanales leaned against the back wall of Large Marge's. The warped aluminum screen door was inches from his right hand. The smell from the garbage bin was much worse on this side of the picnic area.

Either that or it was wafting out of the kitchen.

He could hear the flat whine of silenced heavy-caliber rifle rounds zinging away from the front of the building. The semiauto Dragunov was firing steadily at four- or five-second intervals. Just long enough to ride the recoil wave back on target.

The target was Gadgets.

Blancanales fought down the impulse to boot in the screen and charge the dining room, machine pistol blazing. That course of action was temporarily off the table.

He needed to see around the corner. Slinging his weapon, he broke out the tactical spy camera. He turned it on and inserted the fish-eye camera lens in the crack between the battered aluminum screen door and the wooden door frame. The two-by-three-inch color LCD screen showed a long, narrow, cluttered kitchen—commercial stove, grill and deep fryers on one side and work counter and refrigerators on the other. It was deserted. He had no view into the restaurant proper.

The only window on the back side of the building was blocked by stacked cardboard boxes; the room appeared to be a pantry.

Blancanales shut off the tactical cam and slipped it in his uniform shirt's bellows pocket. If he entered the kitchen through the back door, even in stealth mode, there was no guarantee that Spetsnaz wouldn't hear him. The floor might creak. For all he knew, they had the rear entrance spy-cammed and bugged, or even booby trapped. If they caught him in the act of penetrating the perimeter, the situation would avalanche out of control. The Russians would slaughter the hostages and release the bioweapon, if they had it.

The shooting from the highway side of the building suddenly stopped, replaced by ominous silence.

Had the Spetsnaz bastard managed to hit Gadgets? he wondered. The gunner had expended ten rounds, an entire Dragunov clip. Gadgets was tops at using and evading a long gun, but there was always the chance of a lucky shot. Blancanales pushed the idea out of his head. It served no positive purpose.

He needed to get close enough to the hostiles to do the surveillance job without giving himself away. To his left, along the building's concrete-block foundation was a ventilation screen. The mesh was loose and rusty. He used the point of his multitool to pry the screen out of its plastic frame. The opening was just large enough for him to squirm through. He stuck his head inside the gap in the concrete blocks and was hit by a different smell. Sweet, almost like perfume. It was mold. Weak light streamed into the crawl space through the few other foundation vents spaced around the perimeter.

Blancanales took a miniflashlight from his combat harness, turned it on and put it between his teeth. As he quietly levered himself through the small opening, rifle fire resumed out front. He felt a wave of relief. There was still something to shoot at, so Gadgets was okay. The Russian had just paused to reload. He was firing faster than before, as if trying to track a moving target. Round after round zinged uphill.

Blancanales dropped to his stomach inside the crawl space. It was only about two feet high from the floor joists to the earth. He had to move on his elbows and knees. The dirt felt moist through his clothing. All around him, ragged strips of pink fiberglass insulation dangled from between the joists. Shredded tufts of it lay scattered over the ground.

Rats.

His flashlight spotlighted dead ones in snap traps. Time had reduced them to lumps of moldy gray fuzz with tails. No one had seen to the snap traps in a while. Some were still armed, but the bait was moldy, too.

Blancanales moved the flash's beam around the crawl space, looking for a way into the dining room. When he located the silver heating ducts, he used the light to follow them back to the forced-air electric heater. Getting his bearings vis-à-vis the front of the building, he located the duct that connected to the dining room and started to crawl toward it.

A brick-lined sump pit stood between him and his destination. It was seven feet deep, a twelve-by-eight-foot rectangle, with brick steps leading down. Its concrete floor was dry; the dusty electric sump pump leading to the sewer line was silent. That's why it smelled so moldy, he thought. Either the crawl space flooded whenever it rained, or a subterranean stream occasionally meandered under the structure.

More than half the floor space was filled by an old oil-furnace storage tank, rusting and partially dismantled. Whoever had laid the concrete-block foundation had been too lazy to haul it away.

Blancanales rounded the sump pit and crawled on. The dust and the mold tickled the inside of his nose. He stifled the urge to sneeze.

Above him, he heard muffled, guttural commands. The floor creaked as the hostages changed position.

The heating ductwork was cylindrical aluminum. Blancanales cut the sealing tape and pulled the sections apart, removing the elbow so he could look up the vertical pipe. Two feet above his nose was the floor grate and daylight. The noise-suppressed rifle shots had stopped, but he heard the faint sounds of weeping and moaning. He took off his communication headset and inserted the earpiece connected to the directional microphone on the spy cam's lens housing.

Blancanales fed the fiber-optic cable up to the bottom of the floor grate, careful not to clunk the lens against the side of the duct. The potmetal grate's apertures were big enough for the tiny camera lens to slip through. By twisting and pulling the cable sleeve, he was able to bend the business end of it into an L shape, bringing the room above into view on the LCD screen.

The fish-eye lens produced a distorted image, but he could see two guys in black T-shirts hunkered down below the front windows with Russian sniper rifles. Mid- to late twenties. Well-built. Definitely military products. He couldn't tell at a glance which one was in charge. They were surrounded by tightly packed, living bodies. A couple of the people sitting on the floor were dressed in food-stained white aprons and paper caps, obviously part of the café's kitchen staff.

For an instant, one of the crew-cut Russians glanced across the room, directly into the little lens, as if he had noticed it sticking up above the grate. Blancanales held his breath. His left hand patted the dirt for the pistol grip of his MP-5 SD-3. He was in a very precarious position, caught in a two-foot space, with a long crawl to the only exit. If he was discovered, the Spetsnaz soldiers could pour fire right through the floor and shoot him to pieces.

But picking out the quarter-inch-diameter black housing across the width of the dining room was impossible.

Just as it was impossible for Blancanales to tell through the distorted lens exactly what the Russian was looking at.

Blancanales stopped holding his breath when the sniper turned toward the highway, shouldered the Dragunov and looked through the PSO-1 telescopic sight for more targets of opportunity.

By slowly turning the cable, the Able Team warrior panned the little lens around the dining room. He had to make sure they only had two hostiles to deal with.

The eating area was painted a dingy white, and it was splashed with brilliant red. Red splatters decorated the floor, the walls and the exposed ceiling rafters. He counted six people on the deck; most had their heads blown off.

On the counter beside the cash register was an open

duffel bag. He could see the butts of a pair of 74 Shorty fold-stocks. Rifle grenades and extra mags were lined up. And there was a backpack, set out on its own. Black nylon. It looked full.

Blancanales zoomed in on it.

The top of the main compartment was unzipped, but because of the low camera position he couldn't see inside.

He panned back to the Spetsnaz. With the zoom function enabled, he saw that one of the Russians was eating French fries smothered in ketchup from a red-and-white paper boat. Presumably cold French fries, since the cook staff was either dead or taking an unplanned, extended break.

The backpack was twenty-five to thirty feet from the windows where the Spetsnaz had set up their hide. Blancanales did the math. It was a no-go. He figured he could clear the kitchen and make it through the door to the counter, but he'd never get out alive.

The shot angle for Schwarz looked equally dubious. The counter stood at a ninety-degree angle to the highway, and the backpack was sitting beside the cash register, closer to the rear of the room. Schwarz probably couldn't even see it from his position.

Blancanales had no way to uplink the images to Able and Stony Man. Information transfer was going to have to be verbal. But he couldn't risk using his comm unit so close to the heating vent. He straightened out the cable and eased the camera through the grate and back down the duct.

Crawling across the moist dirt, he headed for the sump pit. When he reached it, he swung his legs around, edged down the brick stairs and took a seat on one of the lower steps. After he put his headset back on, he pushed the transmit button. "Ironman?" he said softly.

Lyons responded at once. "Where are you, Pol?"

"Crawl space."

"What have you got?"

Blancanales hit the spy cam's playback, watching the captured images flow over the little screen. "Two Russian shooters, twelve live hostages, six dead. Lots of grenades and ammo. And there's a backpack. Can't see into it."

"Shit."

"Gadgets, are you okay?" Blancanales asked. "I was offline there for a while."

"Yeah, I'm good," came the reply. "Had to draw some fire. The deputy wasn't in any shape to run. Did a little bop and hop down from the cabins to the farmhouse. Shooter did his best, but I juked him good. The homeowners don't seem too happy about their back door being kicked in, but I'm up in their attic room."

"Can you see the backpack on the counter?" Lyons said.

"Yep," Schwarz replied. "I've got a much better shot from here, a clear KZ, front to middle of the café."

"How the hell are we going to pull this off?" Blancanales said.

CHAPTER EIGHTEEN

G force drove FBI Agent Rick Todd deep into the corner of the Crown Victoria's rear seat as his boss, SAC Al Butterman, slewed the black sedan, lights flashing, siren howling, around a looping, ninety-degree curve on the wrong side of the highway. Todd felt more than a little queasy. He was trying his best not to upchuck into the crown of his brand-new Bureau billcap.

Sitting beside him on the backseat, Special Agent Franklin Merle was looking at him sidelong and grinning up a storm as they were by turns slammed against the inside of the car doors and each other.

Fuckface, Todd thought. Grinning fuckface.

No way could he ask Butterman to slow down a little for the sake of his almost-heaving stomach. Such a request would have been an outright admission of un-Bureaulike unmanliness. The SAC wouldn't have slowed down for him, anyway. Todd had seen him plenty pissed before, but never *this* pissed.

Luckily for the quartet of FBI men, there wasn't much oncoming traffic in the northbound lane. What there was took to the shoulder in a hurry, usually skidding off in a cloud of dust.

Agent Mark Adagio in the front passenger seat was keeping his mouth shut, too. Todd could see his brown fingers on the molded plastic handrail above the door frame. Adagio was squeezing it so hard his knuckles had gone white.

SAC Butterman had started the morning pissed off. He had gotten the word about the sub's grounding at least twenty minutes after the Seattle office, and he hadn't been offered air transportation to the scene. He took having to drive his team all the way from Tacoma as a great big slap in the face. In Todd's opinion, Butterman took everything like a great big slap in the face. Five years short of retirement, the SAC was cranky, short-tempered and a bit too tightly wrapped for comfort.

Todd saw nothing but upside to the present situation, even if they had to drive a couple of hours each way and he barfed into his new hat. Anything was better than the computer-software-piracy detail they had drawn for the past four months. That wasn't what he had signed on with the Bureau for.

It was the old glass-half-empty business.

Todd saw a golden opportunity.

Butterman was furious because of the way it had fallen into his lap.

The high-speed swerving came to an abrupt end when they reached the hamlet of Gardiner. Traffic was parked on both sides of the highway and shoulder—passenger cars, RVs, log trucks, Wal-Mart trucks—which left only a narrow, zigzag open lane down the middle. People were milling around in the road. Butterman had to slow down or run them over.

As they proceeded at five miles per hour with lights and siren blaring, citizens tried to wave them down. They shouted. They wanted updated information. They wanted answers. The evacuees from Port Angeles were trying to get off the Olympic Peninsula, but they were essentially stuck in place until the matter at Large Marge's was resolved and Highway 101 was reopened.

Butterman didn't stop for the pedestrians.

None of the agents rolled down a window.

As they closed on the dogleg right that led down to Discovery Bay, Adagio pointed across the road. "Isn't that the DHS flyboy?" he said.

Todd saw the helicopter pilot kneeling on the shoulder. He was covering a supine body with a yellow plastic sheet. Behind him, a woman stood weeping as she clutched a small child.

"Jumped-up asshole," Butterman muttered. "Probably never paid a minute of serious dues in his whole damn life. Instant golden boys, the lot of them. All because of some lip-service reorganization bullshit."

"Glory hounds," Merle said.

"They tried to squeeze us out of the action," Adagio agreed energetically. "But it doesn't seem to have worked. We've still got a stalemate."

"*That* figures," Merle said, giving Todd a wink.

"What really burns me up is the disrespect," Butterman went on. "They insult us and treat like hayseed chumps. There's got to be payback for that. Serious, mind-fucking payback."

Todd continued to keep his lip zipped. The other two agents liked to bait their boss in the guise of shamelessly sucking up, but he refused to participate. Their juvenile fun and games made him uncomfortable. He was concerned that one day Butterman would catch on. And then the shit would really hit the fan.

As the SAC pulled up to the dogleg, a young, hatless state trooper stepped into their path, his arms outstretched, palms thrust forward. A clear request for a stop, which Butterman complied with. As the trooper approached the driver door, the trunk lid popped up and all the agents bailed from the vehicle.

The trooper didn't ask who they were. The big block letters on the backs of their windbreakers were as plain as day.

"What are you Bureau guys going to do?" he said.

The agents didn't dignify the question with an answer. They busied themselves with gathering up weaponry from the trunk—full-size 12-gauge pump shotguns and a pair of M-16 assault rifles.

As they stripped off their jackets and slipped into armored vests, the trooper said, "I just got word that the National Guard is on the way. Maybe you'd better wait for them to show before you go down there."

The SAC ignored the suggestion, jacking a live, high brass shell into his pump gun's chamber.

"Maybe we should wait for backup," Todd said to Butterman.

"Bureau presence is required at the scene," the SAC said.

Todd looked to Merle and Adagio for support. And got none. They wouldn't even look him in the eye. From the reports they'd picked up on the radio, there were news crews on the south side of the restaurant, news crews in transmission vans that could broadcast live coverage of the stand-off's heroes. Arguing with SAC Butterman was a complete waste of breath.

"The hostage negotiator was wounded," the trooper said, still trying to make his case for caution.

"Is he hurt bad?" Todd said.

"A she, actually. But, no, she wasn't hurt that badly. Her bullhorn got hit by a bullet. She got cut by pieces of it."

"The Bureau wrote the book on hostage negotiation and stand-off resolution," Butterman informed him. "We'll take it from here."

"The perps aren't talking, they're shooting," the trooper said. "The DHS guys who went down there drew some hellacious fire from the restaurant. Only one of them made it back."

"Why doesn't that surprise me?" Butterman said. "Come on, let's roll."

As they walked by, the trooper just stared at them in disbelief.

For his part, Todd was feeling decidedly soft in the knees. Sure, he was carrying a fully automatic M-16. Sure, they had all passed the required live-fire circuit at Quantico, but that didn't make any of them antiterror specialists. Todd was by training a certified public accountant. Even if he questioned the reasonableness and prudence of the SAC's order, no way would he refuse to obey it and let his fellow agents down. In for a penny, in for a pound.

They started down the grade, single file. With Butterman in the lead, they zigzagged around the rows of hastily abandoned vehicles. They had only gone about one hundred yards when a big, blond-haired guy in black appeared below them, loping up the hill with a machine pistol in hand.

"Son of a bitch," Butterman exclaimed. "Would you look at who's throwing in the towel."

The man from DHS waved for them to get behind cover as he closed the gap. Todd could see something wet smeared on the chest and sleeves of his uniform. It looked like blood.

"How many shooters?" Butterman asked him as they crouched behind the rear of a Winnebago.

"Just two," the big guy said.

"Weren't there four of you?" the SAC asked. "I thought you guys were supposed to be such hot shit."

Todd had been taught how to read facial expressions as part of his Bureau interrogation training. In this case, there was none to read. The DHS guy didn't react. No wrinkles in the forehead. No flushing of the skin. No tightening of the mouth. No narrowing of the eyes. That blank stare was truly unnerving.

"I think we can do a little better," Butterman said with confidence.

"Take it from me," the guy in black said, "you boys don't want to go down there."

"Too much for you, was it?" The SAC snorted.

The big man still didn't rise to the bait. In a level, matter-of-fact tone he said, "These guys aren't common criminals. They're Russian special forces. Cream of the crop. They've got long guns and they're experts. Seven hundred yards is inside their comfort zone."

"Where the hell are you going?" Butterman asked as the DHS man rose and started back up the hill. "Are you running away?"

The blond guy didn't respond.

Butterman raised a middle finger to his retreating back.

Todd thought it a rather feeble gesture.

"Come on," the SAC growled at his agents. "We

know what we're doing. That meathead was just trying to psych us out."

At his order, the three men spread out a little and began moving down through the maze of cars and trucks. On the slope closer to the bottom of the grade, they encountered scattered wreckage and bodies. Too many bodies to stop and count.

From the hilltop behind them came the sound of the DHS helicopter revving up. It took off from the hilltop and headed away from the stand-off, banking to the southwest.

"Turning tail," Butterman said with satisfaction.

As Todd scooted from cover to cover, running low and quick, the big guy's last comment about a seven-hundred-yard "comfort zone" kept replaying in his head. Unpleasantly. He kept wondering if they were that close yet. Because of the grade's incline, he couldn't estimate the exact distance.

Then it was done for him.

A double set of almost simultaneous zip-thwacks!

To his right, both Adagio and Merle went down hard. Adagio caught a round through the front of the throat. He didn't reach for his neck as he fell. The shot blew out his spinal cord at the base of his skull. He was dead before he hit the ground. Merle was struck center chest and knocked sprawling across the median stripe. Even though he was wearing trauma plate inside his Kevlar vest, the shock of the bullet impact had to have been tremendous. He lay there, flat on his back, arms thrashing, heels drumming on the asphalt.

Butterman and Todd dived behind a burned-out sedan. In the middle of the highway, Merle was a sitting duck.

"Roll under the car!" the SAC shouted at him. "Get to cover!"

Too late.

There was another awful zip-thwack! Chunks of skull skittered up the roadway, followed by a splatter of liquefied brains.

"Shoot back!" the SAC yelled at his sole surviving agent.

Todd braced himself on the right front fender of the sedan, looking downrange over the iron sights of the M-16.

"Return fire!" Butterman said. "Shoot them!"

"I can't see anyone to shoot!" Todd protested. "It's too far away."

Incoming rounds whizzed past his head, slamming into the sedan's smoke-stained windshield, spiderwebbing it just above the steering wheel.

"Pull back!" Butterman cried from behind the rear of the vehicle. "We've got to pull back!"

As Todd turned to follow the SAC, he was struck from behind. The impact against the top of his right shoulder twisted him, slamming him against the side of the car and bouncing him onto his knees. Arm dead to the fingertips, M-16 lost, billcap lost, Todd crawled under the Ford SUV opposite. The wound was a through-and-through; he could see the exit hole in the front of his shoulder. As he applied hand pressure to the bloody mess, the pain really hit him.

Before he could puke and pass out, he heard that horrible, now familiar sound, punctuated by a low groan. He looked under the back bumper and saw Butterman go down between the line of cars. He was hit in the middle of the back and driven flat onto his face. Before he could regain his feet, he was hit again. And again.

Two rifles turned the SAC into a meat puppet, animated by a string of 7.62 mm slugs.

The snipers hit him five more times before they blew his bald head into jigsaw-puzzle pieces.

CHAPTER NINETEEN

Tre Rupert cringed as the sniper rifle's action cycled and rained down smoking, 7.62 mm hulls on top of his head. He couldn't raise a hand to deflect the hot casings. Both of his wrists were looped with nylon cable ties to the wrists of the people sitting on either side of him. He couldn't raise his arms over his head without forcing the others to raise theirs. Even though the man-woman pair was of Asian extraction, and slight of stature, his fellow hostages had gone rigid and wouldn't be budged.

The men behind the silenced military rifles worked methodically, firing through the glassless front windows of the restaurant, aiming at someone or something up the highway, in the direction of the grade. Each of the shooters was surrounded by six daisy-chained hostages.

A hot casing hit Rupert on the nose; unburned gunpowder peppered his face. The part-time corrections officer for the Clallam County jail didn't make a peep of protest.

None of the other human shields made a peep, either.

There was a good reason for that.

After one of the shooters had used grenades and autofire on the state patrol, he had returned to the café and reloaded his stubby assault rifle with a full magazine he had pulled from the black duffel bag. He had then announced to all the hostages in thickly accented English, "Sit still and you will live. Move and…"

As if his point hadn't already been made by the killings of Large Marge and the runner, he shot the defenseless man sitting next to Ruport once in the face.

Just like that.

Execution.

The stunning, unprovoked murder turned the rest of the hostages, Rupert included, into shellshocked zombies.

From the moment hot brains had splattered the sleeve of his uniform shirt and the right side of his face, Rupert's monumental, four-thousand-calorie, Large Marge eye-opener breakfast ceased to sit so well. His stomach began to rumble ominously; his bowels churned and whistled. When he had gotten up that morning it had never crossed his mind that this might be his last day on Earth. Now it looked like the breakfast he hadn't quite finished might have been his last meal. He had a horrible vision of the two muscle guys in T-shirts just opening up wholesale on the hostages, machine-gunning them to bits where they sat.

Or blowing them up with grenades.

From the moment the brains hit the sleeve, Rupert could see this whole deal working out badly. In fact, he couldn't see any way it was going to work out well.

Heart pounding, guts gurgling, he had watched the Russians start hauling military gear out of the big duffel. With fixed, emotionless expressions they began assembling their sniper rifles. They didn't act like psychos. They acted like guys with jobs to do. Jobs they knew by heart. They put together the long-barreled weapons with speed and precision. The rifles had strange-looking, cutout skeleton stocks with pistol grips, thumb grooves and detachable cheek pieces. The killers slapped home box magazines and screwed on fat, blue-steel silencer tubes.

When they had finished preparing their guns, one of them carefully moved the heavy-looking black backpack along the counter, depositing it near the cash register, closer to the front windows. Then he slowly unzipped the main compartment.

Rupert didn't like the look of that one bit.

Either the pack contained something superfragile or superdeadly.

Or both.

Putting the backpack at that end of the counter and leaving it open gave the Russians quick access to whatever was inside.

The killers had then used a couple of Large Marge's metal-framed chairs to bash out the restaurant's front windows.

While they had been thus occupied, Rupert had quickly unbuttoned and removed his corrections officer shirt, revealing an untucked, tentlike, white V-neck T-shirt with permanent orange chili stains down the front. He had two reasons for getting rid of the uniform. First, the sharp, coppery smell of the blowback on the shirtsleeve was making him sick. Second, and more importantly, he didn't want to be singled out as the next to die just because he was wearing a uniform.

Unfortunately, one of the Russians had caught him wadding up his jailer's uniform. A long rifle barrel swung around and pointed at the space between his eyes.

"Are you in the military?" the killer had demanded of him.

"What?" Rupert said, trying to play dumb.

The rifleman had dropped the weapon's thumb safety. It made a faint but audible click. "Are you with the police?" he demanded as he stepped closer.

Rupert's fantasy of being in law enforcement had instantly evaporated. The truth was, thirty-five hours a week he supervised the incarceration of misdemeanor offenders. Driving with license suspended. Petty theft. Tweakers. Drunks. Potheads. He babysat idiots in hot orange jumpsuits, for pete's sake, and for *that* he was going to die?

At that moment, Rupert had been prepared to deny everything. His citizenship. His parentage. His sexual orientation. Anything to keep his brains from being sprayed all over the cobwebbed ceiling.

"Bus driver for Clallam County," Rupert had said, mopping his sweating face with the clean part of his uniform.

The shooter had used the end of the fat silencer to uncover the shirt's embroidered shoulder patch. "Liar," he said, scowling in disgust. Then he had gestured with the gun barrel. "Put it back on—you stink."

Rupert had done as he was told, never so relieved in his life. But as soon as the Russians started tying the hostages together, it had become obvious why they were keeping him alive, and what purpose he was to serve. His gross size and weight made him the perfect bullet sponge.

The rifle braced on the window ledge above his head coughed, its action clacked, and another hot hull whacked him on the head.

The snipers spoke to each other as they fired at will up the grade. From the tone of the comments, it sounded to Rupert as if they were complimenting each other on their accuracy.

Above the counter, the café's TV was still on. The only live-feed video of Port Angeles was from Victoria, B.C. The screen was filled with a blurry, indistinct telephoto shot of the grounded submarine. The voice-over CNN news reader had no idea what was happening on the ground there. He kept repeating over and over what had already been broadcast.

Then the scene suddenly shifted.

A big green sign with white letters behind a very excited woman reporter read Highway 101 North. As the camera panned away, Rupert recognized the location; he had driven by it five hundred times to and from work. It was just past a wide curve in the road about a quarter mile south of Large Marge's. There were no pictures of the embattled restaurant or the destruction and chaos on the highway around it. There was live video of the back side of the massive police department and county sheriff's roadblock. The camera panned back to the wide-eyed local channel newswoman.

Looking at the TV, at the world of safety and normality that lay just around a turn in the road, walking distance away, Rupert felt absolutely, utterly lost, as if he had been transported against his will to some nightmare of a parallel universe. He wasn't alone in that regard.

Some of the hostages around him quietly, helplessly wept. Others whispered rapid-fire prayers in languages Rupert couldn't understand. The collection of foreigners on holiday had come a very long way just to die. The married couples who were tied together held hands.

What did their future hold?

At some point, Rupert thought, the Russians would either kill them on purpose, or the good guys would kill them by accident. There was no middle ground that he could see. Even though they outnumbered their captors, they couldn't rise up as one and overcome them. Not tied as they were, with some hostages immobile, essentially deadweight.

Then the snipers stopped shooting. As they stripped out and replaced the empty magazines, the one looming above Rupert announced, "FBI not so good as on TV and in movies."

Leaving little doubt as to whom they had been firing at.

None of the hostages asked if the government agents had been killed; everyone knew the answer. Not one bullet had been fired back.

Not one.

The sudden ringing of a cell phone sent a violent shudder through the chain of captives. They were all thinking the same thing. If the phone belonged to one of them, it could spur another round of senseless murder.

One of the Russians pulled a silver plastic cell out of his back pocket and flipped it open. Holding his rifle butt braced on the top of his thigh, he listened to whoever was on the other end for about ten seconds, then spoke back. He flipped the phone closed, dropped it on the floor and crushed it under the rifle butt, striking it again and again, pounding it to unrecognizable fragments. Then, astonishingly, miraculously, both captors chucked their sniper rifles over and out the empty window frames.

Rupert couldn't believe his eyes. Was it really all over, just like that? With a phone call? Around him, people were moaning and mumbling thanks to whatever deities they prayed to.

The Russians moved away from the hostages. Hunkered down next to the front wall, they embraced like brothers.

Not a victory celebration, for sure.

Not quite an acceptance of defeat, either.

More like a fond farewell.

Then one of the shooters rose from the floor and started across the room, heading straight for the open backpack.

ON HIS BACK IN THE COOL DIRT beneath Large Marge's, Rosario Blancanales held the spycam propped on his chest and the MP-5 SD-3 across his stomach. He had the spycam's microphone shut off and was wearing his communication headset so he could talk to Schwarz and Lyons.

After slipping the fiber-optic cable and lens back through the heating grate, he had adjusted the fisheye's field of view to take in the hostiles and the counter where the backpack sat. Then he had screwed the cable to the floor joist with a plastic clamp. Moving across the crawl space on elbows and knees, he had carefully uncoiled the spycam extension cable over his shoulder.

Locating the position of the counter and the back-pack from under the floor wasn't entirely blind guess-work. Through the fish-eye he had seen a stainless-steel sink on the wall that separated kitchen from dining room. It was opposite the cash register. From the water and drain pipes bracketed to the joists and disappearing into the subfloor overhead, he could estimate the distance. He positioned himself on the dining-room side of the counter, between the Russians and the back-pack.

His assignment wasn't to take out anyone trying to reach it. Shooting blind through the floor that would have been flat-out impossible. His job was to cut off access to the backpack just long enough for Schwarz to get off two killshots with the Barrett. That and to give Lyons some cover as he dropped onto the back corner of the roof from the helicopter. Because of the terrain and nature of the opposition, Grimaldi couldn't possibly touch down. The roof was the only safe place for Lyons to jump out. Nine millimeter rounds splintering up through the floor would give the Russians something to think about for a few critical seconds. Hopefully Schwarz could intervene before they got it together to fire back.

Blancanales pulled out the MP-5 SD-3's retractable folds-tock, locked it and, holding the pistol grip, braced the butt in the dirt. As he stared at the little color LCD screen, he aimed the machine pistol at the underside of the floor, virtually point-blank. The Spetsnaz were popping up over the window ledge and pouring aimed fire up the grade.

"What's going on out there?" he asked. "What are they shooting at?"

"Can't see from here," Schwarz responded.

"Can't see, either, but it could be the FBI," Lyons said. "They were on their way down the hill as I was coming up. We're airborne, looping around to the south. ETA three or four minutes."

As Blancanales watched, the Russians stopped sniping, dropped back below the line of broken-out windows and stayed there. The FBI had either retreated, or they were all down.

Because the spycam's sound was turned off, he didn't hear the cell phone ring, but he saw the Russian take the phone out of his pocket.

"Something is going down," Blancanales said into the comm set's mike. "Our friends just got a phone call."

"The sleeper," Schwarz said.

"Or the rest of the Spetsnaz crew," Lyons said.

When the guy hung up and then proceeded to bash the cell to bits, Blancanales could hear the gun butt thumping on the floor. That wasn't a good sign. "Uh-oh," he said as he saw the Russians toss their rifles out the front windows.

"Yeah, I see it," Schwarz said.

"What?" Lyons demanded. "What can you see?"

"They just tossed both the Dragunovs," Blancanales told him. "Now they're hugging like their dog just died. I don't like the looks of this, guys. Gadgets?"

"I'm on it."

"Jack, you'd better goose it," Blancanales urged as he thumbed the fire-selector switch to full-auto. "I think it's going down...."

GADGETS SCHWARZ STOOD behind a chipped, thickly blue-enameled child's play table. The other end of the table was positioned in front of the diamond-shaped attic window. He had wedged the legs in place with some opened boxes of yellow-and-green ceramic bath tile and hardened plastic bags of matching kelly-green tile grout. The Barrett was set up on the tabletop, the feet of its bipod tacked in place with a couple of roofing nails he'd brought along. He had used the jaws of his multitool to drive in the nails. The rifle's butt was propped up on a pair of heavy, string-tied shoeboxes. In lieu of a sandbag under the heel, he had neatly folded up his DHS uniform shirt. As he leaned over the small table, he didn't snug the gunbutt into his shoulder. Elbows on the tabletop, his only physical contact with the weapon was the pad of his index finger resting ever so lightly on the trigger.

The Barrett's first shot was lined up, live round chambered, safety off. Ready to rip. The scope's range-finder gave the distance to target as a hair over 900 yards, and Schwarz had set the bullet drop compensator accordingly. He had a flatter shooting angle from the attic: instead of the forty-five degrees up at the cabins, it was closer to thirty degrees from the farmhouse's third story, which allowed him to see deeper into the café.

With no glass reflections to obscure his view he could make out the tops of heads lined up inside the front wall, the tops of some overturned tables and about five feet of the facing end of the counter, right up to the base of the cash register and the opened black backpack.

Even though he had memorized the up/down compensations for the M-2 round out to 1,500 yards, he had reworked the calculations in pencil on the tabletop twice. When hostages were involved and the distances were long, there was no such thing as being too careful. Because of the down-angled shot, he had to aim a little more than a yard low on the building's front wall to make the bullet fly through the broken front windows. He estimated it would take three seconds for one of the Russians to cross the distance from the front wall to the cash register and backpack. The 900-yard flight time of the M-2 bullet was 1.2 seconds. Enough time for a target to move out of the bull's-eye for a clean miss—that's why he hadn't been able to take a shot at the snipers jack-in-the-boxing over the front windows. The Barrett was positioned for a stationary lead three-and-a-half feet to the left of where the nearer sniper had last popped up, almost directly in line with the counter. The .50-caliber slug had to reach its target before the roofline's overhang hid the Russian from Schwarz's view.

The killzone was a narrow, time-limited window.

Schwarz adjusted his comm link earphone and concentrated on his breathing. With no time left on the clock, and the game on the line, he was the kicker. To win he had to score not one but a pair of long-range field goals.

The second shot going to be extradicey. Based on his practice at the Stony Man range, Schwarz figured it would take him three seconds to recover from the recoil, to chamber a fresh round and reacquire the target. Another couple of seconds were required to slow his breathing rhythm and find the space between heartbeats. Lyons's strategy relied on the shock effect of the first shot to paralyze the remaining Spetsnaz. What the guy would do when he recovered was anybody's guess.

On the upside, any hit with the 709-grain M-2 round would be instantly incapacitating, if not lethal. Even a grazing hit to the limbs would do the trick, and give Lyons enough time to jump down from the roof, enter through the kitchen rear door and do the mop-up.

There was a single, soft, resounding thump from the attic floor behind Schwarz. The owners of the farmhouse had resumed banging on the underside of the trapdoor, albeit halfheartedly. To keep them out of his hair, he had dragged heavy boxes over the attic's entrance. Unable to reach him, the homeowners had shouted that they had already called the police, and that they had guns.

When Schwarz yelled back that he was from Department of Homeland Security, the response from below was, "United Nations, you mean!"

"I work for the U.S. government."

"New World Order, you mean!"

"Do you all want to go to jail?" Schwarz had snarled. "We'll drag you out of here in black helicopters and you'll never see the light of day again."

That had shut them up. Temporarily.

So far, the pounding on the trap wasn't loud enough to mess up his timing. If he couldn't hear his heartbeats, he couldn't fire between them.

"He's moving," Blancanales said.

Schwarz let out a breath through his mouth and took up the trigger slack, holding finger pressure just below breakpoint.

He caught a shadow of movement from the right corner of his scope's field of view. His firing cue. A fraction of a second later the trigger broke cleanly. The Light Fifty boomed and bucked, lifting the table's front legs, shaking the floor and bringing down a rain of dirt and dust from the century-old rafters above. Even though he was prepared for it, the report was so loud it made him grimace in pain.

Schwarz worked the butter-smooth bolt behind the pistol grip, and a thumb-diameter hull flipped out. As he slid a fresh round into the chamber, he reacquired the downrange sight picture. He couldn't tell if he'd scored a hit, but the first guy was no longer in view. The second Russian was already halfway to the counter. He had reacted a whole lot faster than expected.

Too fast.

The 1.2-second time window had slammed shut. Unless Blancanales could divert the guy and slow him, there would be no second shot.

As Schwarz fine-tuned his aim and took up the trigger slack, he heard a machine gun's muffled stutter through the headset. He saw the Spetsnaz juke hard left as Blancanales cut loose through the floor. The Russian didn't stop, didn't hesitate; he jumped. A streak in black T-shirt and jeans, he dived flat out over the counter and as he slid over the back side toward the kitchen, he took the backpack with him.

"Shit!" Schwarz exclaimed as he eased off on the trigger pressure and looked downrange, above the scope's eyepiece.

The familiar gray-and-red helicopter was swinging in over the rear corner of the building. Standing on the copilot side's skid, poised to jump to the edge of the roof, was a big man in black.

ON THE SPYCAM'S TINY color screen, Blancanales saw the running Russian take a big-time hit from behind. The

impact of the .50-caliber slug slapped him to the floor
ten feet from the cash register; the bullet caromed on,
plowing through the back wall. With the sonic boom of
the Barrett rolling down the hillside like distant thun-
der, the Spetsnaz tried desperately to get to his feet. He
pushed his upper body from the floor with his right arm.
He couldn't use his left. The bullet had blown through
the shoulder socket, virtually vaporizing muscle, cartilage and bone. His almost severed limb hung through
the torn sleeve of his black T-shirt, held above the floor
by thin strands of white sinew. Blood sheeted down the
inside of the sleeve, pooling under his chest. For a horrible instant the man's body quivered head to foot from
the shock of the destruction, then his supporting arm
gave way and he collapsed onto his face.

Grimaldi was closing fast from the south, the sound
of the rotor blades growing louder and louder.

On the LCD screen Blancanales could see the other
Spetsnaz already moving in a blur for the backpack; he
could hear the thud of his footfalls through the floor.
The Russian had bolted from the front wall like a
sprinter out of the blocks. He took a different route
than the first guy, high-jumping an overturned table.

Two seconds' delay was all Schwarz needed.

Two seconds.

Turning his face to avoid the spray of splinters and
scorching gases, still staring at the little LCD screen in
his left hand, Blancanales opened fire with his right,
pinning the trigger, pouring bullets into the underside
of the floor. As he cut loose, squinting through the
choking dust and cordite smoke, his heart sank. On the
little screen the Spetsnaz cut hard left, then right, never
pausing, never taking his eyes off the prize. As the

MP-5 SD-3's action locked back, Blancanales watched helplessly as the guy threw himself onto the counter and snatched away the backpack.

At that instant, the building was slammed by rotor wash. It whistled and whipped into the foundation vents.

Through the spycam lens, between the back side of the counter and the kitchen entrance, Blancanales saw the Spetsnaz yank a small black box out of the open top of the backpack.

A box connected to the bag's contents by coiled, brightly colored wires.

Rolling onto his stomach, crawling like a madman through the litter of spent brass and rat droppings, Blancanales shouted into his mike, "Peel off, Jack! Abort! Abort!"

CARL LYONS BACKED OUT onto the helicopter's left skid, machine pistol slung, hanging on to the edge of the door frame and headrest of the copilot's seat. With the wind whipping across his face, he bent his knees to keep his center of gravity as low as possible.

Grimaldi turned the chopper a tight 180 degrees and headed north, overflying the law-enforcement roadblock at high speed. The cops and sheriffs stared up at Lyons in astonishment.

As if he were a circus act.

Or a movie stuntman.

It was the dictionary definition of going for broke.

Because of the tactical situation, Able Team couldn't wait for backup, which wouldn't have done them any good, anyway. Overwhelming force couldn't defuse a crisis like this. All it could do was complicate and delay the outcome.

Delay worked in the favor of the bad guys.

Lyons had considered and discarded all other possible plans of action. Like sending Gadgets and Pol into the café with guns blazing while he played moving bull's-eye out on the highway. They couldn't rely on a surprise rear assault to get control of the backpack. The Spetsnaz had been inside the restaurant plenty long enough to have rigged trip wires or infrared triggers. They could be holding remote detonators. Dead man's switches. Under any of those conditions, even flashbang stun grenades couldn't guarantee success.

Getting control of the bioweapon required taking out the Russians, surgically if possible. If they had Red Frost with them, they couldn't be allowed to leave Discovery Bay with it. Hundreds of thousands of potential casualties hung in the balance.

The goal determined the means.

It was as simple as that.

Stony Man had okayed the plan without comment. Lyons would never have proposed it if he hadn't been confident in Gadgets's marksmanship and in Pol's ability to think under fire and on the run.

At an altitude of fifty feet, Grimaldi veered from over the roadway. Avoiding the string of overhead power lines, he scooted across the shoulder. He cut cross-country, skimming the stunted treetops that canopied the creek bed. He was aiming for the corner of the sprawling red building's roof.

In the final few seconds, Lyons ran through his moves: plant both feet on the roof, grab the gutter with his left hand, hang on and jump. His weight and momentum would probably rip the gutter off the side of the building. He wasn't worried about the noise—the rotor wash and sound of his boots on the roof were going to give him away, anyway. What he wanted to do was break his ten-foot fall.

The simplest, neatest solution was for Gadgets and Pol to drop both targets; failing that, he was counting on Gadgets and Pol to slow the Russians down, giving him enough time to kick through the screen door, avoid the kitchen trip wires, if any, and make it into the dining room. The hostages were still tied up on the floor, out of the line of fire. Anyone standing had to be Spetsnaz. Anyone standing when he cleared the kitchen was dead meat.

The whine of a .50-caliber slug shrieking down at them from the hillside was barely audible over the sound of the rotors. Then, much more clearly, Lyons heard the boom of the Barrett off to his right.

One down, he thought.

Grimaldi brought the chopper to a sudden stop, hovering over the corner of the restaurant. Below them, the tall grass and spindly trees were whipped by the rotor wash. Trash blew out of the garbage bin and sailed away.

Then bullets started zipping up through the café's roof.

Pol, Lyons thought.

The second shot from the Light Fifty didn't immediately follow.

Lyons braced himself with a hand, ready to make the five-foot drop anyway.

Pol's desperate warning through the communication headset stopped him cold. It was followed by a shout from Gadgets.

"Hang on!" Grimaldi growled, then he banked the helicopter over hard to the right, climbing fast.

If the Stony Man pilot had banked to the left, the sudden turn would have pitched Lyons out, face-first onto the roof. Because the turn was to the right, it threw his back against the cockpit doorway. He managed to pivot and grab hold of the door frame, stomach dropping down around his ankles as the helicopter shot across the highway. The wrecked cars and trucks became a blur.

Then the restaurant exploded with a tremendous thunderclap.

The blast wave slammed the helicopter from behind and it lurched wildly, tail end lifting, nose forced toward the glassy smooth bay. Lyons's boot soles slipped on the skid, but thanks to his grip strength, he held on. Grimaldi manhandled the controls, instinctively correcting for the sudden, violent yaw.

As the helicopter leveled out, Lyons glanced back over his shoulder. A huge fireball billowed above the reclaimed tidelands. A wide section of the café's roof erupted into the sky, all four bearing walls exploding outward. As he watched, the entire structure collapsed, jetting wood, glass and metal debris in all directions. As the building caved in on itself, as the flash of brilliant orange dwindled, a dense, dirty white mushroom cloud boiled upward.

Lyons scrambled back into the cockpit passenger seat. "Rosario!" he shouted into the comm set.

Grimaldi cut a tight turn, but he didn't head back toward the plume of smoke. He hovered over the water well offshore. It wasn't safe to go closer. Junk blown out the restaurant roof was falling in a wide circle around the footprint of the destroyed building. Some of it landed in the water along the bay's shoreline.

Giant raindrops splashing.

One look at the heap of splintered wreckage that was Large Marge's and Lyons's first thought was no survivors.

"Rosario! Goddammit, answer me!" he shouted into the mike.

CHAPTER TWENTY

Tblisi, Republic of Georgia,
10:38 p.m. GMT

David McCarter was the first man out the Gulfstream's door and into the warm, gusting, southerly wind. The concrete runway was wet, dotted with standing puddles from a passing rain squall. To his right, under mercury-vapor lights on towering steel stanchions, a row of Mi-26 Halo transport helicopters were being loaded from parked, canvas-covered 6x6 trucks. The soldiers in camouflage BDUs doing the loading moved double-time, as if the devil were chasing them.

At the foot of the gangway stairs, more soldiers stood at attention. The reception committee wore black BDUs and matching berets. Their slung AKS-74 U and VSS Vintorez silenced sniper rifles had the Russian equivalent of a Parkerized, nonreflective finish.

With the rest of Phoenix Force following him, McCarter descended the fold-down stairs. As he did, he noted the shoulder patches on the welcoming party. He recognized the insignia by its shape and color: vampire bat rules the world.

An unhappy thought.

This mission was on the extreme edge of McCarter's personal comfort zone. Not only because of the danger Phoenix Force faced, but because of the company they had to keep.

It was a classic case of the enemy of my enemy is my friend.

And there was an additional caveat. A big one, at that. It was something the team had discussed at length on the flight out. During the catastrophic Moscow Opera House siege, and more recently at the fiasco stand-off in Belarus, Russian special operations had demonstrated just what they were capable of.

Phoenix Force was teaming up with a pack of mad dogs.

At the bottom of the gangway, a lean, angular officer stepped forward to greet him. "I am Major Avrogarov," he said, extending a hand. He had a long, taciturn face, heavy brows and deep creases in his tanned cheeks. "You will be David Green."

"That I will," the Briton responded, stone-faced, to his nom de guerre.

The handshake brought to mind a distant memory. The major's fingers rasped his palm like 220-grit sandpaper. It reminded McCarter of the clasp of a mortician's hand, etched by exposure to formalin. Avrogarov was going prematurely gray at the sideburns. He smelled of burned cordite and tobacco, and above all, he smelled of vodka—he was perspiring it, eighty proof. He showed none of the signs of intoxication, however.

The major gestured at the man standing to his left. "This is my second in command, Captain Vasily Ilich. He is seeing to your needs. Now, other duties I am having." He turned to the younger officer, leaned in close and growled something loud enough for the other soldiers to overhear.

It made them smile.

McCarter had no real command of the Russian language, but like most men in his profession he had picked up some street slang here and there over the years, certainly enough to translate the operative obscenity. Given the context, the major wasn't referring to members of the Moscow Ballet.

Insult delivered, Avrogarov about-faced and marched off in the direction of the helicopters. Half the Spetsnaz reception committee followed him.

The captain was ten years junior to his boss. In his late twenties, Ilich was a huge, blond, broad-shouldered, square-jawed farm boy. His hand was callused, McCarter noted, but not embalmer-abrasive.

After McCarter introduced Encizo, Thomas, Hawkins and Manning, the Russian captain asked, "Will you take part in the operation? Or will you merely observe?" His English was much better than the major's.

"If the U.S. government wanted observers," McCarter replied, "it would have sent a delegation from Congress. We brought along our own weapons and combat gear."

The captain shook his head. "No, that's no good," he said. "You must carry Russian weapons tonight. Of course you are aware that much of our ammunition is not interchangeable with yours. In a prolonged battle such as we anticipate, that could be critical."

"Makes sense to me," Manning said.

"We know your gear," McCarter told the Russian. "AN-74, VSS, VSK-94, we've trained with all of your long guns. We've got no objections to the switch. Is there anything else?"

"You will need to wear our uniform, as well," Ilich said.

Hawkins frowned and looked to his team leader.

"Explain," McCarter said.

"For security and political reasons," the captain said, "we don't want to draw attention to your presence in our ranks. We can't do anything about your not speaking Russian, but you will blend in better wearing Spetsnaz uniforms. This is a night operation, with considerable air-to-ground and artillery support. After the initial artillery and air assault, our main force will attack from below, sweeping the road clear of resistance. A smaller force helicoptered to the summit will rappel down the cliff face and secure the building's upper stories. The rest of us will be taking the low road, behind the main force. By the time we reach the site there may still be room-to-room fighting, and most definitely there will be combat in the caves beneath the monastery. In the heat of battle there is bound to be some confusion, which is another reason for you to wear our uniform. We would hate for you to be killed by accident."

"Ditto," McCarter said.

His sarcasm was lost in translation.

"If you will please follow me," the captain said.

As they started off across the runway, McCarter had questions for his counterpart. "We need to know who the opposition is and how many there are," he told the captain. "We also need to know the strategic situation. The nature of the stronghold, the distance from the sea and your tactical plan."

"The Black Sea is twelve kilometers away," Ilich replied. "The opposition is drawn from special operations units from former Soviet and current Russian military services. There could be as many as two hundred or as few as one hundred. We don't have exact numbers. The attack site is perched on a cliff side, elevation roughly six hundred meters. It's a five-hundred-year-old limestone structure with massively thick walls, six stories high. It was originally designed to withstand a prolonged siege.

"According to legend there is a holy spring beneath it, with waters that can cure the sick. That's why the building was constructed. To protect the holy spring from infidels. It is said that the forest on the slopes below the monastery was fertilized with the blood of thousands of Muslims who tried to storm it. Multitudes have died on that mountainside over the centuries. In modern times, it was used as an insane asylum. The lower levels were reserved for the torture of political prisoners. To save bullets, they executed people by throwing them off the upper balconies. After the fall of the Soviet Union, the building was abandoned." Ilich paused, then added, "Strange that God would bless a place with miracles and then curse it."

"You're religious?" McCarter asked.

"Superstitious," Ilich corrected him. "How can a fighting man avoid it?"

It was a point well taken.

"Your battle plan?" McCarter said.

"Reduce the monastery with heavy ordnance, then mop-up the survivors with foot soldiers."

"And the strategy of the defenders?"

"Make the battle as costly and as time-consuming as they can. Shelling and rocketing will provide cover for our uphill advance, but it won't kill many of the opposition because they can retreat to the caves under the monastery."

"Is there an escape route from the caves?"

"Not that we know of. On the existing maps they all deadend in the bowels of the mountain."

"But you're not sure?"

"They could have extended the tunnels in the limestone to create new exits. This conspiracy is well funded and well organized. It involves traitors from all our military and intelligence services. Until recently, they have managed to keep the operation secret. We can only guess how long they've been planning it."

Ilich took them into a hangar where Spetsnaz uniforms, boots, night sights and weapons were neatly laid out on a long, folding table. "Help yourselves, but please hurry," the captain said. "We need to be in the air in ten minutes."

As Phoenix Force stripped off under the harsh lights, Manning grumbled, "Never thought I'd be doing this. Not in a million years."

Hawkins had a more specific concern as he pulled on the black BDU pants. "Couldn't I lose my citizenship over this?" he said. "I'm putting on the uniform of a foreign power."

"If you manage to survive the night," McCarter said dryly, "I think the masquerade will be overlooked."

"Don't worry, T.J., they'll let you back in Texas," Encizo said.

James and Manning grinned.

"Yeah, real funny," Hawkins said.

"These pistols are standard nines," Manning said, picking up one of the side arms laid out on the table. "Makes no sense to switch our Berettas."

McCarter picked up a pistol, too. It was a Gsh-18 semiauto, the putative replacement for the Makarov PM. He dropped the handgun's magazine, cleared the action and then thumbed out the top cartridge in the double stack. "PBP round," he said, translating the stamp on the casing. "Superhot, hotter than +P+, and armor piercing. It will plow through 8 mm of soft steel plate at fifty feet."

Manning immediately changed his mind. "On second thought, let's burn out their barrels instead of ours," he said.

Encizo tried on a pair of the PN-14K night-vision goggles, adjusting the headpiece's chin strap and pulling down the monocular sight.

"We're taking our own vests," McCarter told the Russian. "They're custom fitted, no insignia, and they're SP-6 proof." The latter being the AP, subsonic 9 mm round for the VSS and VSK-94 sniper rifles. The specially designed 9 mm bullet was seated inside a necked down 7.62 mm case. Its hardened steel core could defeat most body armor out to 400 meters.

"No problem," Ilich said.

James held up an olive-brown plastic jump suit he had pulled out of a shoulder bag. "What's this supposed to be? Jammies?"

"Standard-issue biohazard suit," the captain said.

Encizo picked up the matching hood. It had a long shoulder cape and a clear plastic face plate. There was a port in the back for a self-contained air tank. "Have you ever fought inside one of these things?" he asked the Russian.

"We have trained in them extensively."

"Simulated attacks," McCarter said.

"Until now."

Manning tested the weight of the reinforced fabric. "Seems kind of flimsy to me. Seems like it would rip if it got snagged on something."

"They are stronger than they look," the captain said.

"What happens if they do rip?" Encizo said.

"We will have quarantine and decontamination tents set up."

"In other words, kiss your ass goodbye," Hawkins stated.

"Sorry, I do not understand," the captain said.

"It's nothing, just a joke," Hawkins replied.

"If you're issuing germ-warfare suits and setting up decon and quarantine sites," McCarter said, "you must be pretty sure the renegades are holding stockpiles of the bioweapon. And that they are going to release it during the assault."

"We don't know for certain what they have," the captain admitted. "We don't even know how much of the material originally existed. All the records were destroyed. We have to assume they have a quantity of it and that either on purpose or by accident it will be released. We hope they are storing it in the caves. If it is released underground, at least it will be containable."

"If it gets released into the cave system, how are you going to neutralize it?" Manning asked.

"The biological weapon can be destroyed with high heat. We will use flamethrowers and phosphorus grenades to sterilize the catacombs."

"You've got a big problem then," James said. "These plastic suits aren't going to hold up to high temperatures."

"We have a job to do," the Russian said without apparent concern.

"You've served with some of these men, these renegades?" McCarter said.

"Yes."

"And you're going to kill them?"

"Yes."

"Why?"

"Those are my orders."

"Over and above that?" McCarter persisted.

"We have every reason to believe that if the attack in the United States fails to accomplish the desired result," Ilich said, "if it fails to bring about a return of the old cold war tensions and the revival of the former military state, that these conspirators will turn Red Frost loose against the Russian people. This to topple the current regime and bring about martial law."

There was outrage in the captain's tone, but for an instant McCarter thought he also saw sorrow in the man's eyes. For the blood about to be spilled. Blood that would never wash off. Like the killing of a family member. A brother. Something that had to be done without mercy, and quickly, if it was to be done at all.

The sadness vanished as quickly as it appeared, replaced by granite.

"These will help you familiarize yourself with the terrain," Ilich said, handing McCarter a slim plastic pouch packed with topographic and other maps.

Outside, the helicopters' turbines were cranking up.

"We must leave now," the captain said.

Phoenix Force picked up the AKS rifles and extra mags, and shouldered the bags containing their biohazard suits.

Following Captain Ilich, they recrossed the runway and climbed into the nearest of the Mi-26 Halos. The helicopter could carry up to eight-five soldiers, but in this case, the number was closer to forty. The rest of the interior space taken up with stacked, cargo-netted and strapped-down crates of ammo and other supplies.

Manning pulled down a narrow jump seat from the wall next to McCarter. As he belted himself in, he leaned close and said, "Our Spetsnaz handler almost seems seminormal. What do you think?"

"They only foam at the mouth after they're green-lighted," McCarter said as the turbines' whine grew louder and louder.

With a jolt, the big helicopter lifted off.

After take-off, conversation was impossible because of the noise. Like the Spetsnaz troops around them, Phoenix Force pulled on the well-worn ear protectors chained to I-beam struts above the fold-down seats.

McCarter clicked on his flashlight and began studying the sheaf of maps he had been given. The topographical map showed the steepness of the terrain, which was extreme. The maps of the monastery revealed a complex floor plan that had changed countless times over the centuries as the building's ownership and function had shifted. Large dining rooms had been walled in, turned into rows of small cubicles, then re-expanded as the walls were knocked out, only to be walled in again.

The catacombs beneath the structure were mapped in even sketchier detail. Only the main trunk corridors and branches were well-defined. They descended to a depth of a quarter mile under the mountain, where they appeared to end.

As McCarter stared down at the cave map, he wasn't the least bit reassured. Search-and-destroy missions belowground were never easy, not even with good intel. Confined dark spaces were made to order for conventional ambushes, booby traps and antipersonnel mines. And this wasn't good intel, he knew. This was bullshit.

On top of that, Phoenix Force was going up against Russia's best, not regular army. Commandos seasoned in Chechnya and Afghanistan, the antiterrorist and anti insurgent campaigns of the past twenty years. Soldiers trained and expert in unconventional tactics and weapons.

And willing to die for the cause.

CHAPTER TWENTY-ONE

Bainbridge Island, Washington,
10:06 a.m. PDT

Cigarette smoke hung over Sid Slaney's sunken, timber-beamed living room. The acrid, cottony layers partially obscured the view of Eagle Harbor and the Bainbridge ferry dock out the plate-glass rear wall.

Three unwelcome guests lounged on the conversation pit's sofas. For the twentieth time they replayed the recorded destruction at the Discovery Bay restaurant on his plasma TV. The explosion had rocked the local news camera like an earthquake, and the subsequent sonic blast had overloaded the microphone, making it bleat. Talking-head reporters, uniformed EMTs, bystanders and local police ran for cover, but the person behind the camera valiantly kept filming. With screams ringing in the background and the echo of the explosion ringing off the hillsides, the lens had panned upward, catching the jettisoning debris and ascending column of dirty white smoke. The restaurant itself was hidden around a turn and behind a stand of stunted trees.

As the airborne junk rained to earth, the camera swung back to the highway, just in time to catch a brassy-blond woman with a badge and gun clipped to her belt climb out of the back of an ambulance and charge for the county sheriff's roadblock. She was yelling and holding a gory wad of gauze against her cheek.

The guest with the video controller freeze-framed her anguished face. In Russian he called her a "bloody dyke," which made the other two visitors bray with laughter.

Sid Slaney looked on, speechless. After eighteen years under the deepest of deep cover, the sleeper had awakened to an unthinkable nightmare.

Spetsnaz Lieutenant Boris Luria, the comedian and social commentator holding the video control, was a dark-complexioned Tartar, hairy and heavyset, with short, powerful legs. Ovid Balenko, the man sprawled next to him on the couch, had thin knife-fight scars on his shaved head and across both sets of knuckles. Filled-in bullet scars, like nickel-sized and -shaped blobs of pink wax, deformed Balenko's right forearm from wrist to elbow. The third member of the special-forces unit wore his brown hair in a crude burr cut. Olag Raskov's upturned eyes and mouth made him resemble a perpetually gleeful, feral fox.

The three of them chain-smoked Marlboros and drank room-temperature vodka from tall water glasses. Slaney's massive wood-burl coffee table was littered with empty red-and-white-striped Tom's-brand potato chip bags, and crumbs and cardboard packaging from three party-sized heat-and-eat pepperoni pizzas.

These strangers weren't just eating his junk food, smoking his cigarettes and drinking his booze. They had raided his wardrobe, as well, in search of clothes that would allow them to merge into the alien landscape. They had ransacked his closets, appropriating his Pacific Northwest brand-name outerwear. With the exception of Luria, they were more or less his size. Because of the Tartar's short legs, he had to roll up cuffs of the borrowed, Ex Officio climbing pants.

Sid Slaney had been waiting so long for activation that he had stopped believing it would ever come. Even so, his old spy-school training had stuck. He had always followed procedure, notifying his faceless masters in Moscow on a prearranged schedule that he was in position and operational.

He wasn't a sexy, James Bond 007 spy.

More like a James Bland.

He had used the opportunity his covert insertion provided to earn advanced degrees in computer science and business administration at the University of Washington and Seattle U. He had become a highly paid project manager in a wholly owned subsidiary of the local software megalith. Slaney the Russian spy had sucked up the American sweet life like a bottomless ice-cream soda. In almost two decades undercover, he had passed on no secrets to his handlers. He had discovered no secrets. In fact, he hadn't even looked for any secrets. His mission, until today, was to remain hidden and in place, to stay off the FBI radar and wait.

At a little after 7:00 a.m., when he'd received the activation call on his cell phone, complete with secure password verification, the submarine grounding was already all over the television news, as was the White

House cover story about the vessel's scheduled official visit and tragic accident. The caller had told him to expect "relatives" that morning and his orders were to facilitate their "holiday." There was no elaboration, and no question-and-answer session. The call ended abruptly, but not before the authenticating sign-off cues were exchanged.

Slaney had immediately called his secretary at the Redmond corporate campus and taken a rare sick day. He had guessed the operation was a covert rescue. Russian military intelligence was trying to sneak certain select survivors of the naval accident out of the country before they were discovered—and uncovered. Most likely they, too, were spies. Their escape route of choice would probably be through Canada because it was so close, but Mexico was also a possibility.

He thought he was going to be their travel agent.

The moment Slaney's visitors pulled the white Volvo station wagon inside his garage and he saw the automatic weapons in their laps, he knew he was in big trouble.

Spies didn't carry *okuroks*.

Okurok was Russian for "cigarette butt," the nickname for the 74 Stubby.

Inside the house, things went even further downhill, and in a way Slaney had never anticipated.

His visitors proudly opened waterproof, airtight, foam-lined Pelican cases and showed him the sealed glass vials of the biological weapon. Three separate cases for the seeding of Seattle and points south.

The Tartar then boasted that an attack on the United States was under way, conducted by elite elements of special operations. He said the submarine grounding was just the beginning of the assault. That as a result of the master battle plan, the cold war was not only going to be revived, but it was only going to turn suddenly and irreversibly hot.

At that moment Slaney realized the full extent of his own jeopardy. No way would such an operation be sanctioned by Moscow. And his call to participate in it had been a trick and a betrayal.

In the old days, in the old USSR, he had dealt with Spetsnaz agents. The times were much different now. The personnel was different, too. Without a flutter of empathy or regret, this special forces *troika* had watched television coverage of the bioweapon's spread through Port Angeles, with hundreds of innocent people keeling over and dying horribly. They reserved their tearful, overblown sentimentality for toasts to the bravery of fallen comrades in the submarine, and of others—fathers, brothers and friends—lost in Afghanistan, Chechnya and elsewhere.

Heavy drinking prior to battle wasn't characteristic of a crack Russian military unit, but the action they intended wasn't combat. It was terrorism, complete with suicide. When they released the weapon in a population center they, too, would be exposed to the deadly bacteria. Rather than suffer and die from the effects of Red Frost, Luria had told him they planned to kill themselves after the deployment. They were boozing to numb their fear and bolster their courage.

Unlike the 9/11 hijackers, their mission had nothing to do with misinterpretations of "God's will" and the desire for instantaneous transport to heaven. From their conversation, Luria and the others didn't believe in heaven. They didn't believe in political struggle. They didn't believe in communism. They didn't believe in the old Soviet Union, either. They subscribed to much more ancient codes, what Slaney considered to be "lizard brain" codes. Blood for blood. Fire for fire. Pain for pain. Revenge and devastation in the name of what they perceived as lost honor.

They were soldiers of Genghis Khan.

The Spetsnaz made no attempt to hide their contempt for him. In their view he had been corrupted by his prolonged stay in States, by the rich and easy lifestyle. It was the opposite of their experience over the past two decades. While he had wallowed in stock options and waterfront real estate, the true heroes of Mother Russia suffered hardships, ignominy and despair.

The suicide team had shown him the biological weapons to make him afraid and compliant.

Apparently, everything so far had gone like clockwork. The Spetsnaz invaders had kept well ahead of the pursuit, and despite all the hubbub were still an unknown commodity. At least one of their goals was within easy reach: downtown Seattle was a half-hour ferry ride away. All they had to do was to lay low at his house for five hours, then take the 3:50 p.m. boat to be in position for rush hour.

The airtight plastic cases containing megadeath sat on Slaney's gleaming oak floor.

There was no reason to think they would fail.

And Slaney couldn't let them succeed.

For one thing, his ex-wife, Janey, lived in Fremont, a Seattle suburb just north of Lake Union. She was a corporate lawyer for the same software giant he worked for; that's how they had met. They had been separated for three years, but were still close friends. Janey never knew his real past or his secret life. Chances were good that she was going to be among the dead this day.

Twenty years ago, when Slaney had signed on with the intelligence service it had been to defend his country against enemies, foreign and domestic. Slaughter on the scale of Hiroshima and Nagasaki hadn't been part of the bargain. Based on crimes already committed in Port Angeles and Discovery Bay, these conspirators were the biggest mass murderers in U.S. history. Slaney had no doubt they were going to murder him, too, either to cover their trail or maybe just for the hell of it. After all, they hated his guts and had nothing to lose.

He could see only two options: kill all of them before they got on the ferry, or turn them in to authorities. His pistol, a 9 mm SIG-Sauer P-226, was stored in a lockbox on a shelf in the master bedroom closet. Getting to it, and then catching them by surprise, was going to be difficult, if not impossible. He had hoped that the vodka would make them sleepy, but it seemed to have had just the opposite effect, perhaps because of the adrenaline load of impending suicide. The trio remained alert, active, even animated. They kept their own weapons close at hand. If he didn't manage to dispatch them all in one go, the survivors would certainly kill him and then execute the plan on schedule. Because he wasn't that good a shot, and had never fired a weapon in a combat situation, going for the gun wasn't his first choice.

Calling the police was his only realistic option, but he couldn't do it from inside the house for fear of being caught. His best bet was to sneak out when they weren't looking. He had to put enough distance between himself and the Spetsnaz to complete the call, which meant using his car to get away. He could tell the police it was a home invasion by strangers. There was no paper or electronic trail linking him with the rogue Spetsnaz or the submarine grounding. He could skate with U.S. authorities on the bioweapon plot, but skating with his own people was a different story. He had no idea who was behind the operation, and he had already been betrayed once by someone in the Russian establishment. He had to figure that there would be retribution for giving up the conspirators. He was going to have to disappear from his handlers' radar. It was an eventuality he was prepared for, with false documents, offshore bank accounts and valid airline tickets.

"How about some more food?" Luria said. "I'm still hungry."

"Me, too," Balenko said.

"Not pizza, though," Raskov added.

It was the opportunity Slaney had been waiting for. "I've got some guacamole in the freezer in the garage," he told them. "I can defrost it in the microwave."

It was unclear whether his guests knew what guacamole was. Or maybe they didn't care. All that mattered was they didn't get up from the couch to follow him.

Slaney walked into the kitchen, then through the door that led into the garage. On the far side of the stolen Volvo station wagon sat his year-old Acura two-door sedan. He raised the garage door by hand, inching it up very carefully, trying to make as little noise as possible.

When he opened the Acura's door, he cringed at the chiming sound. Before he could get in, the scrape of a boot sole on concrete froze him in place.

"Where do you think you're going?" Luria asked.

As Slaney turned, his gaze dropped to the Gsh-18 semiauto pistol in Luria's right fist. The fat silencer tube was screwed on, and the hand that held the gun was rock steady.

"You don't need me anymore," Slaney told him. "I've fulfilled my part of the mission. I've done my duty."

"We need you to stay until the job is complete, until after we deploy Red Frost. You might give us away."

"I would never do that."

"We can't take the risk," Luria said. "Too many brave men have already died for the sake of this mission."

"I'm on your side. We're all on the same side."

Luria shook his head, then gestured with the handgun. "Pull down the door."

Slaney considered making a break for it, but there was no cover down the driveway. No way to avoid a bullet in the back of the neck. No one would see him die, either. The neighbors' view of his property was screened by fir trees. With his last hope slipping away, Slaney did as he was ordered.

They started back to the kitchen, but Luria stopped him in front of the chest freezer. "Open it," he said.

After he had done so, the Spetsnaz ordered him to start unloading it.

Slaney reached in and began tossing bagged ravioli, pizzas, guacamole, chicken breasts and bulk coffee beans onto the floor.

The reason was all too obvious.

To make room—for him.

"Don't do this," Slaney said, his voice cracking.

"Please. You don't have to go through with it. You can still stop it. We can stop it together. We can take down the others, if they don't agree. Afterward you can vanish. I have plenty of money hidden away. I can supply you with false documents. You can disappear into Mexico or Guatemala and live like a king. No one will ever find you. The people of Seattle don't deserve to die. They're innocent."

"No one is innocent," Luria said.

"You don't believe that. You couldn't believe that!"

Luria put a hand in the middle of his back and pushed his upper body over the edge of the freezer. Frigid air burned the inside of his nostrils.

"What about the little kids? What are they guilty of?"

Slaney never heard the shot that killed him.

He never felt it, either.

It took nanoseconds for sound and pain to register in the brain. By that time, there was no brain to receive the signals.

CHAPTER TWENTY-TWO

Stony Man Farm, Virginia,
1:11 p.m. EDT

"Rosario! Goddammit, answer me!"

Lyons's shout blasted through the command center's audio speakers, cutting through the funereal silence.

The cyberteam sat on the edges of their chairs, praying for an affirmative response, but interminable seconds passed and none came.

Meanwhile, one of the wallscreens was filled with the live TV feed from behind the roadblock on Highway 101. They didn't have a direct view of the restaurant's destruction. They could see some of the aftermath, though. A thinning pall of smoke drifted over the treetops. Downwind, lighter and lighter objects dropped to Earth like black confetti. When the camera panned to the right, they saw Able Team's helicopter hovering over the mud flats of Discovery Bay.

Hal Brognola stared at the screen, unblinking.

Barbara Price gently put her hand on his shoulder and said, "He may not be dead, Hal. We don't know what happened yet."

The head Fed shook his head and rose to his feet. "We have to prepare ourselves for the worst," he told the others.

"Based on his last reported position," Kurtzman said, "I don't see how he could have gotten out of the crawl space in time."

"Even if he did," Kissinger added, "he couldn't have made it to solid cover before the explosion."

"Based on the ejecta and the concussion," Wethers said, "there couldn't be much left of the building."

"Wait a minute!" Carmen Delahunt objected strenuously. "Like Barbara said, we can't see what's happened down there. We can't write Rosario off! Not until his body's found."

"Nobody's writing him off," Kurtzman assured her. "But it doesn't look good. And that's something we've all got to face up to, ASAP. A lot of other lives depend on us. This mission isn't over, not by a long shot."

Brognola turned away from the screen, a great, painful weight pressing down on his chest. He had to remind himself to breathe. Blancanales's death, if that was what had come to pass, was ultimately his responsibility. He was the man in charge. Circumstances beyond his control had forced him to make decisions based on fragmentary information, under incredible time constraints.

Under those conditions, awful outcomes were to be expected.

Friends, comrades lost in the bargain.

But in the end, there was one simple, sustaining

truth. Every member of Stony Man, Able Team and Phoenix Force was expendable if the fate of the nation hung in the balance. None of them had any reservations about dying for their country.

The grieving for the loss of Blancanales would have to wait. As Kurtzman had said, it wasn't over.

"We have another issue on the table here," Brognola said gravely. "And unfortunately it takes precedence over everything else. It's entirely possible that Red Frost has just been deployed at Discovery Bay."

"The blast certainly could have spread it in a wide radius," Kissinger said.

"Why wouldn't the explosion have destroyed it?" Price said.

"Only extreme heat could do that," Kissinger answered. "Bacteria in an encysted state are tough little bastards. Boiling water isn't hot enough to do the trick. We're talking a prolonged burn of a thousand, fifteen hundred degrees at least, which would require thermite or some chemical accelerant. And there's no evidence of that from what we've seen so far. Based on the color of the smoke and the dispersal rate, it looks like a large quantity of conventional explosive was used."

"So, how are we going to determine whether a biological has been released?" Delahunt asked. "Wait for the military HazMat to show up? Wait while they grow cultures in petri dishes?"

"That could easily take the rest of the day," Price said. "We don't have time for that. We have to know what we're up against."

"There already are plenty of petri dishes on site," Kurtzman said ruefully. "Live ones on two legs. Everyone downwind of the explosion was potentially exposed."

"Based on what happened at Port Angeles, in about an hour we'll know, one way or another," Tokaido said.

"Have DHS contact the local police manning the roadblock," Brognola told Price. "They're going to have to secure the highway to the south, behind the backed-up cars, and keep them there until we know for sure it's safe. They can tell the drivers that there's been a major accident to the south and that they have to wait until it's been cleared before they can turn around. The bottom line is this—no one leaves the scene under any circumstances. No one."

"That's going to be hard to enforce," Wethers said. "Especially if the drivers start to panic."

"Tell the police to use whatever means are necessary."

"That includes shoot to kill?" Price asked.

"We have no choice," Brognola replied.

"I don't believe I'm hearing this," Delahunt said.

"Hal's right," Kissinger told her. "If infected people leave the scene, we're going to have secondary spread on our hands. From the data the Russians have sent us, this bacteria multiplies on and in the body and can be transferred by any kind of person-to-person contact. Even by breathing the same air."

"If people who are contaminated with the bacteria make it back to Seattle," Price said, "the game is over. And we lose."

"We can't let it get out of control," Brognola said. "If it has been turned loose, we've got to contain it."

"But what about Able Team?" Delahunt asked. "They're at ground zero. We could lose them all. What are we going to tell them?"

"The truth," Price said.

"If the biological weapon was released, they've probably been exposed, too," Tokaido said.

"They're going to have to wait it out with the others," Brognola said. "There's no way around it."

"Canaries in a coal mine," Kurtzman said.

CHAPTER TWENTY-THREE

Black Sea coast, Republic of Georgia,
10:20 p.m. GMT

As Dr. Vorostov watched, Druspenskya Sokolova drew ten cc's of pharmaceutical grade morphine into a large hypodermic syringe. Other than the two of them, the yawning, littered banquet room was deserted. It was empty of weapons and ammunition, as well. The other conspirators had taken up or were in the process of taking up positions in the catacombs for the final battle.

Sokolova flicked the syringe's plastic body with a fingertip, then cleared the air bubble with the plunger, squirting a fine stream of fluid into the air. Snatching a cotton ball from her injection kit, she met his gaze.

Words were unnecessary under the circumstances.

Arching one black-penciled eyebrow, with a faintly amused gleam in her eyes, the former GRU officer silently asked the question.

If Vorostov sought an easy exit from his suffering, Sokolova was more than willing to do the honors. But he didn't want to give her that power, or the pleasure she would take in exercising it. He didn't want to take any more morphine to ease his pain, either. Morphine fogged his brain and dulled his wits. Opposing forces were massing along the seacoast below; the pain would be over soon enough.

Vorostov waved off the lethal overdose.

The short woman shrugged as if it didn't matter to her one way or another. She left the loaded syringe and a length of brown neoprene tubing among the debris on the uncleared table so he could inject himself if he changed his mind.

Anticipating the close-quarters combat to come, Sokolova had strapped on a side arm. She carried a battered, 9 mm semiautomatic pistol in a high-riding, ballistic nylon hip holster. Across her uniform jacket and wide chest hung an olive-drab shoulder bag, bulging with antipersonnel grenades.

"See you in hell, old man," she said in her gravelly, chain-smoker's voice.

"Looking forward to it, my dear," he replied. The doctor couldn't imagine that hell's agonies could hold a candle to what he had already endured.

The woman marched out of the room in her oxblood Oxfords, leaving him to die alone. She hadn't offered to wheel him down into the catacombs. That would have meant a slow, difficult, multistory, stairway traverse.

The abandonment to a certain death was no shock to Dr. Vorostov. It wasn't a big disappointment, either. He had no interest in extending what remained of his so-called life. The natural end to his suffering was going to be a long time in coming, and all the more unpleasant for it.

Vorostov flicked his butane lighter and held the blue flame over a well-packed bowl of gummy, black hashish. He inhaled, sucking down the pungent smoke. Its heat burned deep into the center of his chest, then, as the drug passed from lungs to bloodstream, from bloodstream to brain, wave after wave of chills coursed through his body. And as the hash kicked in, his ambient level of pain faded a bit. The dull spear point twisting in his bowels and rectum became a mere splintery broom handle.

He was still puffing on his pipe when the first volley of artillery shells screamed down on the building. They slammed into the lower stories, rocking the floor beneath him and making his wheelchair hop in place. Dirty plates and glasses vibrated off the long table. Then came a blinding flash and roar, and the tall, stately windows facing the Black Sea imploded and the balcony's French doors cartwheeled off their hinges. A wave of blistering heat, broken glass and shattered wood swept across the room.

Vorostov instinctively averted his face and shielded his eyes with the back of his free hand, which did nothing to muffle the thunderclaps of dozens of bursting shells. The pain in his eardrums made him squeal. He dropped the hash pipe in his lap, shut his eyes tight and clapped both hands over his ears.

The power of the chain of explosions was astounding, humbling. Like an angry god stomping, grinding, crushing the massive limestone blocks to powder, kicking out the cornerstones, collapsing the roof. Vorostov's wheelchair hopped about wildly as the floor turned from solid to liquid, a raging sea of buckling, swaying boards. He could feel the shock waves of the detonations traveling through him, shaking his very bones, slapping his innards against the inside of his body cavity. Great, yawning cracks opened in the ceiling; plaster and ancient dust rained down on his head. The air became chokingly, raspingly thick and unbreathable.

With a blinding flash, an artillery round landed square on the balcony. The blast made him black out for a moment. Its concussion swung his wheelchair around ninety degrees, nearly tipping it over, but he never felt the movement. Nor did he feel the wake of the steel shrapnel flying past his head. When he opened his eyes, he was facing the wide rents it had chopped through the wall plaster.

Somehow he had been spared.

As the pounding of shells continued, coarse, acrid smoke billowed in through the doorless doorway. Rounds burst high on the limestone cliffs above the monastery, cracking loose vast blocks of rock, which crashed like vertical battering rams into the roof and rear walls. The floor of the room still quaked, but it had taken on a decided slant, tipping toward the balcony, which was slanted even farther downward. It appeared that the entire front of the building was about to cave in.

But that didn't happen.

The artillery barrage lasted another five minutes—five eternal minutes of concentrated fire, of disorientation, of pure terror. It was followed by an ominous silence that Vorostov could barely make out over the ringing in his ears.

Surely his countrymen hadn't run out of shells, he thought.

Then the floor suddenly groaned, shifting, dropping

farther, timbers cracking as stone gave way, tipping down toward the ruined balcony and hundreds of feet of free fall.

Fate was beckoning to him, urging him to come out to play.

Vorostov wasn't afraid of death. He had made a career of studying it, perfecting it. He was curious, though. Would dying hurt more than he already hurt? Was that even possible? If it was, it was probably only fair. He had killed thousands in the name of research and national defense, soon to be hundreds of thousands.

Dr. Amirani Vorostov wheeled himself over the rubble, through the boiling smoke, onto the sloping balcony. Avoiding the shell crater, he carefully rolled to the edge of the shrapnel-pocked, limestone balustrade.

It was checkout time.

He was ready to receive the answer to the great question: what, if anything, comes after?

From the direction of the sea, Vorostov thought he could hear the steady sound of approaching helicopter gunships. Lots of gunships. Through the smoke, the night was inky-black, the water reflecting dim starlight. The wind had died down to nothing.

He stared so hard that he began to hallucinate. He saw flocks of immense, black-winged angels rising out of the shadows of the treetops. And the muffled ringing in his ears turned to melancholy music, gypsy violins dripping ethno-sentimentality.

Much farther away than he anticipated, lines of tracer fire streamed from low in the sky into hardsites along the access road. The Russian helicopters were only just starting to sweep up the slope.

The churning, grinding sounds of battle rolled over

him. Automatic cannon and small arms sawed back and forth for long minutes. And then he saw a missile track erupt from the trees, ground to air, shoulder fired.

One of the helicopters materialized as it exploded with a piercing shriek. In a brilliant orange fireball, the aircraft tumbled to Earth at the foot of the mountain and continued to burn.

The other gunships poured heavy rocket fire onto the position, setting stands of tall trees ablaze.

Then the shooting from both sides dwindled and stopped. The roadside defenders had either all been killed or they had retreated to better cover.

The beating of rotors grew louder and louder as the helicopters climbed the grade in tight formation, lining up to deliver destruction to the monastery and oblivion to the doctor of death.

Rockets whooshed from their undercarriage pods, knifing through the already blown-out windows in the lower stories, exploding deep in the bowels of the building. Then the gunships opened up with their automatic cannons, strafing the facade with 20 mm rounds.

To Vorostov's left, the stone rail and its support posts disintegrated as AP projectiles detonated on impact. Then he was hit, his lap robe went flying and his wheelchair spun around in a wild 180-degree pivot.

There was no pain.

And no blood.

Across the littered balcony, he saw his right leg lying against the foot of the wall.

No pain.

No blood.

Just pressure. A terrible pressure above the knee, as if a tourniquet had been torqued down too tight. The shell's explosive impact had crushed the tissue, squeezing shut the vessels and arteries. The massive wound hardly leaked a drop.

Dr. Vorostov turned his chair back to face the night.

Gunship cannons winked at him, sharing a private joke as they hovered. Automatic fire walked across the balcony, hurling him out of his chair, taking out his lungs and heart in a single go.

CHAPTER TWENTY-FOUR

Discovery Bay, Washington,
10:24 a.m. PDT

Gadgets Schwarz raced down the slope with the long gun slung over his right shoulder, and all twenty-five pounds of it slapping hard against his back. Below him, smoke still boiled from the ruins of the café, but the heavier debris had fallen to Earth.

He hadn't gone back through the attic trapdoor because he'd anticipated being delayed by a confrontation with the irate homeowners. Seconds after the explosion, he had pulled the sniper rifle's bipod free from the table, scrambled through the diamond-shaped window and dropped onto the gently sloping roof of the front porch. From there, he swung down onto the shaky porch rail.

As he sprinted on the unmowed grass, he replayed the horrendous blast in his mind's eye. All four walls had blown out sideways, even as the roof blew upward, trademarks of high explosive, and in quantity. He couldn't imagine how any of the hostages could have lived through it.

He couldn't imagine how Rosario could have lived through it, either.

Even as he was jumping out the attic window, Schwarz got orders from Stony Man to remain in the farmhouse. The cyberteam figured there was a chance that Red Frost had been released in the explosion. Schwarz was the only member of Able Team who was far enough from the blast's epicenter to have avoided exposure to the bacteria. He didn't think twice about disobeying the command.

Blancanales was likely dead. Lyons and Grimaldi were possibly infected by the bioweapon.

No way could he stay in the farmhouse and twiddle his thumbs for hours waiting for the all-clear...or evacuation.

At the bottom of the pasture he jumped the wire fence and headed across the highway. To his right, about a quarter mile away, Grimaldi was setting down the helicopter. He was descending on the marshy flat on the water side of Highway 101, roughly opposite the restaurant, which was now hidden from Schwarz's line of sight by treetops and the curve of the two-lane road.

Detective Dewitt, her cheek covered with a wad of bloody gauze bandage, rose from behind the barrier of parked squad cars and moved to cut him off.

"You can't go down there," she said. "We just got orders from your people to keep everyone back from the blast site and the highway closed until the HazMat people from the state patrol show up."

Schwarz wanted to warn her about the possible bioweapon release and the mortal danger, but his hands were tied. That information was classified; she didn't have the proper clearance. Besides, if the detective had been exposed, she was already dead. They were all already dead.

"Were any of your guys at ground zero?" Dewitt asked him.

"Yeah, one guy."

"I hope he escaped."

"That's what I need to find out."

"Like I just said, you can't do that," she told him. "Don't make me use force to restrain you." Dewitt waved over a couple of sheriff's deputies who looked even more uncomfortable at the prospect than she did.

"Sorry, ma'am," Schwarz said, "but I have different orders."

When he walked on, she said nothing and nobody tried to stop him.

Maybe it was the expression on his face.

Maybe it was the Barrett.

As Schwarz rounded the bend in the highway, he saw Lyons and Grimaldi cross the road below on a dead run. Darting around the wrecked and abandoned vehicles, they vanished behind the mound of debris where Large Marge's had once stood. The café had been turned into an eight-foot-high, flattened doughnut of wood splinters, shredded pink fiberglass insulation and shattered glass. The pall of smoke had thinned down to a few scattered wisps.

Schwarz broke into a trot.

He reached the outermost edge of the blast ring. Mixed in with the ejecta, sticking to the crumpled sections of aluminum gutter, the ripped-off roofing material and the chunks of wallboard were tiny, wet shreds of pink flesh. Because he had seen that particular, haphazard dice many times before, he recognized it at once. It wasn't pork and it sure wasn't chicken. He hoped against hope it wasn't Rosario.

Lyons and Grimaldi didn't look at all happy to see him, but they didn't look very surprised, either.

"You're not supposed to be here," Lyons said. "You were supposed to stay uprange."

"As if that was going to happen," Grimaldi remarked.

"What's done is done," Schwarz said. "If you're dosed, I'm dosed. We've got to find Rosario, and fast. He could be buried alive under there."

"For crying out loud," Grimaldi said, staring at the pancaked debris pile, "where do we even start looking?"

"Last word we had he was still in the crawl space under the floor," Lyons said. "Blast went sideways and up, not so much down. For all we know the foundation may still be intact below the rubble. Let's pull away some of this junk and find out."

It took the better part of five minutes for the three of them to clear the wreckage from a section of the foundation. It was still intact.

Schwarz squatted and peered through a screened vent. Because debris was blocking the vents on the far side, there wasn't much light coming through. He couldn't see all the way across the crawl space.

"Subfloor is partly caved in," he told the others. "Looks like the damage is directly under the center of the blast."

"Where's Pol?" Lyons said.

"Rosario!" Schwarz yelled into the crawl space. "Make some noise, goddammit! Let us know where you are!"

There was no response.

"Could he have survived under there?" Grimaldi said. "That was a hell of an explosion. Just the concussion—"

"The floor and subfloor would have given him some protection if he wasn't right under the blast," Lyons said.

"Maybe he's not in there," Schwarz suggested. "Maybe he made it out? Maybe he made it into the creek bed behind the café before the explosion. If he did get out, that's where he would have gone, guaranteed. It's the nearest cover."

"He could be lying in the creek bed," Grimaldi agreed. "The concussion could have knocked him out. That's why he isn't answering. Or maybe he got hit by some of the flying crap."

"Better check the creek first," Lyons said. "On the double."

Schwarz led the way around what had once been the rear of the building. The picnic table had vanished. So had the overflowing garbage bin. Lighter debris obscured the swath of tall grass: exploded cardboard boxes of paper napkins, broken bags of flour, pots and pans, a buckled refrigerator door. The stand of alder saplings along edge of the creek bank had been uprooted or snapped off at the base.

When Schwarz looked over the edge, he saw the garbage bin on its side at the bottom. It had been blown clear of the building. Its smelly contents decorated the tree branches all along the opposite bank.

"Let's split up," Lyons said. "Check the far side of the creek, too, in case he managed to crawl out."

The hasty search and shouting turned up nothing. No sign of him.

They returned to the corner of the building they had already cleared of wreckage.

Schwarz immediately wrenched the screen from the foundation vent. "I'm going in after him," he said.

"Be careful," Lyons said. "The debris pile is anything but stable. You make one wrong move and we're going to have to dig you out, too."

"Rosario!" Schwarz yelled into the crawl space through cupped hands. "Dammit, make some noise if you're in there!"

From deep under the foundation they heard something.

Faint.

Muffled.

It sounded like swearing.

CHAPTER TWENTY-FIVE

Black Sea coast, Republic of Georgia,
10:31 a.m. local time

The four-wheel-drive pickup truck lurched forward, then yawed hard right. Even with a boot sole braced against the wheel well, Gary Manning's back slammed against the inside of the bed's wall. He wasn't the only one having trouble staying put. The other members of Phoenix Force hung on to the bed rim as the full-sized truck climbed, one wheel at a time, over the dirt track's deep ruts and exposed boulder tops. Their official minder, the tall, blond Captain Ilich, rode in the truck's cab, in the shotgun seat, his AKS-74 propped on his thigh.

Thirty yards ahead of them, a second commandeered pickup led the way up a narrow lane, past a field where a quartet of howitzers stood silent, its gun crews temporarily idle. In the glare of the pickup's headlights, Manning could barely make out the Spetsnaz huddled in the bed of the lead truck. They were obscured by the swirling cloud of dust raised by its tires.

Behind them was a third pickup loaded with Russian special forces, eating their dust in turn.

Ilich had kept Phoenix Force well back from the action until the artillery had laid the groundwork for the main assault. Now that the cannons were momentarily stilled, the big Canadian could hear the crackle of small-arms fire from the dimly outlined village ahead, and the much more intense exchange of automatic weapons from high up on the road leading to the monastery.

Manning was relieved to be moving forward, into the teeth of it. He wasn't used to cooling his heels while others took the battle to the enemy. Inactivity under such circumstances made him feel antsy.

It had already been a very long day.

And there was a lot more sitting on the table now.

Megadeath, in fact.

The following headlights intermittently lit up David McCarter's face. He didn't look any happier than Manning felt. The Briton was leaning over the side of the bed, the barrel of his PN-14K night sight tipped up. He grimly searched the road ahead, his AKS-74 in his fist. Manning knew what his team leader was thinking, because he was thinking exactly the same thing: they were no longer in control of their own destiny.

Because of the engine and road noise, conversation was impossible.

Not that there was much to say.

And trying to talk while bouncing over foot-deep ruts was a good way to lose the tip of your tongue or crack off a tooth.

The weak side glare of the trucks' headlights swept over cramped, lumpy fields bordered by crude rockpile fences. Everything was colorless, cast in tones of black and gray and off-white. The grass inside the crooked fences was trimmed golf course close by sheep or goats.

As they reached the edge of the ramshackle, medieval hamlet, the cannons behind them resumed firing, lobbing rounds in screaming high arcs onto the ancient fortress, which was miles away. On the mountainside far ahead of them, half screened by the tops of the tall trees, the monastery was already ablaze from the initial high-explosive barrage. Compared to the impenetrable dark mass of cliff and forest, it looked small, but that was an illusion of distance.

A large contingent of Spetsnaz foot soldiers had set off a good hour before the artillery barrage had commenced. This was a battle that couldn't be turned with shelling and air assault alone. It required concerted ground pounding. Roadside ambushes by the conspirators had to be rooted out and neutralized. Cave entrances along the route had to be located and permanently sealed. The good Russians didn't want the bad Russians popping up behind them on the only access road, thereby sandwiching them between a rear attack and the monastery's defenders on the high ground.

As the artillery shells rained down on their tiny target, bright flashes lit up the face of the cliff above, like matchheads igniting on a field of black, then winking out. Only they weren't matchheads. Explosions echoed from high on the mountainside. Explosions followed by the crack and rumble of avalanches. Up there in the dark, massive blocks of limestone broke free of the cliff face and crashed down on the monastery.

There was no discernible return fire from the fortress. No rockets, mortars or cannon. Small-arms clatter from the depths of the forest continued, however. Multiple, heated skirmishes were under way.

The three-pickup convoy bounced onward, up the two-rut lane, into the heart of the unnamed Georgian village. The central cluster of primitive fieldstone buildings looked as if it could have easily been a thousand years old. The mortarless walls were stained by blotches of moss and lichen. The makeshift roofs supported by peeled log rafters.

There was electricity, though.

Sagging black power lines snaked through tiny, narrow windows cot in the stone, windows originally designed to shoot arrows through. As there were no transmission lines along the road, Manning guessed the electricity came from portable generators. Generators that were shut down. All the lights in the village were out. The power lines snaked up to the tops of the medieval towers, too. The towers loomed high over the village's other structures; they were made to repel invaders and withstand prolonged siege. The modern additions to the village's ancient dwellings, porches and sheds were made of rusting sheet tin and scrap lumber.

The place reeked of sheep dung and wood smoke, and dust raised from the road coated everything, reflecting almost white, like dirty snow.

In the monochrome of bouncing headlights, the village reminded Manning of something out of Bram Stoker—a remote, desperately struggling, Eastern European hamlet invaded by well-organized and ruthless high-tech vampires.

A squadron of Russian helicopters swept overhead, flying low and fast toward the foot of the forested mountain. He could tell they weren't Mi-26 Halos. They were smaller, and much faster. Attack aircraft.

Without warning a grenade exploded on the other side of a two-story stone farmhouse, the explosion followed by the frenzied clatter of autofire. When the shooting ended, in the dim perimeter of the truck's headlights, Manning glimpsed a half-dozen Spetsnaz running from between the house and an outbuilding. Evidently, they were still clearing the village of opposition.

With the shriek of locked-up brakes, the pickup convoy skidded to a stop. The driver of their truck jumped out of the cab, as did Ilich. The soldiers in the other two pickups were abandoning ship, too.

"Out, quick!" the captain yelled at the men of Phoenix Force, slapping the outside of the bed with the flat of his hand to hurry them up. "This way!"

Manning flipped down his night sight and headed after McCarter, who followed the Russian. James, Hawkins and Encizo brought up the rear. They vaulted over a low piled-rock wall, then double-timed up a sloping pasture toward a tower perched on a low, rolling hill. Through the sight the world was cast in eerie shades of lime-green.

The Spetsnaz had trained IR spotlights on the slit in the tower's stonework just below the wooden eaves. The slit was two feet tall and about a foot wide. The tower itself was about forty feet high. On the ground in front of it was a ladder, clearly meant to reach the lowermost window or door opening, which was perhaps fifteen feet up.

As they reached cover behind the inside of the pasture fence, Spetsnaz troops already in position opened up with their AKMs along the top of the rock wall, pouring autofire into the narrow window, a hellacious barrage, complete with tracer rounds. Glow-in-the-dark slugs, like luminous minimeteors, zipped through the opening and gnawed at its edges.

There was no return fire.

Someone ten feet down the line of fence shouted a hoarse command over the autofire. Manning recognized their official greeter, and the mission commander, Special Forces Major Avrogarov.

The small-arms fire abruptly stopped. Some of the soldiers shouldered armed RPGs and took aim at the top of the tower. They fired at will. Multiple HE rockets whooshed away, thundercracking as they detonated not 150 away. At least two of the rockets cleared the sides of the narrow window. The subsequent explosions lifted the sheet-metal-and-plywood roof completely off the tower, and blew out basketball-sized chunks of the ancient rock walls, which came crashing to Earth, and bounced, smoking, over the sloping, grassy field.

After the RPG attack, there was no more firing from Spctsnaz.

There was no more need.

The tower was rendered topless, and its five-hundred-year-old floor timbers were burning.

"Who was inside up there?" Manning asked the captain.

Ilich shrugged, as if the question was not worth consideration. Then he waved for his men to follow him back to the road.

As they trudged down toward the idling trucks, McCarter made a sharp detour. Manning detoured with him, as did James, Hawkins and Encizo. They ducked in behind the two-story farmhouse, into the little lane between it and the outbuilding, which appeared to be a livestock shed.

"Son of a bitch," Hawkins said as he flipped up his night sight and looked around Manning's shoulder.

In the weak, dancing light thrown by the burning tower, they could see heaped bodies without their PN-14Ks. They could also see they weren't the bodies of uniformed combatants, the identified enemy. They were old men, women, children, all dressed in rags. Freshly killed, they were stacked like cordwood between the facing stone walls.

"These bastards are shooting anything that moves," Manning growled in anger and disgust.

"Be putting away your tears," Avrogarov said to their backs. "You are knowing nothing of these people. They are being bandits and thieves since the Holy Crusades. They are making deals with the Spetsnaz traitors, helping to move in supplies and ammunition, helping them in the caves under the monastery. That's how they are getting these electricity generators and trucks and gasoline to be running them. They are being warned by us to leave this place at once. They are deciding to stay."

"Do they even speak Russian?" McCarter asked.

"That is whose problem?" the major asked. "You will be going back to the trucks now."

After Avrogarov had walked out of earshot, Encizo said, "How do these guys sleep at night?"

"Goddamn butchers," Hawkins agreed.

"Didn't leave anybody alive to bury the bodies, either," James said.

"Is it just me," Encizo said, "or do you get the feeling that we don't matter any more than the locals did?"

"It isn't just you," Manning replied.

"Stay on your toes," the Briton warned them all. "Whatever happens we stick together. We fight together. We fight the lot of them if we have to. Keep a live round chambered, and don't take anything for granted."

As Phoenix Force climbed grimly back into the pickup's bed, in the distance they all heard the familiar squeal of a rocket launch, followed an instant later by an explosion. They looked up to see a flaming helicopter falling out of the sky at the base of the mountain. The other gunships returned fire immediately, saturating the ground-to-air missile-launch site with their own air-to-ground HEAP rockets. Fireballs bloomed along the tree line, overlapping. The sounds of multiple detonations overlapped, as well.

With a swath of forest burning below them, the gunships took the battle up to the monastery. Rumbling echoes of sustained cannon fire rolled down the mountainside. Exploding conventional warheads flashed deep inside the building, lighting it up from within like a jack-o'-lantern.

After four or five minutes of concentrated, entirely one-sided attack, the helicopters peeled off in formation and headed back for the seaside staging area to replenish their empty magazines and rocket pods.

Even after the attack choppers had passed, Manning could still hear the *whup-whup-whup* of multiple rotors beating over the mountaintop. He guessed that black-clad Spetsnaz troopers, perhaps commanded by Major Avrogarov, were at that moment rappelling out of

Mi-26 Halos hovering above the cliff's summit. Phoenix Force was still a long, uncomfortable way from joining the action.

The trio of pickups lumbered over the unpaved road, climbing a very gradual grade. Rock-fenced pastures on either side gave way to stands of trees. In short order, the road became a ditch fifty feet deep, framed by walls of densely packed, peckerpole firs. The trees' lower branches were flocked with layers of dust. In broad daylight it would have been difficult to see more than ten feet into the boonies. At night the visibility was more like ten inches.

There were no signs of combat on the road. As they neared the foot of the mountain, and the one-lane track got suddenly steeper, that changed.

The headlight beams of the lead truck reflected off a pale haze caught between the bracketing trees. As they drove through it, Manning smelled burned cordite and wood smoke. The latter was from forest fires started by the helicopter crash and rocket blasts. On the right, bleached of color, clusters of skinny trunks canted, half uprooted. Their trunks were shattered, stringy cores splintered and shredded by HE and shrapnel. Their fringed tops had toppled over and were lost in heaps of jumbled branches.

Manning thought he saw a pair of boot soles sticking out from under the fallen limbs. They weren't moving.

Seventy-five feet farther along, at least a dozen bodies lay along the shoulder, facedown amid a scattering of spent brass. Fresh blood glistened as black as crude oil on their camouflage uniforms. This time they weren't civilians. They were bad Spetsnaz. There were a few corpses in black uniforms, too. The good Spetsnaz hadn't escaped the firefight unscathed.

Manning had no idea how many loyal Russian soldiers were ahead of them on the road. He couldn't tell where they were, either, but the sounds of pitched battle rattled from high on the slope above.

At the foot of the mountain, the two-rut road turned parallel to the flank and began to climb upward through a series of tight, steep switchbacks. As the drivers slowed to a crawl to negotiate the first turn, McCarter dropped his night sight's cyclops barrel and said, "Party time."

Manning and the others followed suit, switching on their night sights and switching off the thumb safeties on their rifles. They leveled their weapons at their respective sides of the road and braced for an attack.

All three sets of truck headlights winked out.

Presumably the good Spetsnaz had cleared the road during its advance, but that didn't keep enemy troops from filtering out of their hidey-holes and taking up attack positions after they had passed.

The zigzag grade was an ideal spot for an ambush. Not only did the trucks have to virtually creep around the bends, but also, even with four-wheel-drive, their tires spun on the polished boulder tops that stuck out of the road. When tires hit the boulders they lost traction, and the trucks slewed sideways, actually rolling backward on the grade until their treads could grip. To keep from running into one another, and to keep their forward momentum, the three drivers had to maintain a twenty-yard separation.

A necessity, which as it turned out, saved most of their lives.

Without meeting resistance, or coming across any but dead fighters, the convoy had already climbed well above the plain, to within a quarter mile of the summit. The truck carrying Phoenix Force had just rounded another hairpin right turn, and the lead truck was barreling up the straight grade ahead, engine roaring. Through the dust, the variegated green world uphill went blindingly, uniformly lime.

A fraction of an instant of nothingness.

As the earsplitting concussion and blistering wind of the mine slammed the cab of Phoenix Force's pickup, after a hesitation of no more than half a second, the lead truck's twin gas tanks exploded, as well. The road above them was swept from shoulder to shoulder by green flame. The plume of fire licked at the treetops overhanging the road.

Phoenix Force reacted instantly, jolting into high gear.

Manning turned to bail over the tailgate on McCarter's heels. His mind's eye held an afterimage of a silhouetted truck body violently deconstructing from its chassis. Weld by weld. Bolt by bolt. Doors flying off the hinges, spinning off sideways through the treetops. Window glass vanishing. Hood, fenders, bed vaulting up into the air.

The helpless men in the back of the truck went flying, too.

Springboarded upward and out, bodies were hurled over the shoulder on the downhill side, into the bordering trees.

Some of the Spetsnaz crashed onto the road.

All of them were burning.

As Manning's boots hit the ground, incoming fire

hammered the front of the pickup. Metal-jackets spiderwebbed the windshield and the cab's rear window. The driver and Captain Ilich banged back the doors as they bailed; Hawkins was caught with one leg over the tailgate. The big Canadian grabbed him by the shirtfront and jerked him bodily out of the bed. The awkward, off-balance effort landed them both on their knees on the road behind the back bumper.

Bullets screamed along the sides of the truck, thudded into the radiator and engine block and skipped off the road.

From around and below the rear bumper, Manning saw the apparent sole survivor of the explosion madly crawling down the hill on his hands and knees. His head, the back of his shirt, and the seat of his pants were shooting flames and smoke. He was screaming.

Unable to bring his own weapon to bear, Manning shouted to the others, "Give him cover!"

James and Encizo were already one-handing their AKS 74s over the truck's doors and roof. They opened up on full-auto, trying to turn back or at least blunt the attack.

Enemy assault rifles barked from upgrade, from the slope above the road and from the road beyond the blazing wreck, zeroing in on the human fireball. The Spetsnaz was hit by savage triangulated fire, at least a dozen rounds smacking into and through him. Still burning, smoking like a pile of wet leaves, he collapsed in the middle of the track.

Seizing the opportunity provided, Ilich and the driver stood and ran. They didn't take off down the zigzag road; they jumped across the shoulder and crashed downhill through the trees and underbrush, presumably attempting to join up with the Spetsnaz in the third pickup.

"So much for the coalition of the willing," James said as he stripped out and discarded an empty magazine. He slapped home a fresh one with the heel of his hand.

Incoming fire rattled the front of the truck and whined off the road on either side of them.

"This cover's no good!" McCarter shouted to the others. "We've got to follow Ilich and get off the road. Rafe, take point!"

James and Manning put up defensive fire while the others sprinted across the shoulder, then over the edge and down a ten-foot-wide slope of loose gravel and dirt.

Manning was the last man off the road. As he skidded into the line of densely packed fir trees, their truck exploded above and behind him, bull's-eyed by either a rifle grenade or an RPG. Shrapnel whipped through the treetops high overhead, clipping off branches.

The Canadian plunged into the forest, his left hand thrust out to protect his face, following the trail broken by his four comrades in arms. He was moving too fast to see James ahead on the dimly discernible track. The dense trees and the winding route blocked and diffused telltale body heat. Over the sound of his own clothing brushing the branches, the crunch of his boots on the forest litter, the rasp of his own breath in his throat, he couldn't hear James, either. Inhaling the dust of countless ages, he descended headlong down the sixty-degree grade, hurtling through the thicket of skinny tree trunks and brittle, stunted branches. The distance to the road below was only 150 feet. Running a surreal, infrared obstacle course it seemed a whole lot longer.

Then Manning caught sight of the others: man-shaped blobs of brighter green huddled around a low boulder outcrop. The bedrock formed a tiny clearing on the otherwise solidly treed slope. He put on the brakes, grabbing hold of a tree with his free arm to stop himself before he crashed into them.

Just short of linking up with Ilich and the good Spetsnaz in the last pickup, McCarter had called a halt to their retreat.

Along with the others clustered around the rock, Manning stopped breathing and listened hard over the beating of his heart. He heard a rustle of movement from high on the road above. Men busting brush.

"They're coming," James said.

No further explanation was necessary. It didn't take a brain trust to deduce their enemies' next move. They had split up their force. At least half of them were short-cutting through the woods, trying to get below and behind the surviving truck. This while the rest staged a frontal assault from the road.

McCarter touched Encizo on the shoulder and spoke rapid fire. "Get down to the road. Hook up with Ilich. Tell him what's coming. We'll cut the head off the file in the woods and run the survivors back the way they came. Ilich and his crew need to advance up the hill in the truck and turn back the enemy coming down the road. We'll meet him at what's left of our truck."

As Encizo vanished through the trees, the rest of the Phoenix Force quickly spread out in a skirmish line thirty feet wide. Manning took the lowest position on the slope. McCarter was in the middle and slightly ahead of the others as they advanced across the side of the hill on an intercept course.

The brush-busting noise from above grew louder.

At McCarter's signal, they stopped and dropped to their bellies in the dry leaf litter. The bad Spetsnaz had to be wearing infrared night sights, too. There were no boulders for Phoenix Force to hide behind. Their defense was the maze of peckerpole firs, which would confuse the IR bounce-back and the low angle of sight with them on their stomachs at ground level. Neither guaranteed that the ambush would be successful.

Discovery and disaster depended on how close the enemy passed by.

And how much of a hurry they were in.

A big hurry, as it turned out.

The bad Spetsnaz weren't anticipating an ambush. They were thinking Phoenix Force had sprinted down the hillside to join Ilich and regroup. They were thinking speed was more important than stealth. They wanted to get into position ASAP.

Manning had just enough time to set an extra loaded 74 assault rifle mag close to hand and line up his gunsights before the pointman for the enemy file appeared to his left. Luminous green man-shapes moved rapidly behind a screen of darker verticals—the intervening tree trunks. James, Hawkins and McCarter held their fire. As the lowest gun on the slope, Manning had the responsibility of springing the trap and closing the downhill end.

When the lead man rushed into the Canadian's killzone, he opened up, full-auto. Even though the range was no more than twenty-five feet, he had to shoot through the trees to hit his targets. Manning was glad they were firing rifle not pistol rounds. A split second after he touched off the burst, even as the pointman stumbled to his knees, McCarter and the others followed suit. The air was full of flying splinters, gun smoke, dust and the seething clatter of autofire.

Manning scored multiple hits on the first three men as he swept his sights and blazing gun barrel uphill. The bad Spetsnaz were blown off their feet, or trapped and momentarily held upright in the maze of trees. Caught flat-footed, they never managed to bring their own weapons to bear; they fired into the ground or the air, hands clenching reflexively. Their ghoulish green faces were lit up by staccato muzzle-flashes, faces full of pain.

Manning's rifle locked back empty. He dumped the spent mag and slapped in the full one, pushing to his feet. McCarter, James and Hawkins jumped up, as well.

With the head of their file mowed down, those farther up the hill, not yet in the killzone, managed to stop, turn and reverse course.

A panicked retreat.

For a moment all shooting ceased. Then from the road behind and below Phoenix Force's position, the last truck's engine roared to life and automatic fire once again raged back and forth.

Encizo and Ilich were on the move, advancing up the grade, clearing the way as they went.

"Let's go get them!" McCarter said, taking the lead and charging up the slope.

Manning followed hard on his heels. The path was well trampled, the going much easier, even if uphill. The pursued were now the pursuers, driving home their advantage.

As Phoenix Force mounted the grade, the enemy above cut loose with wild, unaimed fire, intended to slow them down.

It didn't work.

McCarter, Manning, James and Hawkins leap-frogged their way to the edge of the trees, firing short bursts to keep the opposition moving.

By the time they reached the shoulder of the road, Ilich's crew was rampaging up the grade toward them. They were shooting from behind the moving cover of the truck. When Phoenix Force appeared on the shoulder downrange, at Ilich's shouted command they held their fire. There were dead enemy Spetsnaz facedown in the road, far more than there had been before, some of them still bleeding, their corpses illuminated by the dancing light of the burning trucks.

To the right, past the first pickup, Manning glimpsed the last of a handful of conspirators sprinting up the road. "We didn't get them all," he said.

As the driver of Ilich's pickup squeezed past the lowermost flaming wreck, scraping between its side and the side of the road cut, McCarter waved Phoenix Force up the hill, continuing the pursuit.

Suddenly outnumbered and outgunned, the bad Spetsnaz were running for all they were worth.

Gary Manning was the first around the pickup that had hit the road mine. He got off a 3-round burst at a lime-green figure that was half in, half out of a dark cleft in the bedrock on the uphill side of the road. It was a difficult, if not impossible shot. His rounds whacked into the limestone on either side of the opening, bracketing but not hitting his intended target.

"Did you mark that?" he growled over his shoulder at James, keeping his sights trained on the crawly hole and his finger on the outside of the trigger guard as he continued to walk up the road.

"Yeah, I got it," James said, covering the cave entrance with his own shouldered assault rifle.

The pickup truck rammed the blown-up wreck out of the way, battering it onto the shoulder, then flashed on its high beams, lighting up the cleft in the rock.

Phoenix Force flipped up their PN-14Ks.

As Encizo and Ilich joined them, gunfire erupted from inside the opening, bullets whining across the road.

Manning and James shot back, saturating the entrance with autofire, giving the others a chance to move closer to the hillside, out of harm's way.

"Are we going in after them?" Manning asked, tossing away the empty clip and reaching for a fresh one.

"What point would that serve?" Ilich said. "They're not going anywhere." He hand-signaled to his troops. "You had better get to cover now."

As the five-man team moved behind the pickup, two of the Spetsnaz unlimbered RPGs. One of them took a kneeling position in the middle of the road, aimed and touched off a rocket. It hit the outcrop at an angle, blowing the entrance open wider, sending chunks of limestone flying.

Out of the launcher's rearward blast zone, the second man raced along the shoulder. Before the conspirators inside the cave could recover and return fire, he put an RPG right up the proverbial pipe. The subsequent detonation shook the ground like an earthquake. Twenty feet of hillside jumped in the air, and a stand of trees was uprooted and toppled over onto the road.

The cleft in the rock vanished under the landslide.

When the dust cleared, the combined force continued up the road ahead of the truck, checking for more mines as they went.

"At least there won't be any more of them coming out of that particular hole," Encizo said.

"Which only leaves ten thousand more?" Manning said.

"The place is a sieve," Hawkins agreed.

"Who planned this offensive?" James said.

"What makes you think it was planned?" McCarter queried.

"It's planned at the bad boys' end," Manning said. "That land mine had to be remote detonated. Otherwise it would have gone off when the first wave of Spetsnaz headed up the hill. Bastards popped out of their hidey-hole just long enough to touch it off."

"It's a safe bet they've got all sorts of other surprises waiting for us," McCarter said. "Eyes wide open."

They trudged up the zigzag, looking for disturbed earth on the road, for movement in the trees. They found neither. The conspirators had either shot their wad, or they had already pulled back to the catacombs.

The closer they got to the summit, the louder the crackle of autofire became. They couldn't see the monastery for the steep hillside and the walls of trees.

The last straight stretch of grade ended in what looked like an enormous cave mouth. It was easily twenty feet high and twice that distance across. It was also apparently deserted.

Guns up, Phoenix Force and Spetsnaz approached it cautiously. Only after they reached the threshold did Manning realize it wasn't a cave, but a natural arch hewn by wind and water from the native rock. From the far end of the opening, they looked down on the ancient building; they were a few hundred yards above the massive, naked outcrop on which it sat. The monastery's sea-facing balconies and most of its facade had been blown off by the shelling. The din of automatic-weapons' fire was nonstop. Fire engulfed an entire wing. It was too bright for night sights.

Manning flipped up his PN-14K. The descent to the monastery was steep and no wider than the road leading up.

"This was the pilgrims' route to the holy spring," Ilich said. "Through the arch and down. It was improved for the construction of the monastery."

"Looks like a sniper's paradise," James remarked. "Every window at this end has a clear shot onto the path."

"Major Avrogarov's men on the cliff above have complete control of the situation," Ilich assured him.

Inside the building the pitched battle continued. Through the blown-out windows of the lower floor, they could see men running back and forth. "Complete control" seemed a bit of an exaggeration to Manning.

Ilich waved his troops and the pick up onward. "Shall we go, then?" he asked his guests.

"Yeah, sure," McCarter said, turning away. To the men of Phoenix Force he added under his breath, "No bloody sight-seeing. Keep moving until we reach hard cover."

CHAPTER TWENTY-SIX

Discovery Bay, Washington,
10:32 a.m. PDT

Rosario Blancanales came to in the pitch dark, at the bottom of Large Marge's sump pit, inside the derelict oil tank. He couldn't feel his limbs and he couldn't make them move. Commands from brain to arms and legs somehow got scrambled or never arrived. He could think, but nothing else seemed to work.

As the numbness persisted he started to worry.

Am I paralyzed? Blancanales asked himself. *Have I got some awful spinal injury?*

Then, *am I dead?*

Slowly, inexorably, sensation returned to his body, and he knew he was still alive. The recovery of feeling was welcome but not the least bit pleasant. His body ached all over and it burned, as if his skin had been scalded down to the muscle. Under the circumstances, any sort of injury was possible. Broken bones. Ruptured internal organs. Concussion. The outside of the tank had protected him from the crush force of the explosion's pressure wave, but the inner surface was pitted with rust and he had been bounced around inside it like a marble in a tin can.

He couldn't remember the explosion, per se. He could remember trying to get out from under it. He could remember shouting a warning to Lyons and Grimaldi. He knew he had banged his head because he tasted blood in his mouth—from a broken nose or a cut inside his mouth, it was impossible to tell. Blood was smeared all over his face. As he shifted his weight in the tank, there was no sound. All he could hear was a dull roar. It felt as if his head were stuffed with cotton. The white noise was so loud he couldn't hear his own heartbeat.

When he was able to make a fist, Blancanales dragged himself out of the tank and flopped onto the concrete floor of the sump. It was very dark under the restaurant. Much darker than before. He couldn't see his hand in front of his face.

Am I blind? he thought.

He fumbled for his miniflashlight but it was gone. His wristwatch was still there. He flipped up the cover and was relieved to see the glowing hands and face. He had been unconscious for about ten minutes. He didn't pause to check himself for injuries; all he wanted was out, and as quickly as possible. He had to find Lyons and Grimaldi. He knew they could have been in much worse shape than he was.

When he pulled himself up to the top of the sump pit's steps, he realized why it was so impenetrably dark. The joists and subfloor above had partially collapsed onto the rim of the pit.

He found just enough space to squirm through. And when he was through it, belly down on the cool dirt of the crawl space, he saw more fallen subfloor, dropped pipes and heating ducts, and on the other side of all that, a small, familiar rectangle of light. It looked very far away. Hand over hand, swearing a blue streak, he dragged himself over the dirt and around the debris toward the foundation vent.

At least he thought he was cursing.

He could feel his lips moving, his vocal cords were vibrating, but he couldn't hear his own words.

When he reached the inside of the foundation vent, he saw the screen was missing. Then a familiar face appeared in the gap in the cinder blocks.

"Carl, you lucky bastard," he said. Or shouted. He couldn't tell if he was forming the words correctly, or what volume he was producing.

Lyons grabbed his outstretched hand and helped him out from under the restaurant and onto the grass.

Lyons, Schwarz and Grimaldi looked glad to see him. They actually high-fived. Then all of them were leaning over him, talking at once. He knew that they were talking because their lips were moving.

Blancanales pointed his fingers at his ears and bellowed up at them, enunciating every word, "I can't hear a fucking thing."

CARL LYONS FELT a terrible weight lift from his shoulders when he saw Blancanales's bloodied face through the foundation vent.

"Son of a bitch!" he crowed, amazed and heartened by the fact that his teammate had had the strength to drag himself out from under the wreckage.

When they got him spread out on the grass, Lyons's relief faded. Blancanales looked bad. It was hard to tell where the dirt and rust ended and the gore began. There were big flakes of orange scale in his white hair and on his face.

Then Blancanales pointed at his ears and shouted up at them.

Really, really shouted.

"Okay, okay," Lyons said, making a two-handed calm-down gesture.

"He's lost his hearing?" Grimaldi said.

"Looks like," Lyons said.

"Damn, how did he survive that blast?" Schwarz asked.

Lyons repeated the calm-down hand gestures as he spoke, hoping that between them and lip reading, Blancanales would get the picture. "Just stay still, Rosario," he said. "We'll get the EMTs over here."

"I'm on it," Schwarz said. With that, he took off running for the corner of the ruined restaurant.

At Lyons's direction, he and Grimaldi carefully looked Blancanales over for obvious serious wounds. They didn't want him to bleed to death before help arrived. And they couldn't move him around for fear of making things worse.

"I don't see any bleeders, but he could be badly busted up inside," Grimaldi said.

"Yeah, I know."

"He could go into shock any second," Grimaldi said. "We've got nothing to wrap him up with."

"He's not shaking," Lyons said. "That's a good sign. He seems to be alert. We've got to keep him that way. Keep him talking."

Lyons leaned over his old friend and with exaggerated mouth movements said, "What happened?"

Blancanales nodded that he understood the question. "Old oil tank!" he shouted up at them. "Steel tank in a concrete well. End of it was cut out. I crawled inside before it all blew."

After a pause for breath, Blancanales yelled, "Who else made it out?"

"Just you," Lyons said.

When Blancanales looked puzzled, Lyons pointed a finger at him and shook his head.

With Schwarz in the lead, three EMTs showed up carrying a folded-up stretcher and their medical kits.

"Please step back," the head EMT said. He was a small, wiry guy with a thick brown mustache.

"Give them room to work," Schwarz said.

As Lyons and Grimaldi backed away, the EMTs knelt around Blancanales. They immediately began taking his vital signs. The head guy checked his pupils for a possible brain injury. When one of the crew started cutting off his DHS uniform shirt with a pair of blunt-tipped scissors, Blancanales reached out and stopped him.

With an effort, he sat himself up. "Just a goddamn minute!" he bellowed, pushing away the six latex-gloved hands that were trying to make him lie back down.

"Don't make us restrain you, sir," the head EMT said. "You have to lie still so we can examine you."

"He can't hear a word you're saying," Grimaldi said. "The explosion messed up his ears."

"And you better watch out because he can still kick your asses one-handed," Schwarz added.

The EMTs drew back a bit and kept their hands to themselves.

"Is he going to lose his hearing permanently?" Lyons asked them.

"No way to tell at this point," the head EMT told him. "Your friend needs to go to the hospital immediately. Nobody walks away from a blast like that without sustaining serious injury."

"I don't know, he looks pretty lively to me," Schwarz said.

"He could have critical internal injuries," the EMT said. "And his combativeness could be the result of brain trauma. We have no way of telling until he starts to go downhill, and by then it might be too late to reverse things. You've got a helicopter sitting over there on the marsh. We'll stabilize him for transport. You can fly him to Harbor View, land on their helipad. We'll radio ahead that you're coming. There'll be an E.R. team on standby, waiting for your arrival."

Lyons frowned. He knew Blancanales could be dying. Hell, they all could be dying if Red Frost had been released.

In point of fact, he didn't have a choice in the matter.

"Nobody's leaving until we get the all-clear," he said.

"I don't understand," the head EMT said. "What 'all-clear'?"

"You don't have to understand anything," Lyons told him. "It's Homeland Security procedure. That's all you need to know. Take him back to the EMT truck. Work on him there. Make him as comfortable as you can until we can airlift him out."

He gave Blancanales the thumbs-up sign.

Blancanales nodded and returned the gesture.

As they carried him off on the stretcher, Lyons contacted Stony Man via the secure link, giving Brognola the news that Blancanales had survived.

UNDER ANY OTHER circumstances there would have been wild cheering in the background.

Under these circumstances, cheering seemed more than a little premature.

Nobody was out of the woods yet.

"In another hour or so we'll know if we were exposed to the bioweapon," Lyons told Brognola. "In the meantime, we're not going to just sit on our hands. We're going to start sifting through the wreckage and see what we can dig out. Maybe recover something from the bodies of the dead Spetsnaz. You don't have a live video feed of the aftermath, but it's a real mess. The building was reduced to a pile of splinters by C-4."

"Wait a minute!" Kissinger piped up. "You're sure it was C-4?"

"Yep, it had to be. All signs point to it."

"HE is not a good way to disperse this particular bioweapon," Kissinger said. "In fact, it's a real bad way. The extreme temperatures produced at the point of the explosion would destroy most of the encysted bacteria before spreading it. High heat is about the only thing that can reliably kill this puppy."

"That's a positive, then," Barbara Price said. "There's a good chance that either the hostage takers didn't have any Red Frost with them or if they did, it was destroyed in the blast."

Everyone was trying to look on the bright side. Trying very hard.

"Keep us posted on developments," Brognola said.

"Roger, that." Lyons signed off.

The Able Team leader stared at the flattened mass of debris. It looked like a giant pile of toothpicks. Or the middle of a landfill. He figured fifteen pounds of C-4 was needed to do that much structural damage. The shock wave produced by the high explosive would have killed everyone inside instantly, literally blowing them apart.

"What are we looking for?" Grimaldi asked him.

"Where do we even start?" Schwarz said. "There's not going to be anything left of the backpack or the bio-weapon. Or the guy who detonated the C-4. That blast turned him into red mist."

"We're looking for what's left of the other guy," Lyons said. "The one Gadgets shot from the farmhouse. He was down on the far side of the counter when the C-4 went off. He would have been partially shielded. His body could have been thrown clear. It's a long shot, but there might be something in his clothes. Something that we can use to figure out how many of these bastards are left and what their next move is."

"We're on the wrong side of the building, then," Schwarz said.

"He's right," Grimaldi said. "The blast would have tossed him the other way, toward the highway."

They rounded the blast perimeter, walking on the edge of the strewed rubbish to the far side.

"What we need is some heavy equipment to shift the wreckage," Grimaldi said, prodding a disconnected, caved-in water heater with the toe of his boot. "Doing it by hand is going to be slower than slow."

"Even if we had bulldozers to help us it could take a couple of days to sift through all this crap," Lyons said. "We don't have that kind of time. And we can't wait until the Feds get around to sending in a crime-scene unit. We have to do it ourselves."

They started ripping barehanded into the pile of trash, peeling it back until they exposed the floor of the restaurant.

"Got clothing here. Bodies, too," Schwarz said.

Lyons and Grimaldi hurried over to help him pull off the debris. They uncovered several badly mangled corpses at the foot of the front wall.

"Not our guy," Schwarz said.

It took them the better part of forty-five minutes of picking through the rubbish to find what was left of "their guy."

The dead Spetsnaz looked as if he had been hit by a tank or dropped from a great height. Inside his skin everything was crushed, every bone broken, his organs liquefied. They identified him by the vampire tattoo on his forearm and the all-black clothing. He was missing an arm, too, but that didn't distinguish him from the other victims.

When they turned him face up, they could see that the force of the explosion had driven jagged pieces of wood from the service counter through his torso. The bloody spike ends stuck out through what was left of his T-shirt.

A thorough check turned up nothing in his pockets or shoes.

He carried no ID.

All the labels had been torn out of his clothing.

"Shit," Grimaldi said in exasperation as he straightened. "We got zip."

"Maybe if we searched again," Schwarz said. "Maybe we could find something we missed."

Lyons didn't respond. Even if they sifted everything through a fine mesh screen, it was needle-in-a-haystack time.

Grimaldi looked over his shoulder at the carnage their search had revealed and shook his head. "We couldn't save any of them," he said.

"There was nothing we could do," Lyons told him. "Whoever called them on that cell phone gave them the pull-the-plug signal. At that point it was taken out of our hands. I've got to check in with Stony Man."

When he linked up with Brognola, he broke the bad news. "Hal, we've got nothing," he said. "Everything looks like it was run through a wood chipper. Maybe there's something here somewhere—maybe if we had a month and twenty trained technicians helping us we could reconstruct what body part goes to what person, and what shred of paper might belong to that person. What I'm saying is, without a complete crime-scene reconstruction, whatever we find we can't tie directly to the dead Spetsnaz."

"So we've still got no way to pin down the real target, if there is one," Brognola said grimly. "No way to tell how many bad guys are involved or how much Red Frost they've got."

"There's still Phoenix," Lyons said. "They could come up with something at their end."

"How are you feeling?" Brognola asked.

"We're all fine," Lyons told him.

"If you were infected, you should have started feeling the symptoms by now," Kissinger interjected. "Joint pain, fever, disorientation."

"Like I said, we're fine."

"That's great news," Price said.

"What about Rosario?" Brognola asked. "How's he doing?"

"According to the last word we got from the EMTs he's stable," Lyons said. "His vitals are all good, but his hearing is still impaired. Could take days for it to come back to a 100 percent."

"That makes him a liability on the mission," Brognola said. "As long as he's not in danger, get him ambulanced to a hospital."

"He's not going to be happy about being left out."

"Happy has nothing to do with it."

"I'd hand him the phone so you could tell him that yourself," Lyons said, "but he can't hear anything."

"That's what's known as a silver lining," Brognola said.

CHAPTER TWENTY-SEVEN

Black Sea coast, Republic of Georgia,
10:40 p.m. local time

David McCarter led his men down the unprotected
slope and across the monastery's terrace to the single
flight of wide stone steps. He waved them past him,
through the open arched doorway and into the ground
floor. The building's upper stories were either cleared
of hostiles or on fire, thanks to the artillery and rocket
barrages. All the shooting had stopped, but it was anything but quiet on the hillside cliff. The blaze in the far
wing crackled and popped; there were loud crashes
from above as ceilings, walls and floors caved in on
themselves.

When McCarter entered the wide foyer after Hawkins, he noticed wisps of smoke hanging around the
ceiling. It was suddenly, noticeably warmer inside, and
not from the central heating.

That gave the Briton pause.

Once again he got the distinct feeling that Spetsnaz

had no master plan, that they didn't have everything under control. He didn't like the idea of taking his men deep belowground with a fire raging in the structure that stood over them. A fire that perhaps could block their only way out.

McCarter could see similar concern, if not doubt, written on Manning's tanned, weathered face. The Canadian looked at him and smiled grimly. They had no choice. They had to continue. To do or die.

They had met no opposition thus far. The bad Spetsnaz had either been beaten back or had retreated to the catacombs. Following Ilich and his crew, who seemed to know where they were going, they trotted through wide, deserted rooms and narrow hallways with towering ceilings. What furniture there was, was shattered. The floor underfoot was covered with grit from fallen ceiling plaster and littered with spent cartridge casings. Bullet and gren shrapnel holes marked the walls, doors and moldings. There were dead guys, too. Dead bad guys in woodland camouflage. Their bodies had been dragged out of the way and thrown into the nearest corners, leaving shoulder-wide blood smears on the scarred wood parquet.

Moving in the mass of Spetsnaz, McCarter, Manning, James, Encizo and Hawkins passed through a double doorway and entered a great hall with a two-story ceiling. Inside were many more troops, and they were assembled at the far corner. They had their biohazard suits on, but they held their protective hoods in their hands. Major Avrogarov stood with them, also in the body part of his hazard suit. He was wearing a black throat microphone and earpiece. Some of the other troopers were likewise wired, presumably the officers and noncoms.

A crude decontamination unit had been set up along the left side of the room. It consisted of a row of portable showers and hoses connecting them to opaque plastic barrels of bluish liquid.

There were no live prisoners that McCarter could see. The conspirators were fighting to the bitter end. Not that they had anything to lose. Based on what he'd seen of the major's work so far this night, surrender served no purpose except to facilitate death.

Some of the Spetsnaz were aiming their AKS assault rifles through a doorless archway. As McCarter got closer, he realized they were guarding the entrance to the stairs leading down. It appeared that no one on Avrogarov's side had yet descended into the monastery's catacombs. The major had waited for the full complement of troops to arrive before he initiated the assault.

Avrogarov rattled off a command in Russian to his captain.

Way too fast for McCarter to translate.

"Put on your biohazard suits now," Ilich told the men of Phoenix Force. "Leave the night sights behind. They can't be used with the suits because of the face plate. There are high-intensity headlamps built into the helmets."

McCarter and the others took their suits from the bags and slipped them on. They had double lapels with double zippers and built-in boots and gauntlets. They stank of uncured plastic, like cheap inflatable air mattresses, and they were very hot. On the upside, the legs and shoulders were baggy enough to provide a full range of movement. Phoenix Force waited with the others for the order to put on their head protection.

At Ilich's direction, his men passed out small air tanks, and showed Phoenix Force how to connect them to the suits' built-in nipple.

"How much air time do we have on these tanks?" McCarter asked the captain.

"Half an hour per tank," Ilich said as he adjusted his throat mike. "We will be carrying some spares with us. Check your watches when you turn them on. You will have to keep track of the time yourselves."

At a signal from the major, everyone in the hall donned their hoods and prepared for the attack, turning on the canned air supply. When Avrogarov signaled again, four of his troopers armed and chucked a clutch of HEAP grenades through the doorway opening, down the hidden staircase. The men guarding the entrance, moved well back but kept their weapons leveled.

The grenades clunked as they bounced down the steps. After dozens of bounces, each one growing ever more faint, came the familiar, solid whump of antipersonnel ordnance.

The floor shook as the grenades detonated, one after another.

After the last one went off, Avrogarov gave the signal to advance. With Captain Ilich in the lead, the Spetsnaz rushed through the doorway double file, through the rising smoke of the grenade detonations.

Phoenix Force fell in line behind the first contingent. There were at least thirty soldiers ahead of McCarter, including the major. Some of the Spetsnaz carried flamethrower tanks strapped on their backs; most carried AKS-74s. The stairwell was circular and made of yellowish limestone. The rock was dished out, polished by centuries of boot soles. As they descended the well, the tramp of feet on the steps sounded like a cattle stampede. Through the haze of smoke left by the grenades, torches still burned greasily in the iron wall stanchions.

McCarter automatically started counting the steps. It was a reflexive gesture. In the plastic helmet, it was hard to see his feet. Counting made him concentrate. At about step forty-five, he saw the first scorch marks from the grenades. The blasts had put out the torches. At step sixty-four, he had to jump over a dead bad guy, his chest torn open from collarbone to belly by hot shrapnel, his shredded uniform still smoking. The Briton lost count around step 120. It was a hell of a long way down.

He had no doubt that Avrogarov would have gassed his opponents underground like moles or rats if that had been a viable option. The opposition in this case probably had its own breathing gear, which could negate the effects of a poison-gas attack. And the penetration and saturation of any sort of gas was dependent on the volume introduced, the size of the target area and temperature variations within it.

In the light of dozens of bouncing headlamps, McCarter could see the plastic-suited men below him disappearing two at a time through a hole in the wall. The stairs ended in a stone archway.

The entrance to the catacombs had no door.

It also had no guard.

On the heels of the Spetsnaz, McCarter entered a rough-hewed, curving passage about seven feet wide. Its irregular walls had been polished and lubricated by the passing of countless human hands, thousands upon thousands of outstretched sweaty palms over centuries, feeling their way to safety, to a cure. The ceiling was angled upward, like the peak of a tent, and blackened by torch soot. It varied in height, making him think that great blocks of stone had fallen away. Clearly, these caves weren't man-made. They had been hollowed out by water percolating down from above.

There was water standing in puddles on the gritty limestone floor. Here and there it seeped through the walls in tiny beads like sweat, or tears.

Shallow side rooms had been carved out on either side of the corridor. They looked ancient, probably cut by hand chisels. McCarter glimpsed sleeping benches. Niches for holy statues. Places for penitents to rest and to pray. Even through the biosuit, he could feel the pervasive dampness.

Ahead of him, men were occasionally peeling off from the file. They were disappearing into side passages, even narrower seams in the rock that ran perpendicular to the main corridor. Some of them were barely wide enough for a person to slide through sideways. They were moving quickly, though. By the time McCarter passed the entrances the glow of their headlamps was already gone.

Evidently Avrogarov's plan was to clear the entire maze chamber by chamber, crossroad by crossroad. From the crude map McCarter had seen he knew that the central hub of the spiderweb of natural and man-made passages was the shrine of the Holy Spring. That was where the conspirators would keep Red Frost. That's where they would release it, too. In the very heart of the catacombs.

As McCarter glanced back to check on his men, the corridor was jolted by a tremendous bang, and he went down. He barely had time to put his arm out before the floor flew up and hit him. Bits of metal sang over his head, skipping off the tunnel's walls and ceiling. The explosion did more than bowl over the Spetsnaz in front of him. It tore them apart. The middle of the file was gone in an instant, in a brilliant flash and roiling cloud of smoke and dust. Those in front of the blast, including Avrogarov and Ilich, were cut off from the rest.

AP mine in the floor, he thought as he pushed himself up to his knees. Rigged with a remote detonator or a timed delay. Meant to cut off the head and divide the force. And it had succeeded.

The next part was inevitable.

Men in camouflage burst from a cross passage on the other side of the explosion, jumping into the main corridor with guns blazing.

McCarter returned fire through the boiling dust, staying low and bracing himself by pressing his shoulder against the wall. Manning did the same from the other side of the passage. James, Encizo and Hawkins had to duck for cover behind them. In the narrow tunnel, without a clear firing lane, they couldn't shoot back.

Muzzle-flashes winked at them, autoweapons clattered and a torrent of steel-jacketed rounds howled down the tunnel.

McCarter aimed just above the flashes and pinned the AKS trigger. He put half a dozen shots into an imaginary circle the size of a dinner plate. With the low recoil round, and the resulting lack of muzzle climb on full-auto, it was a piece of cake.

One of the dark shapes slumped to the floor.

The Briton followed up, the trigger still pinned, taking out a second man.

Through the smoke two more fell at once, blown off

their feet, either by Manning's gun or good guys firing from the other side of the breach.

Then as suddenly as they had appeared the crouching figures were gone, vanished back into the rockwork like a pack of cockroaches.

McCarter and Manning stood up.

"You okay?" the Briton asked. His voice sounded extraloud to him inside the protective head gear.

"Never better," Manning said. "But you're kind of a mess, aren't you?"

For the first time McCarter noticed that something had sprayed over his visor. Gobs of red, like bits of raw hamburger. It was gore from the blown-up Spetsnaz. He bent down, scooped up some water from a puddle and rinsed it off.

"These suits are total bullshit," Hawkins said.

"Maybe so," McCarter said, "but they keep us from being mistaken for the enemy and getting shot in the back."

"A definite plus," Encizo agreed.

On the far side of the crater in the floor, a soldier in a biohazard suit appeared through the smoke. He shouted in Russian and waved them onward.

The troopers behind Phoenix Force started forward again.

McCarter and the others advanced, stepping around and over the bodies of the fallen of both sides. They were about twenty yards down the corridor when from the rear came a few scattered, single gunshots. They all turned to look.

The Spetsnaz were firing into the bodies point-blank, flash-hiders to temples, making sure their sworn enemies were extradead.

CHAPTER TWENTY-EIGHT

Admiral Anatoli Rukov sat beside Captain Yeveshenko on a bench hacked out of the rock. Behind them in the low-ceilinged chamber a sweet spring trickled into a small limestone catch pool: Karamiso's grotto, deep in the bowels of the catacombs.

The place of miracles.

Both men were stone cold sober. The sounds of the attack in progress, coming ever closer, had negated the effect of all the vodka they'd consumed.

Rukov didn't enjoy the close proximity of his younger, taller, much more vital counterpart. The admiral felt diminished, even a bit unmanned by the unavoidable comparison. It made him feel like the stout, ruddy-faced little seventy-year-old man he was. That great displeasure he managed to successfully conceal.

The Christian iconography taken down from the chamber walls and out of the niches during Soviet rule had returned with a vengeance. Dozens of faceted rosary beads hung draped over jutting points of rock. Half-burned votive candles sat in hardened puddles of wax. Water-stained saint cards and discolored color photos of nameless loved ones were propped up behind them. There were sad little stuffed animals. Dead flowers. Unopened half-pint bottles of vodka. And ceramic and metal cups to drink the spring water from. Someone had even whitewashed away the antireligious graffiti.

To Rukov, there was a sour smell to the place.

Familiar, though.

Fishy.

It reminded him of uncooked, dead frogs.

Muffled by the layers of intervening rock, the explosions and gunfire were almost constant.

Neither of the officers had put on their biohazard suits yet, but the suits were laid out and waiting.

Rukov slipped a hand in his coat pocket and found the small plastic bottle hidden there. He shook the bottle and it rattled reassuringly. It contained a single cyanide pill. Just in case things went badly. Death was an acceptable outcome as far as he was concerned, even desirable if it was glorious and heroic, but he would not willingly submit to Dr. Vorostov's microscopic monster, Red Frost. After seeing what it could do to a human being, no one in their right mind would.

The plan developed by Rukov and the senior staff of conspirators was simple: break the vials of bioweapon, seal off the tunnels and trap all of the opposition inside the central hub.

After that, it was just a waiting game.

Waiting until the enemies' air supply ran out.

Sooner or later they would have to come out from under their protective hoods, and when they did that, Red Frost would be everywhere to greet them.

Rukov and his comrades intended from the start to kill them all, which would force the Russian government to send even more men in after them.

And more after that.

All the while, the conspirators would be sowing their invisible seeds of death, and moving deeper and deeper into the mountainside.

One of the first projects undertaken by the renegades was the construction of a secret route out of the catacombs' central hub. They hadn't used local labor for the job, even though it was readily and cheaply available. They had excavated it themselves so no one outside the cadre would know of its existence. Their escape tunnel was a tight, claustrophobic crawl on hands and knees, but its exit put them well outside the ring of high explosives already wired and ready to blow. Massive rockfalls from the corridor ceilings would block every other exit from the shrine.

Druspenskya Sokolova entered the chamber. She had put on the body part of her biohazard suit. Because she was so short, its midsection was a mass of pendulous horizontal folds. "The enemy is closing in," she announced to the seated men. "Our troops are making contact, then drawing back, and the enemy is following…right into the trap."

The former GRU interrogator was clearly excited at the prospect.

Not jumping up and down with glee.

But damn close to it.

The gleam in her eye wasn't sexual, but it was lustful, brought on by the prospect of other people's suffering.

It gave Rukov heartburn to look into those eyes.

Sokolova was at the monastery only because the conspirators had needed someone with her skills to attend to and control Dr. Vorostov. With the doctor dispensed with, they didn't need her anymore. The admiral recalled that similar, infamous "nurses" had attended the inmates at the Nazi death camps. No one would mourn the loss of the sadistic bitch. Not her sexual partners, whom she had threatened into participation. Not her close relatives, who had long ago disowned her. Certainly not the hundreds of her victims who had died screaming.

"Let them come," Yeveshenko said with confidence and resolve. "See what they get."

Rukov picked up the aluminum case at his feet and carefully opened it on his lap. Inside, packed in custom-fitted, closed-cell foam, were the seven remaining glass vials of bacterial strain B39547. He stroked them gently with his fingertips.

Cold to the touch.

"There is enough concentrated death here to bring down entire nations," the admiral said.

"Shouldn't we divide them up between the three of us now?" Sokolova asked. "Isn't that the best way to preserve the weapon?"

The hopeful expression on her face once again made bile rise in the back of Rukov's throat. It tasted like battery acid. Red Frost was a toy the woman would never be allowed to touch. He and Yeveshenko had already agreed to that. If she ever made a move to grab a vial, whoever was closer and had the better shot would put her down without hesitation.

"We will not be dividing up the vials," Rukov told her. "When the time comes we will break two of them here on the floor. That should be sufficient to infect every attacker. The rest we will take in the protective case with us. We'll need them when the government's reinforcements arrive."

CHAPTER TWENTY-NINE

As the men of Phoenix Force continued down the winding passage, they were overtaken by more Spetsnaz troops. McCarter and the others stepped aside to let the long, double-time column pass. Then they swung in behind a trooper with a flamethrower tank on his back, and picked up their own pace to keep up.

The lights of their headlamps swept over a shelf hacked into the right-hand wall of the tunnel. It stretched on and on ahead of them. The catacombs had been used as a crypt to bury the bones of the local dead. Piled on the shelf, stacked in a pyramid like bowling balls, were fleshless human skulls.

Hundreds, maybe thousands of them.

As McCarter walked by, he noted that on each skull's crown a name and a date had been painted. There were also decorations. Garlands of painted flowers and Christian symbols.

The long bones of the deceased were separately stacked, by size and shape.

The tunnel ahead doglegged hard right. A fraction

of a second after the Spetsnaz with the flamethrower rounded the turn and disappeared, the entire corridor was rocked by a tremendous explosion. McCarter and the others dived for cover in the narrow side passages as a floor-to-ceiling ball of fire rolled down the passage.

After the smoke cleared, they took turns checking one another's suits for tears. There was no way of telling for sure short of inflating them.

Out in the main corridor, the shelf had given way. There were skulls and femurs and vertebrae all over the floor.

McCarter led them through the litter. It was obvious that something had ignited the flamethrower tank. A tracer bullet? A Claymore mine set in the wall or floor? There wasn't enough left of the Spetsnaz trooper to puzzle it out.

As the Briton picked up the pace, intending to close the gap with the men ahead of them, there was a low, rumbling, grinding roar. Ten seconds later a powerful whoosh of air and a blinding cloud of dust hit them head-on.

As it turned out, all of the catacombs' hazards weren't explosive.

Proceeding with caution until the visibility cleared, they came upon the aftermath of a deadfall trap. The enemy had dropped massive blocks of stone from the ceiling, crushing five troopers. Their legs stuck out from under the rockfall, but they weren't kicking. They weren't even twitching. Their heads and torsos were concealed by boulders too heavy to lift. Pancaked.

There was no one mourning their loss. The survivors of the attack had already moved on.

Two suited troopers appeared through the dust,

walking against the flow. Through faceplates, McCarter recognized the major and his captain. Avrogarov seemed very pleased, which surprised McCarter.

"We are having them now," the major boasted.

"Having them?" the Briton said, glancing at the bodies broken under the stones. "In what way are you having them?"

"These criminals think they are fooling with us," Avrogarov continued. "They think they are drawing us into trap, but we know of their plans. A renegade we captured in Tblisi two days ago is telling us everything, after some hard efforts. We had to bring his family into the torture chamber and working on them in front of him before he betrayed his criminal comrades."

Manning turned on the captain and said, "You told us in Tblisi you had no hard evidence of secret tunnels or specific plans."

"You will please forgive me," Ilich said. "I was obeying orders."

"What is their plan?" McCarter asked him.

"To lure us to the center of the catacombs," Ilich said, "seal off the escape routes and kill us with Red Frost."

"How are they going to get out themselves?" McCarter said. "Or do they plan to commit suicide?"

"No suicide," the captain said. "There is a secret tunnel. No longer secret now. Our traitor drew us a detailed map. We are already in control of the exit."

"My troops have located the explosive charges, as well," Avrogarov said. "The ones being used to close off the tunnels. We will be detonating them and trap the renegades inside the center of the catacombs."

"If you do that, they could still release the bioweapon down here," Manning said.

"That's why you are all wearing excellent Russian protective suits," Ilich said.

"Come, this way, my American friends," the major said, "to our victory."

McCarter and the others followed the Spetsnaz officers. As they moved slightly, steadily downhill, they saw troopers pulling wires from the peak of the ceiling, presumably from packs of hidden explosives.

Fifty yards or so farther on, a contingent of Spetsnaz troops stood waiting. Avrogarov and Ilich walked between them and stopped a few feet from a sharp left-hand bend in the passage. The major waved his guests around the bend to have a look.

McCarter couldn't see the escape tunnel exit until Ilich pointed it out to him. A little more than a yard wide, and circular, it stood at the foot of the cavern wall. It was plugged by an artfully camouflaged disk of plywood.

"All the charges are prepared," the major told them. He waved for his men to line up, ready to spring the trap. "When we detonate the explosives, the rats will flee. Hopefully the biggest rats coming out first."

The troopers started turning off their headlamps. Phoenix Force followed suit. When the last one winked out, the corridor was plunged in pitch darkness. For a moment there was silence. The combination of darkness and quiet was disorienting; it took concentration for McCarter to maintain his bearings.

Then Avrogarov uttered a terse command into his throat mike, a command relayed around the perimeter.

The walls and floor shuddered. Rock and dust avalanched from the ceiling, cascading onto their heads. The HE roared and roared.

McCarter reached for the wall with his weak hand to keep his balance.

It seemed to take a very long time for the explosions to end. That was an illusion, McCarter knew, born of fear. Fear of being crushed to death by an inadvertent cave-in.

After the floor stopped shaking, more long minutes passed. The Spetsnaz stood like statues in the dark, their automatic weapons raised, their fingers close to but not yet pressing on the triggers.

With a rasping sound, the camouflage disk rolled away from the opening. At the same instant, a headlight beam cut through the still-falling dust.

The rats were coming out. And they were lit up like Christmas.

From what McCarter had seen, they had to exit the tunnel on hands and knees.

Avrogarov didn't give the signal to fire until many, many renegades had crawled out of the hole. When he did give the signal, absolute mayhem broke loose. A dozen autoweapons fired simultaneously in the enclosed space.

But the battle wasn't one-sided.

The conspirators instantly returned fire.

In front of the Briton, in the light of their enemies' headlamps, three of the good Spetsnaz shooters jerked backward, propelled by multiple chest hits. Even as the men were falling, just around the bend in the corridor, a grenade exploded with an earsplitting boom. McCarter and the others were on the inside of the bend, out of the line of fire, but the shrapnel cut down three more of the good guys. The rest of the soldiers, including the two officers, drew back to cover.

McCarter stepped into the breach, rounding the turn and opening fire on the men below the headlamps. James and Hawkins darted under his cover to the other side of the tunnel. As they knelt, two men in hazard suits scrambled from the exit. One was shooting from the hip, full-auto; the other one was carrying a silver case. They were running away down the passage, angling for a side seam on the opposite wall. James and Hawkins left those two to McCarter and poured autofire on the escape exit, keeping more of the rats from joining the fight.

Swinging a moving lead, the Briton deftly cut the legs out from under the guy with the case. He crashed to his chest and his property skidded onward.

The taller man snatched up the case up by the handle and kept on running. He wasn't moving in slow-mo but the baggy biohazard suit really held him back, as if he were dragging a thirty-pound anchor. Except for the running guy everyone else was down for the moment; at least thirty bodies littered the floor. The field of fire was clear.

"Got him!" Manning growled.

Before McCarter could put out a hand to stop him, the Canadian was off in pursuit.

"Hold fire!" the Briton shouted to the others. "Hold fire!"

Manning crossed the open ground with incredible speed, considering what he was wearing, and he took the big man down from behind in a bone-crushing rugby tackle. Their combined momentum carried the target headfirst into the stone wall. The aluminum suitcase once again skittered away.

"I'll handle the backup," McCarter told James and Hawkins. "You keep that escape hole covered."

By the time he caught up to the two combatants, the show was over. Manning had pulled the helmet off the man's head, revealing a split, badly bleeding skull. The guy was breathing, but unconscious. The tackle had ripped out both knees of Manning's excellent Russian protective suit.

As McCarter bent to retrieve the case, Avrogarov stopped him with a hand on his shoulder. "I'll be having that, thank you," he said as he reached past him and grabbed it up. "I am seeing your comrade has torn his suit. Perhaps he should be standing well back from me now."

After Manning had moved away, the major turned on his headlamp and opened the case on the floor in front of Ilich and McCarter.

There were seven niches cut in the four-inch-thick, gray foam liner. In each niche was a gleaming glass vial, sealed to a point at either end.

Apparently none of the bioweapon had been released.

Captain Ilich rocked back on his heels and let out a whoop of triumph, muffled by his headgear.

"This is being a very good day," the major said. He admired his prize for a moment more, then carefully closed and locked the case.

Two Spetsnaz troopers took hold of the unconscious man's arms and dragged his limp body past them, up the corridor. There were lots of enemy wounded on the ground. The troopers started separating the living from the dead.

An urgent shout from one of the soldiers brought the officers forward on the run. McCarter trotted along after them.

The soldier waved them over to a man without a helmet sitting on the floor with his back against the wall. His legs stuck out straight in front of him; there were bullet holes in the plastic fabric. It was the first guy out with the case.

"Admiral Rukov," the major said to the white-haired man. "It has coming to this. How so sad."

McCarter puzzled briefly over Avrogarov's continuing use of English, then he realized what was going on. Gloating was pointless unless it was intelligible to the people you were trying to impress.

"All the other traitors are trapped inside the holy shrine," the major said. "Your efforts were wasted. Tell us what we are wanting to know and they will be having a merciful death."

The admiral snarled something back in Russian.

"He says," Ilich translated, "I will tell you nothing. They will tell you nothing. They will not surrender to you."

"I am not wanting them to surrender, Rukov. I have enough of your people to be extracting information." He gestured at the renegade prisoners in the passage, already in the process of being hooded and bound, and forced to kneel with their heads resting against the wall. "I will be extracting information from you, too, Admiral. Those inside the shrine I am wanting to die."

Rukov seemed to deflate at this. His head slumped forward and he raised a hand to his face. His fingers passed briefly in front of his lips.

"What did he just do?" McCarter said. "He put something in his mouth!"

The admiral lifted his head, glared fiercely and clenched his jaws.

"Open his mouth!" Avrogarov cried. "Making him spit it out!"

Too late.

The admiral went rigid, eyes bulging, and moments later his heels started drumming on the floor. Pink froth poured from his lips and out his nostrils. As hands caught hold of his chin and nose and tried to unlock his jaws, his face turned dark. Then he fell into violent head-to-foot convulsions.

The troopers let him slump onto his side.

In twenty seconds the conspirator was dead.

"He took the coward's way out," Ilich said.

Avrogarov barked an order in Russian. The captain didn't translate it, but the meaning was obvious when the soldiers set to work. Check the other prisoners for poison pills.

"Do you be wanting to observe our information gathering?" Avrogarov asked his American guests.

"That would be a lot like seeing how sausage is made," Manning said.

"I'm sorry?"

"We'll let you get on with whatever it is that you're going to have to do," McCarter told the major. "But I remind you, time is of the essence here. Our country is still under threat of an unprecedented mass attack."

"We will be getting your answers," Avrogarov promised him.

As Phoenix Force started back up the tunnel, Encizo said, "This is what's called 'plausible deniability.' What we don't see we can't testify to."

"Yeah, as if *that* would ever happen," James said. "It's more like who gives a good goddamn?"

PERHAPS BECAUSE there were a lot of prisoners to interrogate or because the prisoners were uncooperative, the underground interrogations took a long time. McCarter and the others cooled their heels on the terrace for hours before Avrogarov and Ilich marched a short, stocky captive in a hazard suit out of the building.

On closer inspection, McCarter saw that it was a middle-aged woman with mannishly cropped, lanky iron-gray hair and a very large mole on her cheek. She had a gunshot crease along her jawline, and the bone looked broken. Her nose was bloodied and swollen, like someone had repeatedly punched or gunbutted her. She couldn't backhand the blood away because her hands were bound behind her back with cable ties. Despite her facial injuries and the weight of her impending doom, she wasn't crying. She stood there, chin up, stolid, emotionless.

Even without the busted nose and spilled blood she was one of the ugliest women McCarter had ever seen. Stop-a-clock ugly.

And as it turned out, her ugly started on the inside.

"Who is she?" he asked the major.

"A former interrogator with GRU," Avrogarov said. "Her name is Druspenskya Sokolova. Her torture skills are being legendary. In the old days, her specialty was to introduce foreign chemicals into the bodies of the people undergoing questioning. She injected the substances with hypodermics, force-feeding them with funnels and administered them up the behind. She used all sorts of interesting chemicals, intending to produce different, highly unpleasant effects. Caustics. Narcotics. Psychoactives. Laxatives. Her interview subjects used to begging her for death. Druspenskya Sokolova has agreed to cooperate with your inquiries, and provide information about the ongoing mission in your country."

"She's cooperating in exchange for what?" Manning said.

"An easier exit from this plane," the major said.

"We're going to fix these traitors," Ilich said. "Give them some of their own poison medicine."

"You're not talking about releasing the bioweapon?" McCarter said.

"Of course we are. We're going to seal them underground with it. Let them die in the dark."

"We can sacrifice one vial of Red Frost for the sake of justice," Avrogarov said. "Just one vial."

"You're going to kill all of the captives?" James said.

"And the ones still trapped in the shrine," Ilich said. "It's what they deserve. It's what they planned to do to us."

McCarter wasn't in the position to prevent, nor did he have much interest in preventing what the Russians were proposing to do to their prisoners and enemies. Hundreds of Americans had already lost their lives as a result of the actions of these renegades. Many, many more were still at terrible risk. "Whatever you do, you can't let the bacteria escape," he said.

"We'll be sending in flamethrowers afterward to sterilize everything," Avrogarov said.

"And the GRU torturer?" McCarter asked the major. "What does she get?"

"Our Druspenskya knows exactly how this bacteria operates. She has seen the results with her own eyes. And she doesn't want any part of it. She was offered a choice. A bullet in the back of the head or Red Frost with all the others."

"She took the bullet," Ilich said.

"Don't kill her until the information she gives us is checked out," the Briton said.

"We don't intend to."

"And if it turns out to be a lie?" Manning said.

"In that case," Avrogarov said, "she will join her fellow traitors in the chamber of the holy spring. All of her comrades are getting a stay of execution until we verify your information."

"You got that? Do you understand English?" Hawkins asked her.

The woman nodded. "I will tell you true," she said in a gravelly voice.

"Spill it, then," McCarter said. "All the details you have."

"Cigarette?"

"Afterward," the major told her.

"There were six Spetsnaz who landed west of Port Angeles," she said.

"Three are dead," James said. "Where were the others headed?"

"They were to meet a Russian agent named Slaney on the island of Bainbridge. He has a house there. It is nearby to the ferry to Seattle."

"Do they have Red Frost?" Manning said.

"Yes, they have it."

"Do you know what they look like?" Encizo said.

"No. I've never seen them."

"What ferry are they going to take?" McCarter said.

"Three-fifty p.m., Seattle time."

Encizo checked his watch. "That's about forty minutes from now," he said. "Not much in the way of wiggle room."

"This agent, he's in on it?" Manning said. "He's part of the attack?"

The woman shook her head. "He's a sleeper. He has no idea who called him up. He thinks it was an official contact. The Spetsnaz will kill him before they leave his house."

"What are their designated targets?" McCarter said.

The former GRU interrogator shrugged. "They will pick targets of their own choosing. Targets of opportunity. They know how to deploy the bioweapon for maximum effect. If they get to the Seattle side, they will split up and you will never stop them. You must catch them before they leave the island, or before they get off the ship."

McCarter stepped away from the prisoner. Using a secure-link satellite phone, he relayed all the information to Stony Man.

Kurtzman repeated every word back to him for confirmation. There could be no mistakes, no oversights, no miscommunication. When the bounce-back was complete, he put Brognola on the horn.

"How solid is this intel?" the big Fed asked.

"It looks solid to me," McCarter said. "A quick check should turn up this guy Slaney's address on Bainbridge. If he isn't living where our source says he is, give me an immediate call. If it isn't solid, our source is going to die very hard. These Russians are right mean bastards."

"Roger that, we'll get right back to you on the basic info."

"Is it enough for Able to get the job done?" Mc-Carter said.

"Don't worry, we'll make it work," Brognola said, then he broke the connection.

CHAPTER THIRTY

Bainbridge Island, Washington,
3:30 p.m. PDT

Spetsnaz Lieutenant Boris Luria found his dead host's spare car keys hanging on a hook by the kitchen door. The kitchen itself was turned upside down. Luria and his two-man crew had gotten hungry after an hour or two and, half-drunk, had cooked for themselves. The nearly emptied refrigerator door was still open. There were greasy fry pans sitting on the stove and counter, broken glass in the sink and scattered across the quarry tile floor. Boxes and canisters taken down from the cupboards had been opened, then tossed aside. What they had spilled and broken they hadn't bothered cleaning up.

The Tartar's boot soles crunched on broken glass as he returned to the spacious American living room. He waggled the keys at Balenko and Raskov, who were lounging on the sofa with their feet propped up on the burl coffee table next to empty vodka bottles and frozen-pizza boxes. At the sound of jingling keys, they turned away from the giant plasma TV and looked over the sofa back at him.

"Time to go," he told them. "Time to make history."

"So early?" the bald Balenko said.

The dock was only five minutes away, but Luria wasn't taking any chances. It was better to be fifteen minutes early and make the 3:50 p.m. boat than be late and miss it. Too much was at stake. From what the dead spy had said, sometimes there were lots of cars in line and you had to take the next boat. The next boat was less than optimum for catching rush hour.

"We go now," Luria said.

Balenko and Raskov rose to their feet. They gathered up their automatic weapons from the floor and walked over to the credenza where the three Pelican cases sat. Solemnly, they each took one. Luria took the last, then he shouldered his flat-black AKS-74 by its fabric sling.

As Luria turned back toward the kitchen, Balenko stopped him.

"Wait a minute," he said. "We leave TV on." He put down his bioweapon case, walked back to the burl coffee table.

On the screen an on-scene reporter was repeating for the hundredth time what little was known about the explosion and loss of life. Behind her, in the background, the site was crawling with uniformed National Guard.

Instead of picking up the remote, Balenko grabbed an empty bottle of vodka by the neck. He cocked back his arm and threw the bottle through the middle of the plasma TV screen. With a crash, the picture winked out.

"Now off!" he said.

Raskov grinned at his comrade's antics. "Crazy man."

"Like rock star," Balenko corrected him.

Loaded down with guns, extra loaded mags and the bioweapon, the three Russians moved through the ransacked kitchen and into the garage.

Luria knew that Homeland Security might be looking for the Volvo station wagon they had stolen in Sequim. The make, model and license plates could already be on the system watch list. He had decided to take Slaney's two-door Acura sedan, even though it was smaller. Stealing another, bigger car from the neighborhood raised unnecessary risk this late in the game.

The Tartar opened the garage door, then got behind the wheel. Raskov, the smaller of the two other men, slipped into the cramped backseat. Balenko took the shotgun seat.

"Keep your weapons down and out of sight," Luria reminded his crew as he tucked his AKS-74 muzzle first, halfway under the driver seat. "We don't want to draw any attention to ourselves."

Balenko wedged his gun between the side of the seat and the inside of the passenger door. Raskov put his on the floor and covered it with a jacket he found on the seat.

Luria backed the Acura down the driveway and onto the street, then headed west toward the ferry landing. He felt on top of everything, way ahead of pursuit, coasting to the finish.

The American mission had gone like clockwork. Every stage had been completed according to plan. The submerged submarine had entered Puget Sound unchallenged. The strike team had successfully evacuated and landed ashore in the wave skimmers. The submarine's crew had been poisoned with the bioweapon by a member of the conspiracy's inner circle. That same person then destroyed the stealth technology modules that allowed the sub's penetration of ASW defenses. He surfaced the ship, set it on a collision course for Ediz Hook, then killed himself. As expected, the strike team had found everything they needed to move the operation forward—America was the Land of Plenty. The Discovery Bay attack had accomplished its twin goals: to divert attention and resources from the rest of the team and keep all eyes focused on events well to the west of Seattle.

The rest of the mission was fairly simple. Two team members would be dropped off in Seattle, and the third would drive on to Tacoma. By the time the first victims of Red Frost were starting to drop all of the vials would have been dispersed, two major population centers would have been struck, and it would be too late to do anything about it.

Balenko pulled out a dog-eared photograph and kissed it. There were tears in his eyes.

Luria had seen the picture many times. It was of Balenko's father and his two uncles in their Soviet army uniforms. They had been war heroes, much decorated, wounded in battle, and they all died in the gutter. One of the uncles had frozen to death in a Moscow park; one had killed himself with heroin. His father had blown his brains out. That was Balenko's legacy.

In the Russian soul there is a special place reserved for revenge.

In the Russian soul there is poetry in destruction, the more absolute, the more exquisite.

"Where are your pictures?' Raskov said from the backseat.

"I have already said my goodbyes," Luria told him. Indeed, he had drained himself of all emotion in preparation for the attack. He was in charge; he had to maintain a Zenlike detachment. He had to keep the others on track and on mission.

"They will not forget this day," Balenko said.

Luria waited at a stoplight until the signal turned green with an arrow, then he turned left into the entrance to the ferry terminal. Down the hill, he could see the big, white, wedding-cake boat had already docked, but hadn't started off-loading its vehicles. Directly ahead the road diverted and divided into multiple lanes, each feeding past a separate white toll booth. There was no one in front of him so he pulled up to the nearest window.

The uniformed toll collector slid back the glass and looked down at them. He counted heads, and said, "One driver, two passengers." Then he tapped in the total on his keyboard, which appeared on a little electronic screen below the window for Luria to read.

The Tartar paid with cash from a thick wad of bills.

As he took back his change and receipt, the collector said, "Stay in lane 2 and have a nice trip."

Luria gave the Acura some gas and pulled past the booth. The loading lanes were clearly marked with huge white numbers. A ponytailed woman in a dark blue uniform, Day-Glo vest, and Washington State Ferries billcap waved him into the second lane from the left. He obeyed, then drove down the slope. As he did so, the ferry began disgorging its car and trucks. A steady stream poured up the hill, on the other side of a low, concrete barrier. He parked the Acura behind a dark green SUV and turned off the engine. Through the

Ford Expedition's back window, he could see a big, goofy-looking red dog. It had long hair and floppy ears, and it appeared to be smiling.

On the left was a car packed full of high-school students. They had rolled down all the windows of the scruffy-looking, half-primered Honda four-door and were playing loud rap music and smoking cigarettes.

Luria tapped in time on the steering wheel. "I like," he said.

He looked up in the rearview mirror as a Volvo station wagon pulled in behind. Not a new one like the car they had stolen from Sequim. This one was big and boxy. It had a cracked windshield. There were four people in the station wagon; two of them were strapped into kiddie seats.

The sun streaming in through the Acura's windshield made it too warm in a hurry. The Spetsnaz rolled down their windows. They lit up more of Sid Slaney's cigarettes and enjoyed the rap rhythm.

"Good music," Luria shouted to the blond boy in the Honda's front passenger seat.

The boy nodded and smiled automatically, then he looked more closely at the three men in the car. His expression went blank, and he quickly looked away.

"You are scaring the children, Balenko," Raskov said from the backseat. "Cover your arms."

Balenko glanced at Luria for a countermand. When it was not forthcoming, he jerked the sleeves of Slaney's Patagonia shirt down over his bullet scars. "Now you'd better cover your face," he said over the seat.

Raskov leaned forward.

Before he could spit out a comeback Luria said, "Enough. Enjoy the sunshine. Smell the salt air."

On the right, in lane 3, an unmarked, silver semi-trailer with a red tractor pulled past them and coasted down to the front of that row. It stopped with a whoosh and squeal of brakes.

As the departure time approached, many more cars and trucks pulled into line, quickly filling up all the available lanes. Travelers had waited until the last minute to take their boat ride.

Luria looked around at all the waiting cars and all the waiting people. He waved at the big red dog as he blew a puff of smoke out the window.

All dead, he thought.

All dead.

CHAPTER THIRTY-ONE

Bainbridge Island, Washington,
3:37 p.m. PDT

As Jack Grimaldi set the helicopter on the tarmac bordering the shore of Eagle Harbor, an unmarked black sedan pulled through the gate in the hurricane fence and barreled straight for them. The ferry terminal storage yard was very large and mostly empty. The trailered inflatable rescue boats, big spools of cable and salvaged equipment on wooden pallets were distributed along the north side of the fence. There was plenty of space in the middle of the asphalt for the helicopter to land.

Lyons was the first one out of the aircraft, lugging his loaded, ballistic nylon duffel toward the oncoming car. When the sedan stopped, the DHS uniformed driver and passenger got out.

Lyons impatiently waved them aside. "We need the wheels," he said as Grimaldi and Schwarz ran to catch up with him, lugging their own gear. "We need them now."

He reached into the car and popped the trunk latch, then rounded the back bumper and dumped in his duffel. Grimaldi and Schwarz added theirs, then slammed down the lid.

By that time Lyons was already in the driver's seat. When his teammates piled in, front and rear, he dropped the car in gear and peeled out, leaving the real DHS agents in a cloud of burned rubber.

Doing a job so important without Rosario Blancanales along for the ride felt weird to Lyons. Not precariously weird, but out-of-balance weird. There was no way Pol could have participated in this one. He knew it. Everyone else knew it. Blancanales was already at the Harbor View E.R. getting thoroughly checked out, top to bottom.

According to Stony Man's research, relayed through the secure channel, audio comm link, the house of the sleeper spy Slaney was very near the terminal. If they could manage it, Lyons wanted to end the battle there, behind closed doors. Inside the house they had containment and afterward they could conceal the whole operation. Inside the house there were no innocent bystanders to worry about.

As Lyons closed on the address, he took his foot off the gas and let the sedan decelerate. Schwarz was reading off the numbers on the even side of the street. "There! That's it!" he said.

At the end of the long, sheltered driveway the garage door was up.

Lyons opened the channel to Stony Man and spoke rapidly into his headset mike. "We're at the subject address," he said. "The stolen white Volvo station wagon is parked in the garage. Looks like we're on to something. Looks like we've hit gold here."

"What about the homeowner's car?" Kurtzman said. "The maroon Acura two-door sedan?"

"The homeowner's car is gone," Lyons told him.

"Clear the house," Brognola reported. "The targeted ferry is scheduled to leave the dock in eight minutes."

"Let's do this quickly," Lyons told his companions as he stopped in the driveway.

All three of them bailed with handguns drawn. Right away they saw the bags of thawing frozen food scattered across the floor.

Schwarz opened the door of the chest freezer.

"Here's our homeowner," he said staring down at the already frosted corpse. "A sleeper forever now."

With Lyons in the lead, they burst into the house through the kitchen access. Fanning out, it took about a minute for them to make the loop from room to room and back to their borrowed car.

As Lyons reversed down the driveway, he filled in Stony Man. "Our friends have already left," he said. "We're en route to the ferry."

Lyons stomped the brakes hard when he hit the street, rode the backward skid to the right, then shifted into Drive and stomped the gas. The resulting g force pushed all three of them deep in their seats.

"We're going to have to go ahead with Plan B," he said into the mike as he switched on the cruiser's flashing lights. "Contact the ferry. Tell them not to load any vehicles until we arrive."

Kurtzman broke in. "The longer we delay the three-fifty sailing the more crowded the boat is going to be."

"That can't be helped," Lyons said as the speedometer needle edged toward eighty. "Another thing—we've got to make sure no one makes a move on our friends, but us. The state patrol's got search dogs working the lines of waiting ferry traffic, looking for explosives and drugs. If they sniff out the gunshot residue on these guys, we could have a problem that we don't need."

"The dogs have already been called off," Brognola said. "Everything else is in position. The military Haz-Mat unit is waiting in the ferry line. It's all set up. When you give the go-ahead, Ironman, they'll be the first vehicle allowed on the boat."

"Gotta go!" Lyons said as the four-way intersection came up very fast in front of them.

Tapping his brakes to reduce speed without losing control and giving the cruiser's siren a little goose for emphasis, the ex-LAPD cop proceeded to bully his way against the light, through the oncoming traffic to make the necessary left turn. Past the intersection, heading downhill toward the water, he didn't pull into the toll booth lanes. He killed the flashing lights and drove on the wrong side of the street, swerving up a driveway meant for Kitsap County buses, and screeched to the stop behind the passenger terminal.

By the time he popped the trunk, Schwarz and Grimaldi had their doors open. They grabbed their gun bags and ran around the front of the single-story building to the covered walkway that led to the elevated passenger loading ramp.

At the bottom of the walkway, a line of ferry passengers waited to be let on board the ship.

An overhead electronic sign read Security Check In Progress. After every crossing, the boat was swept for bombs. Because of the backed-up people, some with luggage, Able Team had to slow down. Through the walkway's open slider windows they could see the rows of vehicles in line. It was going to be a full load.

"That's got to be them!" Schwarz said. "Behind the green SUV, second row. Check it out."

Lyons and Grimaldi stopped and looked closely.

"I make three guys," Grimaldi said. "Two in front, one in back."

"We've got no high-probability shots from up here," Schwarz said. "The angle is too steep, and there are too many noncombatants moving around in the killzone. Even with a long gun the risk is too great."

They hurried on, past a second electronic sign carrying the same warning, then followed a right bend in the windowed walkway. Two turns later, they showed their DHS ID badges to the crewman manning the drawbridge-style passenger loading ramp. He took a good look, then waved them onto the boat.

Lyons raced across the open deck, under the observation deck overhang, and into the main passenger cabin. Before him under a low ceiling was a wide expanse of individual chairs; along the side windows were facing bench seats. Standing at midships, beside the food service area, a female crew member with a long blond ponytail gestured for them to hurry her way.

"I've got your changes of uniform waiting in the crew quarters," the blonde said as they ran up to her.

"We've to stop meeting like this, Kate," Lyons said.

"No, I've got to stop being your wardrobe guy," she said, quickly ushering them through the narrow doorway.

There wasn't any time for modesty. They stripped off in front of her.

"I want to do my bit here," she told them as they

pulled on the short blue jackets and Day-Glo vests. "You might need another gun."

"If you got hurt, Rosario would never forgive us," Schwarz said.

"Bullshit," she said.

Lyons opened his duffel. He put his holstered .357 Magnum wheelgun inside and took out a Beretta 93-R with a noise suppressor already screwed on. After checking the magazine, he jacked a live round under the hammer, then slipped the weapon under the jacket, into the small of his back, hooking the grip over the outside of his uniform trouser waistband. He tested the fit and the ease of draw and was satisfied.

"You're going to try to kill them in the car?" Kate said. "While they're waiting in the ferry line?"

"No, after they get on the boat," Lyons told her. "That's the only place we can isolate them. We can't take them out on the dock. They're sandwiched in, with civilian vehicles all around."

"We can't try to move the civilians out of their cars, either," Grimaldi said as he checked his own suppressor-equipped handgun. "That would tip off the bad guys that something was up."

"But if they've got the bioweapon in the car with them," Kate said, "and you guys open fire, a wild shot or a through-and-through bullet could accidentally hit and break the containers. If that happens, and the slug carries through the vehicle, it could transport some of the bioweapon into the air. We're talking lethal contamination, big-time."

"And your point is?" Schwarz asked.

"The job demands precision, but under the circumstances, that isn't possible."

"That's why we're going to severely limit the field of play," Lyons told her. "Otherwise we face a worst case—the release of Red Frost and a running gun battle with autoweapons in the middle of a crowd of hundreds of innocent people. Kate, we need a link with the HazMat unit. It's critical that they are in position, ready to do their thing, so we can cut down any possible exposure. Will you do it?"

"Of course I'll do it," she said.

"If everybody's ready," Lyons said, "let's load this boat."

They took the stairs down to the cavernous, still deserted main car deck. Kate, Grimaldi and Schwarz immediately headed for the bow of the boat. Lyons went the other way. He pulled aside the mate in charge of balancing the cargo. A quick word in the man's ear and a flash of his DHS credentials got him exactly what he wanted. The mate walked off the boat, onto the dock and waved the red semitractor on board first.

Lyons waved the truck into the second-from-the-left lane and it pulled all the way forward to the bow, where Schwarz stopped it.

When the HazMat unit was in position, Lyons nodded to the mate and he started general boarding. Cars and trucks in lanes 1 and 2 began bumping over the steel ramp and rolling onto the ferry's deck. The uniformed crew directed them to the appropriate lanes to keep the load even and the boat from tipping.

Lyons guided vehicles into the deck's yawning central space, alternating lanes, until the maroon Acura appeared at the foot of the ramp. A glance at the front license plate told him it was Slaney's car. He stepped forward and held out his palm, the universal signal for hold it.

When the car stopped, he walked around to the driver's side. Both side windows were rolled down in front. He leaned down and smiled at the black-haired Spetsnaz behind the wheel. He kept eye contact with the man, even though every fiber of his being screamed for him to glance around the inside of the car, looking for weapons and Red Frost carrying cases. "Go up the ramp on the left," he said. "Please roll your windows all the way up. There may be some spray during the crossing."

The driver just stared at him.

"Windows up, please," he repeated, deadly serious.

It was a stupid request, but the Spetsnaz didn't challenge it. Making a fuss could have cut their mission short.

When the driver and his bald passenger complied, Lyons thanked him. Then he pointed to the first lane on the left-hand side of the deck. It led to a narrow ramp that climbed to a second level where there were two more lanes of additional parking space. Blocked by superstructure and elevation from the view of the rest of the ship, it was Able Team's best option for containment.

After the Acura drove up the ramp and disappeared over the rise, Lyons blocked off the entrance with a row of orange plastic traffic cones. As he ran up the slope after the car, he drew the Beretta from the small of his back and hid it along his thigh. He had been forced to leave his Colt Python behind. A revolver couldn't be effectively silenced, and silence was a requirement.

When he reached the flat stretch of the deck, he saw brake lights flash on. Grimaldi was waving the Acura forward in the right lane. He stopped the car where that lane dead-ended. The left lane continued, turning into the ramp that angled back down to the main deck.

Lyons slowed to a quick walk, moving along the side of the superstructure, toward the bow, closing on the rear of the Acura. He was ten yards away when Schwarz and Grimaldi bent down and blocked the car's front wheels with wooden chocks. The three men inside didn't seem concerned as the blue-uniformed crewmen straightened beside the fenders.

Lyons was even with the back bumper as Grimaldi and Schwarz raised their silenced Berettas and fired through the front cabin's side windows, point-blank, 9 mm double taps. Their shots were angled down, through their target's heads, and toward the rear. The tempered glass imploded around pairs of crazed holes. Blood, glass and brains sprayed over the Acura's leather upholstery and headliner.

The wiry guy sitting in the back wasn't hit by a head shot through and through. He didn't freeze up, either. He immediately ducked down for something hidden on the floor between the seats.

Lyons stepped closer to the car, bringing up his semiauto pistol two-handed. The second before he fired, he got a subliminal glimpse of an orange plastic case and the pistol grip of an AKS-74. Aiming downward, at the top of the man's skull, he shot three times through the rear side window. The window exploded inward and more blood and brains flew over the car's interior.

It was a done deal in less than five seconds.

Slaughterhouse quick.

Able Team backed away from the target vehicle, automatically picking up their brass as they moved upwind.

Lyons heard a thumping sound behind him, from the bow of the boat. That would be Kate, he thought, pounding on the side of the HazMat trailer. Hidden from view on the lower deck, the trailer's side doors swung open. Six men in biohazard suits ran up the ramp. They each carried a four-foot-long roll of what looked like plastic wrap over their shoulders.

The HazMat boys knew what they were doing. Quickly, efficiently, they used the rolls of plastic wrap to cocoon the entire car, sealing the broken windows, undercarriage, passenger compartment in layer upon layer of clear film so absolutely nothing could leak out. Not blood. Not bioweapon.

When they were done the Acura looked as if it had been made the dinner of a giant spider.

To conceal the cocooning, they pulled a car cover over the vehicle and secured it with chain and locks.

As they returned to their trailer, Lyons trotted toward the stern. He left the orange cones in place at the foot of the ramp and stepped up to the chief mate. "It's going to be a light load this trip," he said in the man's ear. "Shut down the boarding and let's shove off."

"We're leaving a lot of cars on the dock," the mate said.

"No skin off yours or mine," Lyons said. "There's always the next boat, and you won't be on it. You'll be in Seattle when it docks."

The mate shrugged. Then he signaled the rest of the crew to stop loading and raise the ramp.

The crossing to Coleman Dock was uneventful. After the ship had tied up, and all the other vehicles had been off-loaded, the HazMat team unchocked the tarped Acura, winched it down the ramp and up into the back of the semitrailer.

Standing on the passenger deck, Lyons, Kate, Schwarz and Grimaldi watched the truck drive off the boat and across the loading dock. The bundled car and its occupants were headed for Fort Lewis, and absolute, high-temperature destruction.

"Too bad we can't call Rosario at the hospital and give him the good news right away," Schwarz said.

"He couldn't hear a word we said," Grimaldi lamented.

"We could call the nursing station," Lyons said. "Get one of the staff to relay the information."

"Yeah, a nurse could write it down and hand it to him," Grimaldi said.

"I got a better idea," Schwarz said. "Kate can go over and tell him in person. Maybe hold his hand a little while."

"Well, Kate?" Lyons said.

"You guys fight good," the blonde said, "but as matchmakers, you really, really suck."

CHAPTER THIRTY-TWO

Black Sea coast, Republic of Georgia,
6:05 a.m. local time

From the terrace of the ruined monastery, David Mc-
Carter stared due west at the wide expanse of the Black
Sea. Whitecaps danced all the way to the gray horizon.
The dawn wind gusted hard against his back, whistling
over the clifftop above, whipping through the trees,
stirring up the fires still burning out of control here and
there on the forested slopes below.

The other members of Phoenix Force were sitting on
the stone steps, keeping out of the wind and the smoke.
They had stripped out of and discarded their biohazard
suits. Their borrowed weapons were still close to hand,
and fully loaded.

Major Avrogarov had kept his promises. He had uncovered the information necessary to stop the renegades' attack against America. He had trapped and
poisoned the surviving conspirators with Red Frost.
His forces were still going through the catacombs with

flamethrowers, frying to a cinder everyone and everything.

Complete sterilization.

The mass poisoning defined a code of conduct that David McCarter wanted no part of. "Do unto others" was right enough, but a firing squad would have had the same result. Minus the prolonged and truly horrifying death agonies.

But literal revenge was part of the time-honored Russian mind set: an eye for an eye, right down to the length of the nail on the thumb used to gouge it out.

He could tell Encizo, James, Hawkins and Manning weren't comfortable with the details of the final outcome, either. Manning seemed in a particularly foul temper.

It had taken close to two hours for the hundred-plus trapped renegade soldiers to become infected, to sicken and die. It had taken even longer to toast the caves before they could be sealed up again. This time forever.

McCarter looked up as the two Spetsnaz officers exited the building's front doorway, still wearing the bottom half of their biohazard suits.

Major Avrogarov gestured magnanimously for the Phoenix Force to gather around him. James, Hawkins, Manning and Encizo rose from the steps. McCarter crossed the windswept courtyard.

"All the renegade traitors are dead," the major told them. "Their bodies have been incinerated to ash. You watched us destroy the last of the deadly vials with fire. Red Frost is no more."

They had indeed witnessed the burning of the bioweapon, but they hadn't observed the cremation of all the bodies. There were too many dead, and they were too scattered. That this was the last of the bioweapon was also problematic. No one knew how many vials existed in the first place.

Avrogarov's summation was way too neat, in Mc-Carter's view. The mop-up wasn't over by a long shot. Secret purges were on the near horizon. Blood purges in Russia, political purges in the States. Clearly the conspiracy in Russia had wide and invasive tentacles. Ultrasecret technology had been appropriated and misused. The existence of that technology revealed catastrophic weaknesses in the defenses of America. The U.S. government could deny that it was an incursion at all, and if it repeated the same lie over and over and over, the press would pick it up and the public would swallow it as truth. In private, however, heads in uniform were going to roll.

And rightly so.

Major Avrogarov cleared his throat meaningfully and glanced past them, in the direction of the terrace wall. A reminder that one more killing was scheduled, after a long night of killing.

Whether it was an anticlimax, or an overdose, Mc-Carter couldn't make up his mind. He turned to look at the former GRU interrogator. Bedraggled. Exhausted. Defeated. Tied to a stanchion like a sacrificial goat.

The information she had given up had saved many lives in the Pacific Northwest. McCarter was grateful for that, but he had no intention of interceding to save her. Like the old way of life that she represented, she had to go.

Phoenix Force followed the two officers across the terrace.

Captain Ilich untied Druspenskya Sokolova from

the post and shoved her over to the low stone wall. On the other side of it was a long, straight, three-hundred-foot drop down the cliff face.

Sokolova leaned over the wall. Head lowered, eyes closed, she began mumbling to herself.

"What's she saying?" James asked. "Is she praying?"

"What the hell do you think she's praying to?" Manning said.

"I shudder to think," McCarter said.

Ilich put the muzzle of his Gsh-18 to the matted back of her head. No preamble. No warning. Just the flat crack of the pistol shot. A puff of blood mist and brains hung in the air for a second before it was blown away by the wind. The twitching body slumped onto the top of the wall.

The captain grabbed the thick ankles and without ceremony dumped her body headfirst over the parapet. That done, he hawked and spit after her.

Unlike the two Spetsnaz officers, the men of Phoenix Force resisted the urge to look over the edge and watch the corpse cartwheel as it plummeted to the ground.

"Well, that is being that," Avrogarov said, brushing off his hands. He took a silver flask from inside his biohazard suit. He unscrewed the top and drank deeply. After he wiped his mouth with the back of his hand, he said, "Perhaps, David Green, we can be doing some sight-seeing in Tblisi this evening?"

The Briton was incredulous.

"There is being some entertaining nightlife there."

Suddenly, miraculously they were all foxhole buddies. Maybe they could even get tattoos together.

"I think we'll take a pass on the local clubbing," McCarter said. "Official duties require us to be elsewhere, you understand. But thanks for the offer, anyway. Perhaps another time?"

"Until that happy day is arriving," Major Avrogarov said, toasting them all in turn with his silver hip flask.

"Yeah, we'll kill you later," Gary Manning announced through a fierce, toothy grin.

Calvin James immediately turned away, as did Hawkins, and Encizo rolled his eyes, aghast.

The Russian major and his captain smiled back winningly, however.

Perhaps another case of lost in translation? McCarter thought.

And then again, perhaps not.

James Axler
Outlanders

DARK GODDESS

Buried deep in the sands of the Sinai, a secret port can unleash the dangerous mysteries of an alien race. Unless the Cerberus rebels can outwit a she-god with an army at her disposal…and the cunning and cruelty to wrest Earth for herself.

Available in November wherever books are sold.